THE
MIND
GAME

THE
MIND
GAME

M. G. HARRIS

First published in 2024 by Darkwater Books
An imprint of Harris Oxford Limited.
41 Cornmarket Street, Oxford, OX1 3HA

ISBN 978-1-909072-57-2

TheMGHarris.com

For everyone who read 'The Joshua Files' and is still reading my books now. Thank you!

TRAILER

Dulles International Airport, Washington DC, five years ago. On a spring morning, the concourse was already rammed with travelers. No one wore masks back then, it was before the pandemic. Remember how things used to be? Everyone breathing the same air, not a thought for microscopic packages of deadly genetic material.

In the line for passport control, twelve-year-old Maxim Santiago clung tightly to his mother's hand. Witnesses say she stared directly ahead. Did Maxim try to catch her eye? Did his mom look away?

Even aged twelve, Maxim didn't think of himself as a kid any more. At school he was afraid of no-one and nothing. His classmates and teachers had never met anyone like him. So maybe he was different. Yet waiting on line that day, beside a mother who trembled with fear, Maxim must have been scared.

It was a busy line, it moved slowly. Scanning tech at the borders was still new, clunky, they didn't trust it. Despite the scanners, half the time guards had to check documents and faces. The line advanced. For just a moment, his mom let go of his hand. Was it for one last check of their documents?

His gaze wandered along the row of people in front of him, settled on a family of five, the Grover-Dysons from Alexandria. When Maxim Santiago looked at you, really looked at you, that wasn't something you easily forgot. Katie Grover-Dyson was thirteen years old at the time and being scooped out of school for a family funeral in Boca Raton. She remembered his eyes, described them as 'haunted."

Did Maxim know what was coming? Did Masha, his mom?

If they were forced to leave their home, Masha must have made Maxim promise to keep it a secret. Because he didn't breathe a word. Not to anyone.

By now you're maybe asking – what's my connection to this case? Well, whereas I only slightly knew the influencer Rich Wonders, from my first series, Who Killed Rich Wonders? this series will be a lot more personal. Because once, before he disappeared, I was pretty close to Maxim Santiago. We both were.

Back when Maxim and I were kids, I knew a boy, let's call him 'Mike.' Mike and I were in a band with Maxim. Basically, we were the closest thing Maxim had to 'friends.' We hung out together outside of band practice, gamed together, told each other the small stuff you share so easily when you're eleven and twelve.

If Maxim had known he and his mom were leaving, he would have given us some hint. Okay, maybe he'd not have come right out and admitted that everything the three of us had worked so hard for in that rehearsal room was basically for nothing. But he'd have said something. Even if it was just "Oh hey, I can't make tomorrow's practice."

If Mike and I had no clue that Maxim was leaving, it's because Maxim didn't breathe a word. We didn't know anything, so we waited a whole hour that afternoon for him to join us for practice. Mike and I played the whole piece through until we had it down. Maxim would have been happy with how good we sounded, which is partly why we were pissed at him. Until we heard the news.

The night before Maxim and Masha Santiago disappeared at Dulles International Airport, I was over at their house. His mom made us fried-egg sandwiches with ketchup. When it got time for me to go home, Maxim didn't even get up from the sofa. He just turned off his Nintendo Switch and headed for the piano. Not a single hint that this was good-bye.

That's how I remember seeing him the last time, five years ago. A twelve-year old kid with short, bronze hair *cut in a faux-hawk, kicking back on the couch, his face lit-up by the TV in a darkened room, seeming kind of irritated because I had to leave before he'd had a chance to even the score. His mom at the kitchen table, studying for her latest English exam.*

Just another weekend. Not what you expect to see from a family on the brink of skipping town. Yet somehow, between eight and nine the next morning, beneath the feet of the Santiagos, the ground shifted.

Where were they headed at the airport? After they were apprehended at Border Control, where did they go? What happened to the Santiagos?

A tad nervously, I watched Kenzie's eyes scan the page, once, twice and then annoyingly a third time, even slower than the previous two. I dropped the hopeful act. "You hate it."

He shook his head, put on a pair of wire-rimmed glasses he occasionally used and stroked his chin so thoughtfully, I began to wonder if he was making fun of me. Then I realized he was probably relishing the fact that his chin-stubble was growing back after the last time he shaved. I watched for a second, unsure what I thought about the slight greasiness of his reddish hair. It'd been months and months since he'd been to the barber and this new look of his, curling ringlets drooping into his eyelids and over his ears, made him appear partway between slob and rock-god.

I grew impatient. "You got any notes?"

Kenzie shook his head, the curls waving a millisecond behind. "I'm still not liking 'Mike,' for me."

"You'd prefer 'Marc?'"

"Obviously not, it's my actual name."

"Like anyone other than your parents knows you as 'Marc.' Even teachers call you 'Kenzie.'"

"Let me pick the pseudonym, something cool. How about 'Pete'?"

I snorted. "'Pete'? That's an old-man cool name. Like, 'Luke' or 'Clint.'"

"And 'Mike' is the straight-edge cop who busted Pete, Luke and Clint for fighting 'The Man.' You can't win this one Padi, so don't even try." He waited for me to give him a grudging laugh. Then, once again he hesitated. "Also, it's a little unconventional. For a crime pod."

I bristled, instantly on defense. "Yeah, cos that's my whole schtick. Remember the opening to *Who Killed Rich Wonders?* I don't just do crime; I do unsolved mysteries, too."

"Fair," he acknowledged. "Also – I probably wouldn't say 'clung tightly to his mother's hand.'"

"Dramatic license, obviously the audience knows I didn't actually see any of this with my own eyes."

"But you spoke to an eyewitness, yes? At least, it reads like you did."

"Yeah, the Grover-Dyson kids, Katie and Celine."

"Right. So the listener might think Katie and Celine saw Maxim 'cling tightly' to his mom. Which I cannot see. With my mind's eye, y'know? And I actually knew him."

Kenzie had a point. Maxim wasn't the clingy type. That part about him being scared of nothing and nobody? That was from me and it was true. I thought about defending 'clingy' for another minute but decided to drop it. Kenzie was usually right about stuff like this, which was why I asked him in the first place.

"Fine, I'll change that up. But otherwise?"

He gave a grudging nod. I've seen more enthusiasm over mandatory vaccines. Yet after a moment he said, "It's good. You're going to trail with this?"

"Yeah. Downloads on *Who Killed Rich Wonders?* just keep going up. Might as well use the attention."

"So you talked to the Grover-Dyson girls. Anyone

else?"

"Nope. I lucked out with them, obviously, since they're seniors at school. They saw everything *and* they were standing next to the Santiagos in the line. That's my next episode, right there."

"But after that?"

I spread my hands on the table at Starbucks. "Nada. Which is why I'm trailing *What Happened to the Santiagos?* for a month at least. With a pretty-please at the end. Hopefully someone else on line that day, or even just at the airport, will see it. A twelve-year-old kid and his mom don't just vanish, like smoke. Not even at Dulles."

"And if the pretty-please goes nowhere?"

I'd be burned, obviously. "Then I'm just another sixteen-year-old with a podcast. Who gives a damn if I fall on my face?"

Kenzie grinned, suddenly. "It was a good decision to stay anonymous."

"Pseudonymous, you mean. 'La Chica Curiosa.'"

"I'm pretty sure you need a normal-sounding name to be pseudonymous."

"Oh yeah, something like 'Roni McCurious'?"

We both laughed. Kenzie was incapable of inventing any name not in the 'FirstName McHilarious' format.

We recorded the trailer later that day, adding Kenzie's changes to the script. I managed the whole thing in one take. With the new mic I'd bought for 'Rich Wonders,' the sound was sharp as a tack, almost zero production needed. Basically, it was done pretty quickly. We didn't think too hard about it, at least I didn't. Just recorded, tweaked and dropped the podcast trailer all on the same night, along with the pretty-please at the end. It was identical to the one that worked so well for 'Rich Wonders,' asking listeners to come forward with thoughts, hints, reactions, theories, whatever. Afterward we went to Wendy's.

Thinking back, Kenzie was kind of quiet at Wendy's. Something was on his mind.

I guessed what it was, but didn't like to say. I was too excited about the new podcast, too eager to experience the rush, the excitement of 'Rich Wonders' all over again. I'd produced that series on a whim and it had done *great*. Kids at school had been talking about it for two weeks now and no sign of slowing up. More were getting on the bandwagon, catching up with binge-listens now that all six episodes were available. I was starting to see comments and downloads from all over the country.

Even so, Kenzie was worried. *What Happened to the Santiagos?* wasn't like 'Rich Wonders,' where basically the whole story was in the public domain. This mystery had the feel of *a can of worms*. Kenzie knew it, I did too.

I knew it when I sensed the jittering of my stomach, when I lay down to sleep. Knew it from the edginess I felt when I checked my phone the next morning and saw fifteen new messages on the podcast trailer. There was something different jangling around my nervous system that day, and it hadn't been there all the time I was dropping new episodes of 'Rich Wonders."

This time, there was fear. Palpable, honest-to-goodness, fear.

Humans have instincts that protect us, that's how come me and Kenzie and Maxim and *you* got to be alive, unlike all the humans that didn't make it to the 21st century. All those non-existent kids of historic humans that let the snake bite them, they didn't even get to be born. Their would-be ancestors lost the human race. But for our ancestors, yours and mine, a rustle in the grass was enough to make them high-tail it out of there. *Our* ancestors didn't wait to see if a poisonous reptile made those sounds, or just the wind. We're not descended from the ones who ignored the danger, who told themselves 'I'm sure everything's fine, probably.' No. We're descended from the ones who *listened* to that frisson of fear. That's why they lived long enough to tell the sorry tale on a cozy night, maybe to someone of the opposite sex, maybe enough to persuade them into making a baby. The kind of baby who'd grow up *paying attention*, when nerves came a-tingling.

Take it from me, we aren't descended from idiots like yours truly, who heard the tingle of fear loud and clear, who saw it in the eyes of a best friend – and just plain *ignored* it.

All of this to admit that what happened was my fault. La Chica Curiosa? A good nickname for me, as it turns out. We know what curiosity did to the cat. That should have been a hint to me, right there.

TWO

Nostalgia Hour

Our final International Baccalaureate exam finished at four in the afternoon. Most seniors were headed home. A lot of people went to after-parties, good if you were into that kind of thing, which I was not. All I wanted to talk about was my podcast, but with the whole pseudonymous thing, I'd have to pretend to be a listener - not, y'know, behind the whole thing. No way for me to be chatty without a) feeling like an idiot pretending to fangirl my own pod and b) being the type of idiot who fangirls their own pod.

Kenzie hung back waiting for me but I made an excuse and wandered. I didn't know exactly what I wanted or needed, just that inside of me was a feeling I didn't recognize; a kind of ache, a yearning. I didn't know for what. Maybe I just wasn't ready to graduate. Without parents or even any relatives to celebrate with me, was there any point?

I strolled the halls of D.C. International School, wandered past classrooms I'd sat inside ever since sixth grade. It was easy to remember why I'd chosen to stay at the school after my parents were gone. I'd been happy at D.C. Inter. I *was* happy. No complaints, other than losing my mom and dad at the height of the pandemic. What did Oscar Wilde say about losing both parents, something about it being careless? *That.* Careless of someone, definitely not me.

I lingered outside what had been our home room. The room where I'd laid my head on the table and sobbed, while the teacher cleared everyone else out and sat with me until I had no more tears. Just questions and the beginnings of fear as I finally allowed myself to ask a question that filled me with terror.

What's going to happen to me?

Had my folks dared to talk to me about how neatly they'd planned the post-them scenario, I'd have experienced less angst. Or not, I guess you can never know. Hence my lingering, that afternoon in the empty, eerily quiet hallway outside of my grade eight home room. I wanted *really* to remember how it'd been back then, how I'd felt when my parents were still around and I was just a regular teenager.

Up until now, I hadn't felt ready to go there. I'd refused therapy, told everyone I preferred to just 'get back to normal.' For some reason, my mind chose that post-exam, summer afternoon to begin to process feelings I hadn't dared to touch for two years. I felt close to tears, but not quite. They bubbled up behind my eyes, yet wouldn't flow. Moving through areas of the school I'd inhabited those days, I was able to walk things back in my mind and was drawn to the very room where I'd last really felt myself to be a child.

No, this isn't going to be one of those grim abuse memoirs, my story isn't in that league. Like I already wrote, it's not about what happened to me, it's about what I *made* happen, by being curious.

And it all began long before the horrible thing with my parents.

The room in question was a music rehearsal room, over in the primary years campus. A short bus ride separated the two campuses and there was a shuttle that teachers could use, which went a few times a day. I spotted the bus in the parking lot on my way out, so I hitched a ride.

The music department in the Georgetown campus had a couple of practice rooms. I'd been back a few times to the hall for concerts or plays, but hadn't returned for years to the main campus. This being late in summer and end-of-year concerts behind us, everywhere was silent apart from the sound of a soccer ball being kicked on the field behind the main buildings. It was as quiet then as during long-gone afternoons when Marc Mackenzie, Maxim Santiago and I used to practice in a sound-proofed room, playing on a baby grand piano, bass guitar and a drum kit.

My own kit now gathered dust in our attic, untouched for years. Revisiting the practice room that day I finally understood why I'd stopped playing. It'd happened almost immediately after Maxim's disappearance. To this day I don't get why we didn't figure it sooner, neither me or my parents. Why don't people ask the right questions when a sad thing happens? Is it because they're afraid of the answer?

But that day, after my final exams at the school, I was ready to revisit the scene of our childhood bliss. The summer break was close and the music practice rooms were empty. Even the elementary schoolers seemed to be running out of steam. Maxim Santiago wouldn't have given us the afternoon off – not for any reason.

It'd been June then too, a little earlier in the month. We'd been in the practice room every day for weeks – Maxim, Kenzie and me. Maxim could be patient or impatient, insistent or relaxed, but he always knew exactly what to say to get us back in the room. Even when we were bored of the whole thing. Let's face it, what twelve-year-old wants to rehearse *the same tune* every day for six weeks?

Thinking about it, there probably are kids like that, but I'd expect to find them in music schools, which D.C. International was not. Maxim should have gone to a school like that. Instead he glommed onto Kenzie and me and pretty much forced us to help him realize his ambition of having a jazz trio. Which is another thing no normal twelve-year-old does, but we've already established that Maxim wasn't ordinary.

It wasn't just Maxim's crazy persuasion skills that brought me and Kenzie back to that room every day. We *wanted* to be there. Playing that music together had a hold on us that I didn't understand at the time, playing *The Forgotten Village*.

Alone in the room that afternoon, I sat down at the piano, placed my hands on the keyboard and closed my eyes. Pictured Maxim there, twelve years old and already the most intense, focused person I ever met. All that mattered to him in those weeks was getting us to sound perfect. Not an easy thing for two mediocre, twelve-year old musicians like me and Kenzie.

Maxim on the other hand, was already a brilliant pianist. The principal would wheel him out to entertain parents, carers and the school board, playing Mozart, Scarlatti and Satie. When we played in the trio with Maxim, even Kenzie and I managed to play well. It felt *incredible* to sound that good, the sensation got into my bones and radiated out all the way to my fingertips, so that every piece of the drumkit seemed in some way connected with me.

Yet that wasn't why we kept showing up to rehearse. It was the music itself. There was something haunting about that tune. I noticed it the first time Maxim played it for us with nothing but a metronome to accompany him. A forgotten melody about a forgotten place, like something buried just under the skin for years, that begins suddenly to itch. We just had to scratch. The opening bars of that music were like a gateway. When you entered, you forgot everything. You were just there, inside all that was forgotten. A memory that you could only cling to when you were within that space. Once the notes faded, so did the feeling, so did the memory. Might as well try to hang on to a dream.

Standing in the empty practice room I selected the same tune on my phone, the original version, plugged in the earbuds and listened. Tears began to flow. Tears for everything we lost when we lost Maxim. Tears for my lost parents. *Finally*. I welcomed them, listened to the piece three or four times, allowing all that sadness to spill out.

Gradually, I became aware of someone else in the room; Marc Mackenzie. I tugged on my earbuds. Was he following me?

He smiled, a little sadly. "I guessed you'd be here. Maxim Santiago, hey? Still talking us into coming back here."

I laughed, wiping tears and feeling a little ridiculous. "I… I don't know why, but I just had this weird feeling of… *nostalgia*."

Kenzie crossed the room to the drum kit. He touched the high-hat lightly, as if to check it was real. "I think it's your podcast trailer. You got me thinking about Maxim. About that time when we thought we were a jazz trio."

"Well, we kind of *were* a jazz trio."

He grinned. "Yeah. We were pretty awesome, for twelve-year-olds."

"We only played one song – *The Forgotten Village*. So I'm not sure that counts as 'good.'"

Kenzie chuckled, then imitating Maxim he complained, "'You lazy jerks! I was stuck on *Twinkle Variations* for five weeks when I started violin! We don't leave until you get it right!'"

We both burst into laughter. "Omigod. Do you remember? He wouldn't shut up about his Suzuki violin training."

"Yeah, like, 'dude, don't blame us if your teacher

was basically OCD.'"

Laughter felt wonderful after my tears. Optimism surged, relief flooded through me. I wanted to grab Kenzie's hand, to hug him tight. But I was careful about stuff like that, for so many reasons *other* than that we lived under the same roof. We'd stayed best friends for years by not crossing any lines. I was eighty-five percent certain Kenzie wasn't into me, saw me as a buddy, the way I saw him. The unknown fifteen percent, however, made me cautious. The last thing I wanted was to hurt my best friend. And fifteen percent is non-trivial. I knew I had to take care not to push him away, but also not to give him the wrong idea.

It was something of a high-wire situation. A lot of people at school assumed we were a couple. We were both aware. Sometimes we had to deny it, which was also something I did *very* carefully. In general it wasn't the easiest, being besties with a cis, straight boy. So many questions. Ugh.

"You came back here out of pure nostalgia," he mused. "You sure about that?"

"Yeah. I was feeling kind of *blah* after the finals. End-of-an-era-ish."

Kenzie stuck his hands in the pockets of his jacket. "Yeah. Hard to believe it but I'll actually miss this place. Is that why you came back here?"

I hesitated. "I wanted to remember our time in this room."

He waited, eyes brimming, expectant, empathic.

"I guess I'm realizing now that everything changed after Maxim disappeared."

He became thoughtful. "I guess it did. What a selfish dick, getting himself abducted, and all."

I had to smile at that. "You and me, we just stopped playing music. Did you ever wonder why?"

He acted uneasy, again. We were near dangerous

ground.

"Maybe that's why I wanted to make the podcast," I suggested.

Kenzie looked straight at me. "Maybe you shouldn't."

"Why not?"

He didn't have an answer for that. I think for Kenzie it was just a feeling, something formless, frictionless, impossible to name. For me, however, it *had* a name: the song title that had popped up, out of the blue, in one of the fifteen private messages I'd received since dropping the trailer for *What Happened to the Santiagos?* The name of the song we'd played as a trio. The only song, as Kenzie had reminded me.

"Remember *The Forgotten Village?*" It was the only message I received that was anonymous. Whoever sent it, they weren't yet ready to show their cards.

THREE

THE FORGOTTEN VILLAGE

In fact, I actually *had* managed to forget *The Forgotten Village*. At least, until I got the idea to produce *What Happened to the Santiagos*. Then, of course I remembered.

It was the tune that brought us together; Kenzie, Maxim and me. Before that, to me and Kenzie, Maxim was just 'Maxim Santiago,' the most famous boy in school, always top in every class, a natural athlete, a kid who oozed such confidence that no-one could believe he was so young. Good-looking, obviously, like all the popular kids. Light-brown-skinned and bronze-blond hair, with a steady gaze from his dark brown eyes.

Maxim was famous and everyone admired him, but in terms of friends he really had none, only kids that lined up to befriend him because he was so cool. These were closer to colleagues; other kids who could help him achieve some goal, like when he created a Jai-Alai team that he got tired of after six months, or to perform a play he'd written and talked a teacher into producing. All this before he turned eleven. *Of course* he was school-famous.

In fifth grade Maxim discovered a new obsession – jazz. Who knows why – he didn't tell us things like that, rarely talked about anything personal. The music department had started up a rock school program across both campuses, putting kids together in six different bands. Everyone was pleasantly surprised to see Maxim show up. Everyone knew he could play like a dream, but at school events he played difficult and strictly classical piano. Suddenly he wanted to be in a band with two dopes like Kenzie and me? Very odd. Yet that's what happened. Then suddenly it wasn't a rock band but a jazz trio. Kenzie and I weren't eager but Maxim persuaded the teacher to basically force us. Persuasion was kind of his thing.

From that day we met every afternoon to rehearse. Literally. Weekdays at school, weekends at Maxim's house. Those weekends, we shifted from being two kids who played in Maxim's band, to being his friends. Met his mom, Masha. Played video games with him, hung out for hours after practice. Two goofballs and the coolest kid in school, who under all that veneer of diffident over-achievement turned out to be just another goofball.

The Forgotten Village by Shai Maestro is a simple enough tune. No fancy runs on the keyboard, although Maxim could do those when needed. The bass and drums just pulse away underneath the main tune on the piano. It took us three weeks to get through the piece without making any mistakes. After that, it was all about getting the mood, the vibe. The tune had a way of casting a spell. The very first to be enchanted were the musicians.

I'd barely thought about that tune since Maxim went. Then, the afternoon after our final exam, a message on the podcast trailer – 'Remember *The Forgotten Village?*' – drew me back to our old practice room.

Who'd sent that message? So far as I knew, only me, Maxim, Kenzie and possibly our parents, (not that they paid much attention to it) knew about *The Forgotten Village*. We hadn't played it in front of anyone yet. Maxim didn't want anyone to hear us until it was 'just right.' This included our music teachers.

Whoever sent the message knew Maxim *personally* – that was for sure. Knew him, knew the name of the tune we'd rehearsed so hard.

When Kenzie showed up a few minutes behind me at the Georgetown campus music department, I instantly assumed *he* was the sender of the message. I asked him right away.

He looked puzzled. "You got a message… about *The Forgotten Village*?"

I gave him a moment to admit he was playing games, but nothing. The expression on his face should have been enough for me. Kenzie was as taken aback as I'd been. We both understood that only someone who knew Maxim extremely well would send that message. If not Kenzie then, who?

We talked about that all the way back home to his moms' house in Falls Church. Zara, his work-from-home mom, a psychotherapist from Chile, opened the front door. She seemed anxious at how late we were. When we walked into the kitchen we understood why. The moment he opened the door a chorus of 'Surprise' rang out.

Kenzie seemed genuinely shocked at the kids' party set out in the kitchen; a table laid with mini sandwiches, pizza, bowls of chips, cans of soda and a blue-frosted sponge-cake with 'Goodbye High School' spelled out in white icing. Sitting around the table were his other four friends. They were a nice bunch, all kind of nerdy, into board games and such. I liked them all. They had on party hats. Balloons had floated up to the ceiling. There was a banner made by his moms, with the inscription – 'SCHOOL'S OUT!'

"It's *ironic*," Zara insisted, like it was only now hitting her that laying on a kids' party for seventeen-year-olds was kind of bizarre.

Kenzie grabbed a paper plate and loaded it with sandwiches and a slice of pizza. He pulled a dippy grin. His friends – I won't name them, they don't appear again in this tale of awful stuff that happened because I poked my nose where it wasn't wanted – looked relieved and started piling their own plates. Zara put on some music and the party began.

I gave in to the festive spirit. After an hour, Bobbie, his work-at-school mom showed up and the wine came out. They let us have a glass, too. It was kind of cool. I like Kenzie's moms, and not only because they invited me to live with them after I was left alone, which saved me from a random foster home. There was a South American vibe in the house, which made it extra-comfy for me. Even though I never lived in Mexico, I always *felt* Latina and yeah, I speak Spanish. Theirs was 30:70 a Spanglish household.

Later after everyone had left me and Kenzie thanked Bobbie and Zara for the party. His moms had planned it so meticulously that we almost didn't come home to enjoy it, that's how little we suspected. When we wanted to go to bed at nine, Kenzie's moms came over as a tad curious. Perhaps they thought this was finally the night we would make a move on each other or whatever.

Hopefully not. Hopefully, by now you've guessed that Kenzie and I were eager to get back to the subject of what happened to the Santiagos and specifically, who sent me that message about *The Forgotten Village*, something that meant so very much to us and Maxim. Something that only an insider would know.

We changed into pjs and reconvened in Kenzie's room, which was farthest from his moms. He'd thoughtfully brought up two more slices of chocolate cake but didn't touch his. Over the next few hours we tried to figure out:
❖   Who sent the message
❖   What to include in the second episode (I already had an outline for the first)

The 'who' of it finally came down to Mr. Garibaldi, the teacher that used to run the rock school. Even though Maxim hadn't allowed anyone in the room when we played, we figured that he might at least have told Garibaldi what we were playing. This seemed like the most innocent possibility.

We agreed it would be kind of creepy for any sender of a friendly message not to sign their name. Who knows, maybe Garibaldi forgot? Apart from him there were no 'innocent' possibilities other than Bobbie and Zara. My folks weren't exactly in a position to send secret Internet messages, and Bobbie and Zara, well, they just wouldn't do a weird thing like that. Our remaining options were between someone who had gotten to know Maxim *after* he disappeared, or Masha, or Maxim himself.

I think that's when I got fully committed to the mystery. Was it possible that Maxim was reaching out, sending out a call for help?

We tracked down Garibaldi – an unusual enough name for a music teacher. We located his new school in Maryland. I emailed him from the podcast account to ask if he'd sent me a message about Maxim.

My phone pinged two minutes later. Garibaldi had responded right away.

Hello, of course I remember Maxim Santiago. And it's great to hear from you too, Veronica! It remains a regret to this day that we never got to witness what I was repeatedly assured by Maxim would be the 'best damn jazz trio' the school would ever see. Such a pity that he and his mother left like that, without telling anyone. But I'm afraid that where it comes to your mysterious interlocutor on the podcast, I'm not your man. I didn't even know you had a podcast. I'll be sure to listen to your podcast trailer about Maxim, and also the other one that I can see has so many listeners. Many congratulations on your burgeoning career in the media, may you go from strength to strength!

Kind regards, Paul Garibaldi.

"Garibaldi didn't send the anon message," Kenzie concluded.

"Are you sure? He replied pretty quickly... And 'what I was repeatedly assured' strikes me as a teentsy bit snarky..."

"Agreed – he's totally dissing us there. But why would he lie about not sending the message? He seems genuinely clueless."

We agreed that Garibaldi wasn't our guy. Which left Maxim and Masha.

"Or some rando we know nothing about, who Maxim or Masha talked to."

I shook my head. "Some 'rando' wouldn't know how important that song was to me. Think about it. To anyone who isn't me, *The Forgotten Village* is meaningless."

"So?"

"So, now we know. The sender *knows* we played that tune with Maxim. Which means they've figured out who I am. They know that 'La Chica Curiosa' is Roni Padilla."

Kenzie propped himself up on his forearms, looking down from his bed towards where I sat cross-legged on the floor. "Ooh. Busted!"

Going Dark

A little way back in this account of what happened, I mentioned how we're mostly evolved from hyper-suspicious, pre-human types, remember? The type who didn't stop to check whether the grass rustled because of a poisonous snake or from the wind. Well, that's one of the things I learned from Maxim Santiago.

He had a lot of interests, knew more about almost everything than any kid I ever met. Evolution was something he talked about a lot. He seemed to know a ton about it, far beyond what we'd been taught in school. He liked to get into arguments with the religious kids, which did not go down well with teachers. They were afraid of upsetting parents and carers, some of whom would get antsy if teachers spoke up about a whole bunch of topics.

But Maxim wasn't afraid to talk about science. He'd look anyone right in the eye and speak very plainly and directly. Even if a belligerent parent showed up afterward, red-cheeked and yelling, after a moment with Maxim they'd walk away, smooth and steady. I don't know how he did it.

When I first heard him tell that story about our hyper-suspicious ancestors, he was replying to another kid who declared that humans were designed to believe in God. I didn't exactly understand the point Maxim was making, so later in the lunch line I asked him to explain. Before replying he observed me for a few seconds, peered real close, as if to determine whether I was another religious kid hankering for an argument. I wasn't, yet for some reason the longer he looked at me, the more suspicious he seemed, until his suspicion morphed into surprise.

"What's wrong?" I said, uneasily. "I'm not even supposed to ask you to explain?"

Then I saw something I never saw again from Maxim. He seemed flustered and at a loss for words. Yeah. If you're thinking 'like he was love-struck' you'd be right. That is *exactly* how he looked.

No boy had ever looked at me that way. I was eleven, close to turning twelve. Definitely the first time, but not the last. So far, so normal, right? Twelve-year-olds can totally feel the first stirrings of a crush. No-one is immune, not even cool, super-smart guys like Maxim.

But this isn't a story about how me and a boy fell for each other when we were twelve. Because that isn't what happened. Maxim *had not* fallen for me. He simply *acted* like he had, for a brief moment in the lunch line.

I didn't imagine it. It was as though I could hear his heart pounding, inches away from mine. As though I could feel the tremor that went through him, because when it was done flowing through him, it jumped across the air between us and surged through me. And then, as suddenly as it had begun, the sensation vanished.

His eyes went back to normal and he answered my question. Normally. "We evolved from human ancestors who saw patterns and meaning in everything. Even when there was nothing there, like the non-existent snake in that story."

I still didn't understand so he tried again.

"We see patterns and meanings in weird stuff, but that doesn't mean there's really anything there. We invent gods and suchlike to explain the unexplained, not because we're designed to 'believe' but because we can't help it."

Remember, we were *twelve*. This was the smartest and most insightful thing I'd heard any kid say, ever, and as *finally* I understood what he was saying, I was in awe. "So… thinking that way is what kept our ancestors alive?"

He grinned, delighted. "Right! Exactly." Then abruptly he asked, "Is it true you play drums?" He pointed across the canteen to the music teacher, Mr. Garibaldi who was seated facing us with two other teachers at their table. "I asked Garibaldi if he knew any drummers, he said you did. You're Veronica Padilla, yeah?"

The sudden swerve caught me by surprise. "Yeah, I am."

"Okay if I call you Padi?"

I didn't know what to say so I probably nodded and that's where *Padi* began.

Maxim asked me if I knew any bassists, I mentioned Marc Mackenzie and he grinned. "Padi and Kenzie. Good jazz names."

"Huh…? I mean, I *guess*…"

Before I knew what happened Maxim was talking me into joining his band. A jazz band! If that sounds odd to you now, then you're close to understanding how strange it seemed to me that day. And yet there I was, nodding and going along as if the previous two minutes hadn't happened. If something like that happened today, I'd be more wary. I would assume the whole thing was a scheme to get to date me without risking being rejected. But I was twelve and not yet wary of rizz, Which is how come I ended up agreeing to be in Maxim's band.

The following morning, after our trip down memory lane and the surprise party, Kenzie and I were on the school bus. I asked him something I'd been musing over all night.

"Was it weird yesterday? That I would do something so nostalgic?"

"Not at all. Why?"

"Cause we're only seventeen. Nostalgia is for, y'know, old people."

Kenzie thought it over and replied, "Nah. I get nostalgic all the time. The top shelf of my closet is full of Playmobil and Legos and old game consoles. Not because I'm collecting them but because I can't stand to get rid. All the memories."

"Like Andy in *Toy Story 3*."

"Uh-huh. That's why I followed you to the primary campus, yesterday." (Primary school being international school lingo for elementary school.)

"You felt it, too?"

He nodded. "Like I said, it's your podcast. Really takes me back. Those were good times. It felt like something ended when Maxim left."

"When he *disappeared*, you mean."

We sat in silence, facing the window as we crossed the Potomac at the Francis Scott Key Memorial bridge. Two rowing eights were racing, almost neck and neck as they passed beneath, the boats slicing neat lines in the smooth, silver surface of the water.

I examined Kenzie's face as it turned away from mine, his eyes following the eights. His jaw was squaring up, the last traces of puppy-fat melting away. His shoulders were broadening and he'd lost a lot of weight, probably from the long bike rides he did a few times a week to unwind.

Kenzie was my brother-from-another-mother, so I didn't think there was anything odd about checking him out while he wasn't watching, but that day I was taken aback at how abruptly he'd stopped looking like a kid. How come I hadn't noticed before? Then I wondered if *he* ever checked *me* out like that, and I looked away. On second thoughts, maybe it *was* a little weird.

"Y'know," he mused, "I could try searching the dark web for leads about the Santiagos. Maybe we can find out who sent that message about *The Forgotten Village*."

I had not even the tiniest idea what he was talking about or how any of that information might be on the dark web. "Or I could just message them back and ask."

"Sure, but right now the sender has the advantage. They know who *you* are but you still don't know who *they* are."

"Are you saying they might lie?"

"Yep. Especially if they had something to do with Maxim and Masha's disappearance."

The possibility had occurred to me, but I didn't take it all that seriously. "Then why would whoever-it-is risk blowing their cover?"

Kenzie shrugged his shoulders. "Could be anything. Maybe for the lulz. Or maybe they want to shut down your mystery pod. Why did you get into this anyhow, Padi? Didn't you figure that maybe there was something sketchy about what happened to the Santiagos? You never wondered if there'd be folks who didn't want the whole drama getting dredged up again?"

I had not. It all happened five years ago. I'd presumed that the cops had stopped investigating the Santiagos' disappearance for a good reason. Honestly, I thought the case was *cold*.

"I can't stop now," I mumbled. "I mean, I trailed it and all. Plus the Grover-Dysons gave me such great interviews. Also, isn't it good that I got the message? It's a lead, right?"

"Maybe. Only if whoever sent the message isn't

trolling you. You could try to get ahead of that, maybe. Especially if I can find something about them on the dark web."

At this stage in our conversation, Kenzie had to explain the dark web. I assumed it was the name of a website. You who're reading this are almost certainly smarter than me and know that it's a lot more than one website – it's a network of computers that don't get indexed by search engines, a network that you can access anonymously via special software. Unlike searching the open internet, which leaves a blazing trail, basically 'Padi was here' over every site I'd clicked.

Kenzie had by then been dipping into the whole 'hacker space' for several months. He'd been inspired by the Anonymous and LulzSec efforts against the Third Russian Empire, ever since the European invasions began. Half the planet was horrified by what was going on and either raising money for refugees or actually hosting one. The other half was waiting to see who won the war. The Third Russian Empire had tendrils everywhere and a lot of folk were happy to play nice with the Czar, if it kept the oil and gas flowing.

Kenzie went a step further, is all. I don't know which citizen cyber-group he'd joined or whether it was all talk. But his cyber-hackery was the main reason why despite living in the same house, we hardly spent time together. Lately especially, he'd had his head down pretty hard in some new project, something I guessed to be very secret. I wasn't sure it his moms realized, but I had noticed that he'd become super-evasive on the entire topic. So we'd lived separate lives for most of the year – until I started my podcast. Then, for the first time since Maxim's jazz trio we had an interest in common – the uncovering of hidden information. That I agreed to his offer should in no way be taken as an indication that I understood *any* part of what Kenzie was doing or how dangerous it might be.

In fact I did not, because – well, I refer you to my previous statements re curiosity. And for now you can relax, because as I keep pointing out, this story is about things that happened because of what I chose to investigate, not Kenzie. We'll just put a pin in the Kenzie thing, for now.

FIVE

DRAWER

The next day was a Saturday. I woke up late after a difficult night with a lot on my mind. Kenzie had already left the house. Bobbie and Zara didn't know where he'd gone. They assumed I did. I had to tell them 'not a clue.' I checked my phone, sure he'd have left a message. But nothing. A little irritated, I sent him a snippy message: **???**

The next hour passed quietly. I ate Cinnamon Grahams, showered and dressed, while checking my phone every couple minutes. The message I'd sent Kenzie didn't even register as read. I could see that he'd used the app a few minutes earlier. He'd almost certainly seen my message but evidently wasn't bothering to go into our message thread. Now I was even more annoyed.

Two hours passed. He was definitely ignoring me. I wracked my brain for any reason he'd do that. Maybe he'd met a girl. Or a boy, someone, a friend, and he'd taken off with them. Maybe it had something to do with his possibly secret, possibly dangerous and illegal cyber project. Or maybe he was on a date and too embarrassed to mention it. Bobbie and Zara decided to go with that theory. Obviously I didn't offer up mine. He was also ignoring their messages. They acted like they found it amusing but I noted some tension in Bobbie's jaw as she tried to laugh it off. I made a conscious effort to ignore my phone and instead worked on the script for the second episode of the podcast.

May 29th was uncharacteristically cool that year. Maxim and his mom had on light winter jackets over their T-shirts and wore jeans and hiking boots. In the line behind them, Celine Grover-Dyson recognized Maxim from D.C. International. She'd moved to the senior school by then but remembered the serious-faced young boy with the faux-hawk haircut, who'd entertained parents at her graduation ceremony. From the look of their clothing, she guessed the Santiagos were bound for a cold-weather location.

"I asked them if they were headed for the Rockies. Maxim's mom seemed kind of put out to see me there. It wasn't an official school vacation; my dad had to beg the principal to let us have the time off, which is why I assumed his mom was also embarrassed about taking him out of school. She hand-waved my question and asked if I liked to ski. Then we were talking about skiing. Maxim didn't say a word. They both kept eyeing the window up ahead, where border guards were checking documents. It was taking a long time. People in the line were getting impatient. You could hear muttering like 'what the heck is going on?'"

That's when Celine began to wonder – were the border guards searching for someone in particular? When Maxim and his mother finally arrived at the window, it seemed to confirm Celine's suspicions, because the guard emerged from a cubicle up on the dais and stepped out, leading Maxim and Masha away.

"They marched the Santiagos past the line, back into the main concourse. Everyone went quiet. I tried to smile at Maxim as he passed me. That's when I saw that the color had totally drained from his face. He didn't look back at me. I don't think he even saw us."

The Santiagos followed the border guard like docile lambs in shock. They rounded the corner and disappeared from view. Where did they go next? Were you in Dulles Airport that day, between eight and nine in the morning? Perhaps you saw Maxim and Masha Santiago? Message me please! Let's talk about what happened to the Santiagos.

I stopped writing and messaged Kenzie again.

Hey, where u at? Working on ep2 script, would love your feedback.

I waited. Nothing. The messaging app said he'd last been seen thirty minutes ago. He was checking in occasionally, but not replying to me. I went downstairs, took an apple from the fridge, chopped it into four pieces and put them on a plate. Kenzie's moms always prepared fruit for us, they did a lot of cute things like that, things my parents never had time to do.

From the day they put me in full-time daycare when I was six-months-old, both my parents worked flat out. Evenings and weekends we often had fun, don't get me wrong, and I loved my kindergarten and school but thinking back I realize that they were always tired, always trying to catch their breath. Only when I saw the different parenting style for people that don't work round the clock, did I notice what I'd missed. Plates of prepared fruit, for example.

I took my plate of apple wedges into our back yard to enjoy, feet up on the deck's rattan furniture. Zara was there too, with a paperback. She gave me a pleasant smile. "What a good idea."

I offered her the apple plate. "Kenzie's still ignoring me."

Zara took the nearest piece and took a delicate bite before replying, "Yes, us too."

"Still think he's on a date?"

"Breakfast was over a while ago. Maybe he's gone to the neighborhood library."

I couldn't think of a single reason he'd do that. The school library was perfectly good enough for our school work or general reading. Not that Kenzie had actually read a book all the way through for years.

"Why would he?"

"Didn't he say something about the library?" Zara frowned. "I feel like he might have."

"When he walked out?"

"Mm-hm. Yes. Definitely. The library."

"So you talked to him?"

"Not really." She paused. "I think Bobbie might be worried. She does that."

"And you're not?"

"Not if he's gone to the library."

I picked up a wedge of apple and set down the plate beside her. "I'll go check."

On the way over to the neighborhood library I thought about what Kenzie had said the night before. He'd intended to hunt for clues about the anonymous sender of the Forgotten Village message. I'd gone ahead with my own idea and replied to the sender with:

Hi, thanks. Would you mind introducing yourself?

So far no reply.

"I'll get ahold of the logs of your podcast host and look at the IP addresses," Kenzie had told me. "Then I'll try a reverse IP-lookup. Might lead to an actual address if we're lucky."

At the time of hearing, this made as much sense to me as white noise. It's only much later that I understood what he was actually trying to do. Hopefully I've learned enough to explain here. I guess we'll see.

So, here it is. Kenzie had confessed that what he planned to do wasn't strictly kosher. Hence the need to source some of the info on the dark web. Don't ask me exactly how it works, something to do with buying data from hackers and paying them with cryptocurrency. I knew Kenzie owned crypto of one flavor or another but not the foggiest idea how much. Later I found out. Oh. My. God. Has the world gone insane? I guess that's another story.

Had Kenzie gone to the library to access the Internet so that his IP address at home wouldn't be detected? That's the theory I went with and frankly it calmed me on my bike ride, all the way to the library. But as some readers will already know, turns out you can hide your IP address by using something called a Virtual Private Network, something that Kenzie would obviously know. He didn't need to leave the house to hide his IP address. Neither did whoever left the message on my podcast. The IT guy at the neighborhood library told me all this while I was searching for Kenzie.

Because as you've probably guessed, he *was* not and *had* not been there.

By now I was worried. Sick-to-the-stomach and drained-in-the-face worried. Apple chunks stirred in the pit of my belly, the burn of acid in my throat. A creeping sensation was rounding on me, as if I were wandering a winding alley somewhere far from home and expecting to stumble upon something that had been waiting for me for a long time. An unopened letter in a forgotten drawer.

Beneath me, the bicycle wobbled. I sailed through a red light. A car's screeching brakes jolted me to my senses. I hardly noticed the furious yelling that followed me as shakily, I climbed off the bike and pushed it to the sidewalk, my whole body shivering.

Even through that fog of dread a tiny part of me recognized that this was too much. I had no rational reason to be so scared, at least not yet. It hadn't even been six hours. You can only fight your own mind if you understand that it's tricking you. I didn't know it yet but I was sinking fast into that fog.

Bobbie saw me come through the front door and knew immediately that I wasn't okay. I was sobbing, barely able to communicate through desperate gulps for air.

"He's… not there. Something's… happened to him. I… I know… Something bad."

SIX

THE RUSSIAN HOUSE

At this time you might want to prepare for an anti-climax, because of course Kenzie eventually showed up. The stress-level of this story only gets worse. If back then I'd known by how much, I'd have made an effort to be more chill.

Bobbie and Zara got me through the next few hours, during which I had some kind of minor breakdown. It didn't take therapy for me to understand why. Behind all those dark thoughts about Kenzie and what might have happened to him, lurked a memory I'd worked hard to avoid.

The memory was of an afternoon two years ago when I'd been called to the principal's office. Bad news, he told me. Things weren't looking good for my mother and father. "You should probably prepare yourself for the worst."

It's not something I want to dwell over. I dealt with it, somehow. Not as well as I thought, perhaps. Which is why I won't be talking about it.

Kenzie evidently has a sadistic streak that made him enjoy the thought of me and his moms suffering for a day, waiting for him to reply to our messages. He claims that he forgot, got stuck in his research and lost track of time. I don't know. Who goes hours without responding to messages from people who are obviously crazy-worried about them? Anyhow, that was the tale told by his wide-eyed-innocent expression, when a couple hours later he sailed through the door. *Forgetfulness.*

I was cried-out by then. Couldn't face him. It took

an intervention from Bobbie and Zara to get me to sit down opposite Kenzie and agree to listen to his excuses.

He shook his head, vehemently. "Oh no, I didn't go to the neighborhood library. I was at the Library of *Congress*."

Then followed five minutes of four-way yelling about why he hadn't bothered to mention that tiny, yet important detail. After that came his account of everything that happened after he got the idea to hack the IP address of my anonymous message-sender.

"I got an early start this morning, while everyone was asleep. Someone in Turkey had dropped me a file with the database I was searching for. It's a log of traffic to your podcast host."

"Someone in Turkey, meaning a professional hacker? That doesn't sound particularly legal," Bobbie said, clearly anxious.

Kenzie looked shifty for a second then dodged the issue, continuing; "I was able to get the IP address they used, based on the timestamp of the message. I did a reverse lookup and traced it to a coffee shop in Russia."

"Russia?!" Obviously, I was a tad alarmed. All you heard those days was Russia this, Russia that, and usually scary stuff.

"Don't freak out. Russia is almost certainly *not* their actual location. Coffee shops are often used in VPNs to bounce a signal so that it can't be traced. In fact, I would bet all my remaining crypto that whoever posted this isn't in Russia. But…" He paused. "On a whim I looked up the address. It's not just any old coffee shop, it's inside a museum. In Perm, Siberia. A historic old house, the Elena Atlas House. I cross-referenced all the other databases I have with website analytics and found that same IP address was used to access three other websites. All of them businesses in Mexico City."

"You're saying that whoever sent me that message is in Mexico City?" It didn't make a lot of sense to me. As an afterthought I added, "What kind of businesses?"

"Just, y'know, nothing special. A tamale restaurant. A spa. And a hotel."

"So the sender was in one of those places, and bounced their signal from a coffee shop in Siberia?"

He nodded. "Most likely. Can't believe there'd be many Mexicans in Siberia. And obviously, not many Russians in Siberia order piping hot tamales from a restaurant in Mexico City. Whereas a VPN makes a lot more sense. It's masking the sender's true location, which is in Mexico City."

"Why?"

"My guess? There's a VPN network node that this person – or persons – in Mexico City is using to mask their real IP address when they access the Internet."

I repeated, "Why?"

His eyes became animated. Even Bobbie and Zara seemed to be interested. "Why hide his IP address? For privacy. I do it all the time. This stuff is interesting, am I right?"

We murmured our general agreement. Kenzie grinned and ran one hand through his red curls, evidently enjoying the attention.

"That's why I went to the Library of Congress. I did a search and found a collection of photos there, including of buildings in Russia. You can only see a high-resolution images if you physically search from inside the library. Well, I went to check it out."

"To see a high-res version?"

From under the table he pulled a brown manila envelope. I sensed the tension in the room as he plucked out four 8 by 10 inch color photos of what appeared to be a gingerbread house made from three different types of wood. The roof and window frames were made from a dark, gingerbread-brown wood, the front and sides were paneled in a pale, coffee-colored wood and the decoration was all in a pale wood, almost white. The eaves and window cornices were intricately carved, very ornate. Each photo showed a different side of the house. It was situated on the corner of a street in Perm and looked to be pretty large, maybe like a six-bedroom house. The only sign that it was a museum was a metal plate to the right of the front door, a three-dimensional portrait of a woman dressed in a Russian fur hat, a style I'd describe as 'benevolent.' The kind of woman who'd donate her house, I imagine.

"Elena Atlas, I presume?"

Kenzie nodded and tapped a finger to the photo. "That's why I wanted a hi-res image. I could see there was something there on the digital photo, but it wasn't clear."

He handed me the photo. In tiny writing below the outline of the woman's face was the inscription 'Elena Arkadyevna Atlas."

Bobbie cleared her throat. "And the relevance to the disappearance of Maxim and Masha Santiago?"

"Apart from that they all have Russian first names? Who knows?"

I gave him a hard-but-friendly shove. "Get outta here!"

Kenzie beamed. He was right, we were onto something.

"Maxim and Masha have *Russian* names," I repeated. "How did we miss that?"

Zara stood up, sighing. "I can't really see how this is progress, but I'm glad to see you two are friends again." She left to make dinner. Bobbie also made an excuse and left us to what she referred to as our 'scavenger hunt.'"

"Maybe Masha got deported to Mexico City," I suggested. "Because she's a Russian spy. That's it, that's the answer."

"Jump to conclusions, much?"

"Hey!" I frowned. "It's a working theory. Mexico's full of Russian spies. It's, like, Spy Central for Chekists. Everyone knows that."

"Do they, though?"

I stuck out my tongue. "Google it. Plus, their second name is 'Santiago.' So they're *Chilean* Russian spies. Working out of Mexico. Totally makes sense."

His nose crinkled in ridicule. "What? Now you're just stringing the names of countries and cities together. And why Chilean? There's a Santiago in Spain and I'm pretty sure there's another in Cuba."

"Cuba? Even better. *Cuban*-Russian spies makes a lot more sense. Mmm, how 'bout this: if Masha's a spy then she'd have a cover identity. 'Santiago' wouldn't be their real name."

"What would a Russian spy be doing in D.C. working as a translator of children's books?"

"Exactly," I said. "Why would a translator of kids' books live in DC? Doesn't make an ounce of sense. Unless Masha was an 'illegal,' like in that TV show about the deep-undercover Russian spies."

"What TV show?" he said, looking confused and irritated.

"*The Americans*. I watched the whole thing with your moms. About Russian undercover spies in the 1980s. They live in Falls Church too, it's pretty neat."

His eyes rolled. "Okay boomer, whatever."

"Your moms are Gen X," I countered, with a haughty blink. "And on my theory Masha was an 'illegal.' Until her cover got blown and she got deported. Poor Maxim."

"Not that it isn't a fun theory," Kenzie admitted. "But the truth is probably way simpler and less exciting. Like, maybe Masha lived in D.C. because of Maxim's dad. And maybe said dad heard she was leaving town and put out a stop on his passport."

"Can you even do that?"

"Oh yeah," he said. "It's called an 'ATRO.' A parent can stop the other parent from leaving the state with their kid. Bobbie did it to her first wife, Nadine."

I was stunned. "Wait, what? You never told me that."

Kenzie began carefully to replace the photos of Elena Atlas House in the envelope. He nodded towards the kitchen, from where we could hear his moms chatting as they cooked dinner. Quietly he continued, "I don't like to bring it up. But yeah. When Nadine did that they were already divorced, I was spending time with both. She went ballistic when she found out about Zara, tried to take me to Baltimore."

"Whoa. How come you never said anything?"

He shrugged. "Nadine died when I was five, so…"

"Dude! What else haven't you told me?"

The look he flashed me then made me snap my mouth shut pretty quick. Kenzie was right; he didn't owe me a story that could still hurt him.

I thought of him a little differently after that. I'd been assuming Kenzie had what I didn't – a history of a blissful childhood with two happy parents, no sadness or loss in his past. In fact, I overlooked quite a few things about him, even though we grew up close. Some things can be so in-your-face that you become blind to them.

SEVEN

LOCKED ROOM MYSTERY

Apart from the embarrassing glitch caused by me losing it a bit when Kenzie went AWOL for most of a day, I was having a blast making *What Happened to the Santiagos*. It'd helped me and Kenzie to reconnect with good times in our childhoods, memories we'd suppressed because of the association with Maxim's disappearance. Now that we were talking about it every day, we were both finding it easier to process whatever it was we felt about him vanishing.

Hey-ho, maybe there's something to therapy after all. (Still not going to see a counsellor about my parents. Thank you for your concern.)

Moreover, with the Russia-Mexico connection and my undercover spy theory, it seemed like the mystery had launched. Who can resist a Cold War conspiracy? Not me. So what happened next was a curveball that came out of left field on my blind side and knocked me sideways.

There are certain things you expect from Cold War conspiracies – secret codes, spies, poison, bombs and what-have-yous. So far as the genre goes, the anonymous message about *The Forgotten Village* was in my wheelhouse. Ghosts, not so much.

(It's no joke. Like a ghost leaving untraceable messages in a haunted house. That's where this story is headed.)

The house in question wasn't old, it wasn't deserted and technically it wasn't a house, more of a museum, but you get my drift. Since the only lead we had was the Elena Atlas House, Kenzie decided to look into it.

I didn't know anything about Russia, but Kenzie had his hacker source now, the Turkish guy.

On this occasion however, no hackery was required. We found a website for lawyers who help people buy property in Russia. On the live chat an agent was perfectly happy to explain how to search the Russian Land Registry. By the next day Kenzie had a page of information: six other properties owned by the Atlas group, as well as some company details. The organization seemed to own a collection of architecturally interesting buildings, all formerly private houses. Two were in Russia, one in Cuba, two in Mexico, one in Miami and one in Washington DC. They were all art museums.

Cuba. Russia. Mexico. The USA. My hunch about Cuban-Russian spies hanging out in Mexico City was looking solid. Oh, I was having fun.

Kenzie sent me a link to the Atlas Studios in DC. It was in Georgetown, near our high school. On my phone I flicked through photos of the house. It was built from gray concrete, all hard lines and boxy, like the architect went out of their way to piss neighbors off in the midst of all their pretty brownstone townhouses and tree-lined avenues. I liked the windows a lot. They occupied most of the surface area of the house and had these thick, brown frames, so wide and ugly that it made a glorious statement.

People have been known to call me a Pollyanna, but even I doubted a place like this could have a connection to the Santiagos. Yet as Kenzie pointed out, what other clue did we have?

We visited after school. It wasn't a big place, a ground floor and a basement. The art was all on the ground floor, the basement was where events and workshops happened.

At the front desk was a young woman, probably in

her twenties, amazing complexion, lightly applied but classy makeup and had on a short, tailored dress and expensive-looking shoes. Her hair was coiffed into some glossy, lacquered creation. Honestly, it was like she'd come from a modelling session. She eyed us sullenly, then handed us a leaflet, a guide to the exhibition. Her fingernails were rather surprisingly, a mess. Bottle-green nail polish, cracked and badly in need of a do-over.

I liked her. Those fingernails struck me as a quiet rebellion. Work from two artists was on display – one painted trees using only blue and white, the others were by a sculptor that worked with glass. Honestly, they just looked like amorphous blobs to me. Glass blobs with a lot of bubbles, like soda in a glass.

So much for the art; we were the only people anywhere close to that exhibit. Everyone else was at the front of the house in the tiny coffee shop, six chairs and a rack of fancy notebooks and postcards. We looked around the whole place, searching for any mention of Russia, Mexico, the Santiagos. Nothing. We asked the boujee rebel in the spiffy shoes for a history of the house or the Atlas group.

She knew nothing of use. "They let artists display here in exchange for a few hours watching the store." Turned out Boujee was the painter of blue-and-white trees.

The trip in from Falls Church seemed to have been a waste of time. I looked longingly at the gorgeous notebooks and wondered if I could justify almost twenty dollars for one. I asked to use the restroom while I thought it over. Boujee handed over a key.

The restroom was the highlight of the place. The rest of the house had been given over to the art or coffee but the restroom was itself. Huge enough that sitting on the toilet in one corner, I felt dwarfed by the boldness of the architecture. A shiny industrial duct ran along the length of the ceiling and two concrete slabs flanked the room, each with a round washbasin made from distressed steel. Two washbasins, only one toilet. There were no windows. Gray slate slabs tiled the floor, narrow gray bricks the wall and ceilings. The basin faucets emerged from a slab of polished stone in the wall. There were no mirrors, so I guess that the stone itself was meant to be the mirror.

Running the hot water, I washed my hands with mandarin-scented liquid soap. As steam rose, it misted over the mirror. I examined the duct work, admiring the aesthetic. This was my kind of place, I decided. Urban chic. I patted my hands on a towel and squirted some of the chamomile- scented lotion provided over my fingers, rubbing it in gently. My skin was so dry.

Perhaps I daydreamed for a moment, maybe realized I was hungry and thought about where we might go for snack nearby. Anyhow, for whatever reason I lost track of time. It couldn't have been for more than a minute or two. Next thing I knew, someone was hammering on the restroom door.

I walked over and unlocked the door. Kenzie was there along with Boujee. Both wore troubled expressions.

She said, "You all right?"

I shrugged. "Yeah, why?"

Boujee flashed me a supercilious smile and stretched out her palm. "Key." But she didn't need to use the room. She just stomped away, back to the front desk.

"Sure you're okay?" asked Kenzie. "You can tell me, she's gone."

"I'm fine."

He shook his head. "If you say so." He seemed reluctant to say more. He paced over to the sink and wet his fingers, wiping his face. "Let's go. Wait." He pointed to the mirror-stone. "What's this?"

"Yeah, not much of a mirror, is it?"

"I meant the writing."

At first I thought I'd misheard him. "Did you say 'writing?'"

He gave me this quirky smile, like he thought we were playing. "Yeah. 'Find unicorns.' Why'd you write that?"

"Me? I didn't write anything."

He continued to point directly at the stone slab. "And yet."

Completely baffled, I closed in for a better look. Then I saw it. The words took a few seconds to register a meaning. An inscription in the fine condensation was fading rapidly but still legible. Traced, very obviously, by finger.

FIND UNICORNS.

My fingertips and nose felt suddenly cold, as if they'd caught a sharp breeze. I swallowed, grasping for a memory that wasn't there.

I repeated, "I didn't write anything."

Kenzie's eyes twinkled. "Then who? Casper the ghost?"

I grabbed his arm, not gently. "I'm being serious, Kenzie. I did not write those words."

He flinched, as if I'd flicked his face. Anger flashed across his face for just a second.

He thinks I'm lying, playing a dumb game.

It's exactly the kind of thing I used to do when we were kids. I would pull scary faces in the mirror and tell him in deadly earnest that there was an evil goblin in the mirror. Then he'd look at my real face and I'd make it as sweet as strawberry pie. Then he'd glance back at the mirror and my face would have changed – you get the idea. Sometimes I'd keep it going for days, until he was scared to glimpse my image in the mirror.

I was sure he enjoyed our game on the quiet, but apparently not. One Halloween when we were eleven he finally yelled at me and admitted that he'd always hated it. So I stopped. And that's what he thought I was doing that day in the restroom of the Atlas Studios; that I'd gone back to playing the Mirror Goblin. As if we were nine years old, again. He was wrong, I wasn't.

But I didn't insist, I didn't talk anymore about the writing on the wall. I was scared enough for both of us. Because that door was properly locked, and they'd been outside, banging on the door for five or six minutes. No-one but me inside and no windows.

A real locked-room mystery.

EIGHT

FIND UNICORNS

Over the next day or two things were frosty between me and Kenzie. I sensed this wasn't going to be anything either of us could persuade each other over, the way it can be with religion, or vaccines.

He believed I was lying about the writing on the wall. I knew I wasn't but I could see his point. The room had been locked, after all. Then there the matter of my 'lost time.' I'd heard of 'lost time' from alien abduction stories. It's a classic component of that mythology; lights go weird, observers zone out and when they come to, time has passed. Minutes or hours for which they can't account. That's what happened to me, although it took me a few days to admit it to myself.

Obviously I didn't tell Kenzie. He was already ticked off and I was ninety-percent certain this would only make it worse. I'd experienced a paranormal event, now I was on my own, at least until I understood more. So I went dark awhile. Quiet. Put my head down and did some research.

Also annoying was that Kenzie began to remind me of the *original* theory for why Maxim and Masha had gone missing, the original reason the cops gave for why the entire mystery was dismissed after a few weeks. Kenzie and I hadn't believed it at the time, yet now he seemed seriously to be considering it.

"It's obvious," he insisted. "The cops said it at the time; they were deported. The Santiagos were here illegally. They got caught at the border. ICE got 'em. Happens all the time."

ICE got 'em.

Yep, that was the b-s theory that did the rounds five years ago, when they disappeared. Until the Grover-Dyson girls told everyone they'd seen US passports in Maxim and Masha's hands as they waited on line. That fresh detail slowed the gossip, but by then too many people had already stopped caring. Calling someone an 'illegal' can have that effect. Well, maybe they were 'illegals' – the kind I'd learned about when Bobbie, Zara and I had binge-watched *The Americans*.

Masha and Maxim's Spanish sounded heavily gringified, while their English was one-hundred-percent American. But still – the Santiagos were brown and had a Spanish last name, so I suppose ICE was always likely to be invoked. Honestly, I was disappointed in Kenzie. I didn't like this theory, not a bit.

Even so, the Santiagos' lack of fluent Spanish combined with a Spanish last name had always intrigued me. They didn't vacation in Cuba, they never talked about having lived there. Not that this was *necessarily* a fly in the ointment of my Cuban-Russian spy theory, because of course, it could have been a secret that they had a connection to Cuba. If Masha really was a Russian spy based out of Cuba you'd expect her Spanish to be a) flawless b) Cuban. And her English, presumably, would have some tinge of a Russian accent. At least so I thought, until I spent some time actually researching the tradecraft that had been featured in the TV show about 'illegals.'

Turns out that the Third Russian Empire's foreign intelligence service – known as the Cheka – was still thought to be running 'illegals.' The irony wasn't lost on me – people had gossiped that the Santiagos disappeared because they were 'illegals' and now it seemed they might in fact have been 'illegal' Chekists –

spies with deeply buried identities. Illegals were given time to build up a history of living in the target country under some humdrum identity. They'd have almost flawless, Standard American English. Then, when their cover identities were solid, they'd start spying. I thought about Masha's job. What could be more humdrum than a sweet-natured occupation like a children's book translator?

Everything was falling into place, except for the inconvenient incident of my 'missing' six minutes alone in a locked restroom, while the words 'FIND UNICORNS' somehow materialized in steam on a wall. I didn't want to talk to Kenzie about it. I was pretty sure he didn't want to hear about it. I didn't even like to *think* about it because when I did, unwelcome thoughts bubbled up.

During the day I tried to ignore those thoughts. I filled my time with my podcast. Aside from the research and scriptwriting, there was so much to produce. I thought about asking Kenzie for help, but he was being weird. Basically I was flat out and reaching my bed each night in a state of exhaustion, so busy I had barely time to drink enough water. It was the happiest I'd been since losing my parents.

Even so, I started waking in the middle of the night to find myself in a dark, quiet house, thoughts racing. *Something* was waking me. A dream, perhaps. I never remembered any dream but I could still feel traces of adrenaline coursing through my veins. And those words were there, they'd wormed their way to the front of my mind until when I closed my eyes that's what I saw.

FIND UNICORNS.

Three days after our visit to the Atlas Studios, after one of these forgotten dreams I went downstairs. I poured myself a glass of chilled water. As I closed the fridge door I almost dropped the glass, startled. Kenzie was standing behind the door, like a serial-killer in a horror movie.

"Kenz! You scared the bejesus out of me."

He glared at me. "Swear to me you really didn't write on that wall."

"Still with that? Jeez, Kenzie! I swear! Now will you believe me?"

Almost triumphantly, he relaxed. "Then I've figured it out. The writing must have been there already. Someone wrote it before you got there. Steam can do that – you write using something waxy or greasy. The writing stays invisible – until steam reveals it."

For a moment I could feel a surge of joy and relief. I wanted to believe he was right. But the memory of the writing was very clear in my mind. I had a mental image of water dribbling in the condensation and trickling down from each letter, which surely wouldn't happen if the steam was just revealing a greasy smear on the stone. Kenzie, however, seemed so eager to convince me. I didn't have the heart to object. More than anything, I wanted us to be friends again.

"Then it's nothing to do with me?" I said.

"Didn't say that. Could be someone followed us to the museum, went into the restroom and left the message for you."

There were a few holes in that theory. I almost had to bite my tongue to keep from listing them. Kenzie wanted to be friends again, that's all that mattered.

"Left a message for me – about 'unicorns?'"

"Right," he agreed. "It can't be meant literally. Obviously 'unicorns' is code. A clue. Have you maybe looked into that?"

Was he kidding? I'd been way too freaked out to do a thing like that. "I've been getting to grips with Cheka tradecraft," I told him, fudging the issue. "My guess is that unicorn mythology is about to turn into another rabbit hole. But yeah… I have to admit it's a solid lead."

"Okay then, can I help?"

"I thought you'd never ask. I'll Google. You do dark web."

A hopeful grin began to spread across his lips. "I'm glad you said that… cos I already took a peek."

"Oh yeah? And?"

"Well… To be honest I did find something. Something pretty dark."

It was around three in the morning. I wondered if he'd lain awake listening out for me. I mainly wanted to get back to bed, but the way he said 'something pretty dark' stopped me even from yawning. I peered into his eyes. No hint of humor.

"You're serious? How 'dark?'"

"Child trafficking, dark." He said it with a mixture of dread and triumph.

"Damn, that is dark."

"Yeah, like I said."

We shuffled across to the kitchen table and he took out his cell phone. Huddling around the glowing blue light of its screen, he showed me what he'd found.

"Your half-assed, 'illegal' Cuban-Russian spy theory might not be so far off-base," Kenzie began.

"That's because it was always *full*-assed. Unlike your ICE theory."

"Not *my* ICE theory, but fair. All I mean is that from the facts you started out with, Cuban-Russian spy in Mexico seemed like a bit of a reach."

"Seemed pretty logical to me."

"Fine, Holmes, whatever. Anyhow, I started from that theory. Then I searched for leaked government documents."

I hesitated. "Is that an especially good way to find

information about spies?"

"For sure. It's why people who leak sensitive government information end up doing serious prison time. Supposedly they're endangering undercover agents. Brixton Fanning. Certainty Marvel. Ted Storm, if they ever get ahold of him."

"Yeah, I don't know who any of those people are."

"They're all US citizens who blew the whistle on military secrets."

"Why would they do that?"

"Because, I don't know, they thought people should know about the shitty things that were being done in foreign countries by the US military. In our name, without our knowledge. That's not the point though. What's important for us, is that every now and then some conscientious intelligence officer or military type dumps a bunch of documents on the Internet. Sometimes they get caught. Either way, the information gets out."

Nodding, I said, "And you found something about 'FIND UNICORNS' in documents like that?"

He pushed his phone closer to me. "I did. On Wikileaks."

I fumbled with his phone. "What exactly *is* 'Wikileaks?'"

NINE

VAULT 7

Obviously I'd heard of Wikileaks! The same way I'd heard about Watergate — I knew vaguely it was a big deal to do with government corruption, but I didn't know the details.

"They can't shut down Wikileaks," he told me, "because of the way it was set up. They'd pretty much have to take down the whole Internet. Secrets that get uploaded tend not to stay secrets very long. The main problem is that there's so much material and too few people to investigate."

"Maybe that's what my podcast should be about?"

Kenzie shot me a warning look. "No. Stick to unsolved crime. Getting into the secrets of the rich and powerful isn't for folks like you and me."

His warning, however, had something of the opposite effect. When I'd started investigating the death of Rich Wonders I'd stumbled across a whole online, citizen detective community. It was a lot of fun, frankly. The most fun was when I'd experienced a frisson of danger. It happened a couple of times in the Rich Wonder case. Far from being deterred, it'd sent me in search of another mystery, until I realized I had one in my own past.

Kenzie's phone screen displayed what he'd discovered on Wikileaks. It was a project that contained multiple mentions of 'unicorns.'

"It's part of a document dump called 'Vault 7' — a huge leak of confidential CIA information. Mostly about CIA hacking techniques — they're known as 'weapons.' Also a lot of the info they hacked from a bunch of sources, like cell phones and TVs that operated as bugging devices."

"'TVs that operated as bugging devices'?"

"Yeh, so next time you 'Netflix and chill,' bear in mind the NSA might be listening."

I couldn't tell if he was joking. I checked the time on his phone. 3:23am. My heart was racing.

"Let me see if I got this straight. The CIA hacked information that mentions 'unicorns' – and it's something to do with child trafficking?"

Kenzie handed me his phone. "Read it for yourself."

I speed-read the page a few times. It was an email, largely redacted. All the to: and from: information was blacked-out as well as much of the content. Kenzie was right; child trafficking was mentioned once. There was a short list of 'interested parties.' This was a bunch of organizations with names I didn't recognize apart from the Mossad, which I'd heard of: Israeli intelligence. The term 'unicorns' popped up twice in one paragraph.

"*Meanwhile the unicorn project will remain at K-FDN. (Redacted) assigned to oversee. Interest in (redacted) unicorns expressed at the highest level, expect contact from (redacted).*"

"What's 'K-FDN?'"

"No clue. There's no other mention of it anywhere, I already checked. But check the list of so-called 'interested parties.' They are *all* secret services. And from a bunch of the worst countries for human rights, at that."

In the unlit kitchen of Kenzie's moms at around three-thirty in the morning, the sheer ridiculousness of what we were doing hit me like a brisk slap. I'd been trying so hard to tell a compelling story, one that would hook my podcast listeners. But now, even I could see how slight were any connections between the facts we'd unearthed.

Could we *really* have chanced upon an international child trafficking ring that had stolen Maxim Santiago one morning at Dulles International Airport? If so, the CIA were probably already involved. Maybe Kenzie was right – Wikileaks stuff might be too spicy for a teenage investigative journalist.

"You know," I said, my voice slow and tired. "Maybe the Santiagos were deported, after all."

Kenzie was silent for a moment. Then – "I don't believe this."

"Why not? Think about it – even if they had US passports like Celine said, those passports could have been fakes. Maybe the border guards figured that out and ICEd them."

"I mean, I don't believe *you*," he said, sighing. "The biggest mystery at this point isn't what happened to the Santiagos. Can't you see that? *Who is sending you these messages*? That's the real question."

I inhaled slowly, blinking. "Omigod. You're right. I'm an idiot."

"Someone wants you to keep on looking into this case. Maybe it's an insider from the CIA."

"Oh sure, the CIA want help from *me*. Fun. You're a funny guy."

Kenzie ignored my smirk and opened a kitchen cupboard. He took out a jar of Skippy peanut butter. From a drawer he took two knives and handed me one. "Pass the bread." He joined me at the kitchen table, still in the dark as we spread peanut butter on soft white bread. I spread mine nice and thick, a layer of nougaty goodness on the spongy bread.

"Mmm. Brain food," I murmured between bites. "Why would a CIA analyst use us to investigate a child trafficking case?"

"Because we actually *knew* Maxim. Has to be that."

I nodded. "It's just wild enough to be plausible. Let's wargame it a bit more. How do we tell this analyst that we're on the case?"

"They could listen to your next episode? We already know they listened to the trailer."

"Do we though?"

He frowned, disappointed that I hadn't caught up with his reasoning yet. Ugh. *You* try being besties with a certified genius.

"Obviously, they're listening to your podcast. They know you're an amateur sleuth but more importantly, they kind of had to listen to your pod if they were able to leave a message on it."

I blushed, glad of the darkness to cover my shame. "I know they *found* my podcast, dummy. What I meant to say is, you think they actually listened to it?"

Thankfully, he didn't knock that down as a silly question. "I'd say they did, yeah. Whoever it is probably has a search alert on 'Masha Santiago.' One day, up pops a link to your trailer. They listen to it. Yeah. Why wouldn't they? They need the information. They have intel on Maxim, that's how they know about *The Forgotten Village*. So they send you a message."

A cold but unmistakable thrill ran through me. A CIA analyst listening to *La Chica Curiosa*! By now I had material for another ten minutes, which was the length of each episode. The story of how our secret informant had sent the first two messages was probably enough, but it would mean disclosing that we had that kind of source.

I wrinkled my nose. "Really? I dunno. Seems a little... *picayune* of them to pick up on a detail like the music we played. No, Kenz, you're cold, very cold. At least, I think so. And even if somehow, someone at the CIA found about our tween jazz band, which I honestly doubt, if the CIA sent me messages, should I really, y'know, talk about them on the pod?"

"About the messages?"

I nodded. "Frankly, I wasn't planning on it."

He paused for thought. "They didn't tell you *not* to. I'm pretty sure you're good."

"It just doesn't make sense. All we've done so far is find the kind of intel that whoever sent the messages *already* knows. For example, a confidential CIA document that mentions 'unicorns.' Or this child trafficking case, 'K-FDN.' We don't know what it means. 'K-FDN' is probably not even important."

"Obviously it's important!"

"Then why wasn't it redacted?" I objected. "Everything else was."

"Well, maybe not. At least according to Wikileaks. Vault 7 docs were only redacted to protect named individuals and hacker secrets. There's plenty of important stuff left."

I licked the final traces of peanut butter off my fingers. "Then I say we go back to our alleged CIA informant and tell them about 'K-FDN.' Then wait for the next hint."

"Sounds like a fantastic second episode."

"Maybe." I sighed. "If they're actually CIA and not someone yanking our chain. Which – think about it – could totally be happening."

"But who'd do that?"

"Not a clue. I'm having a hard time believing this is really happening."

"Why, Padi? You have a great nose for a mystery. We always figured there was something sus about Maxim's disappearance."

"Yeah, but *child trafficking*? Don't you get it? If Maxim was being trafficked then Masha would have to be involved. And that, I cannot see. Masha seemed so, so nice."

The idea that our twelve-year old friend might have been trafficked right under the noses of the school community was pretty grim.

"True," Kenzie agreed. "All those times we were over at theirs, we could have been in danger of…" He left the rest unsaid and concluded, "I think I liked your Cuban-Russian spy theory better."

I picked up the glass of cold water I'd poured and drank it down in one go. Beads of moisture on the outside of the glass trickled down my wrist.

"Well anyway, thanks for hanging out," Kenzie said. "I wasn't sure you were awake, since you were ignoring my messages. But I thought I heard you tossing and turning."

I put down the empty glass and wiped my lips with the back of my hand. "Ignoring *what* messages?"

Kenzie showed me his messaging app. He'd sent me two messages in the past hour. Messages I definitely hadn't received, which I proved by showing him my phone.

"Now that's odd," he said, pensively. He fiddled with my phone for a minute then showed me the app again. Suddenly the missing messages were there.

"That's a relief," I chuckled. "For a second there I thought maybe the CIA had hacked *my* phone."

But Kenzie didn't smile. He tapped my phone. "Spyware? Could be. Only one way to find out."

I gasped. "I was joking! You actually think my phone could be hacked?"

"Open it." He took my phone without any resistance from me and for the next minute or so, examined a few things, don't ask me what. "Whoever is sending the messages seems to know where you are. Did you tell anyone you were going to the Atlas Studios in Georgetown?"

"No. But I may have mentioned it somewhere. In a

message to you, Bobbie or Zara. Jeez." I took a beat to consider. "Now you think the CIA is surveilling us, are you serious?"

I reached for my phone but he pulled back his hand. "Give me time and I can find out if your phone is hacked. But y'know what, Padi? I'm starting to think maybe we should drop this. Maybe this mystery is too big, too weird, too dangerous."

TEN

GUARDIAN

Kenzie hung onto my phone until just before lunch the following day. He stopped by my bedroom to hand it back. "No Pegasus spyware, from what I could tell. I downloaded the Mobile Verification Toolkit from Github and ran various checks. That was kinda fun, thanks, I never did it before."

He lost me at 'Pegasus,' but I was loving his confidence. "Is the phone clean or not?"

"Probably. Or not." He shrugged. "Loan me the phone another day and I can do a more thorough check."

I wiped greasy smudges from the pearly-pink case and the phone screen. "Ugh, Kenzie. Your fingers must be disgusting, gross, all these marks."

Ignoring this, he leaned forward and with sudden earnestness asked, "Can we talk about what happened yesterday? I feel like you're moving kind of fast."

I was totally thrown. "Talk about what?" I managed, eventually.

He sucked in air sharply through his teeth and then paced across the room, dropping heavily onto the end of my unmade bed. With his right foot, he dragged my desk chair around until it was facing him. "C'mon, Padi, I'm just checking in on you."

I racked my brain for another moment, then narrowed both eyes as I realized what was up. "Did Zara put you up to this?"

"What if she did? She cares about you. Obviously."

Sitting down, through gritted teeth I said, "If your mom wants to shrink my head she could have the decency to do it directly."

"She reminded me to check in with you, is all. It's not her fault that I don't get social cues."

I sneered. "Oh, you get them. You just don't want to own that you triggered me."

"So, you admit it."

I threw up both hands. "That you triggered some horrible memory about when I found out about my parents? Yeah, Kenzie, I admit it. I'm not the one who left everyone hanging for hours, sick to their stomachs with worry."

"Do you want to talk about it, though?"

"I literally am!" I exploded.

Kenzie shook his head, eyes downcast. "No. About what happened. About your parents."

My eyes bulged with suppressed rage, for two, three, four seconds. "No. I really don't. How about instead we talk about whatever your mysterious cyber project is, the one you were obsessed by until you decided to get all up in my business?"

"Oh-kay," he replied, briskly. "I respect that, so, let's ah… Let's both agree to respect boundaries." He seemed relieved, after all that. "So, d'you want to get back to your whole…?"

"The investigation, my podcast, the main thing I use to manage my anxiety, would I like to do that? Yeah, I think so, Kenz, think that'd be just awesome."

He leaned back on his hands and nodded. "What are you going to do?"

I'd decided to keep going, for now. The whole point of my podcast was to unearth unsolved mysteries. I wasn't the one with something to hide. Until our anonymous benefactor revealed themselves or begged me to keep their secrets, I was an open book.

I opened the podcast messaging app and replied to

the message thread about *The Forgotten Village*, typing a reply: 'K-FDN?', the clue we'd gotten from the Vault 7 leaked files that mentioned 'the unicorn project.' Guess I could also have written that, but I figured K-FDN was a nice detail, something that'd show we had specific knowledge. I hit 'send.'"

"No going back now," Kenzie announced with an air of finality.

The next day was uneventful. I kept checking my phone, hoping for a reply from our Anonymous Benefactor, our A.B. who we'd taken to referring to as 'Abby.' No activity there.

The following day was also uneventful. I kept working on the script for the second episode, which was going well. I was beginning to wonder if I'd just have to give up and admit to my audience that the trail had gone cold. I'd figured I could probably get away with a third episode to round up and chew over all the different theories to date. It was a stalling tactic I'd also used during 'Rich Wonders.' Yet unless we could glean more information from *someone* or *somewhere*, starved of oxygen the Santiagos podcast series looked like tapping out at episode three.

Which is why, when an unmarked black van turned a corner and screeched to a halt in front of me on Wisconsin Avenue, my first instinct wasn't to panic but instead the fleeting thought: *At least I'll have something for episode four.*

The thought lasted only a second, but it stole away my critical response time. I should already have been running away. Instead, when the door slid open and a figure in a ski-mask jumped out and shoved me into the back of the van, I was too dazed to make anything more than a useless objection – "Hey, what gives?"

In the next instant a cloth bag went over my head. Then everything changed. My nervous system took a few seconds properly to engage with what was a totally new and unexpected situation but when it did, it took ahold of my entire body and made me feel like I'd been injected with some mind-altering substance. I felt disoriented, teetering from side to side as the van made rapid turns. The road sounds became jumbled up, no matter how hard I tried to focus on individual noises, here and gone a second later. Fear of a wholly unprecedented nature grabbed my entire body and seemed to shake it violently. Even my toes seemed alert to the fact that I was in danger. I tried to talk and couldn't. It was as though my jaw had locked.

Someone in the van put a hand on my shoulder. "Breathe."

The hand was firm, with only a reassuring amount of pressure. The voice belonged to a man. It was someone who seemed to want me under control rather than someone who was worried if I was about to have a heart attack. I breathed. After a few minutes my breathing became less ragged and shaky.

"Good," murmured the unseen man. "We'll be there soon."

We were in the van another twenty minutes before it slowed to a halt. In the final five minutes I tried to pay attention to the sounds of the road. We'd left DC, I was certain. Probably ridden the freeway for a little while and then pulled off. I guessed we were somewhere in the country or a quiet, fancy suburb. The van drove into an underground garage, I think. My captor opened the van door and escorted me, still hooded, shuffling up some steps and through a hallway (I know because I touched the walls) until I felt my toes hit something.

"Sit back," said a familiar voice. *Very* familiar. If not for the total disorientation of being abducted I would surely have recognized that voice. But honestly,

I struggled to identify its owner. Isn't that weird? "It's a couch," the woman added, helpfully.

When my unseen escort removed the hood I found myself in the living room of a very simply furnished suburban house. Sitting in a fake-leather tub chair opposite the couch was the person whose voice I knew. It was Olga Garcia, my guardian. To say I was stupefied would be very much too mild.

"Olga? What's happening? Did you do this?"

"I'm sorry, Veronica."

"It's Roni now," I growled.

"Of course. Forgive me, Roni."

I fell silent, seething. Every time I met Olga I wondered why my parents had wanted me to live with someone quite so disinterested in my life. Then again, if she'd liked me more she'd probably have wanted me to live with her in the boonies or wherever this was, and I mightn't have been able to continue at D.C. International.

I surveyed the room, watching Olga send her errand boy, my captor, to bring us some sodas. He'd finally removed his ski mask to reveal a rather sweet face with a chin dimple, tidy, short dark-brown hair, clean-shaven with cheekbones to die for, a slim, lightly-built guy in his twenties. His light brown eyes were soft and gentle, not what I'd have guessed for the tough-guy he was trying to play. He had on what appeared to be box-fresh white sneakers, straight, ankle-length black slacks, a long-sleeved black T-shirt under a thin, charcoal gray, quilted body-warmer, the entire combo screaming 'urban Tokyo style.'

I glared. "Isn't it illegal to abduct a person? Even if they're, y'know, whatever-I-am to you."

The errand boy returned with a tray of Pepsi, Sprite and orange Fanta. I took the Fanta.

"You are my 'ward,' Roni. And yes, technically it's

illegal for me to abduct you. Do you wish to press charges, send me the same way as your folks?"

Scowling, I popped the can of Fanta as aggressively as I could. "Maybe." I peered into the kitchen beyond the living room and to the street beyond. This was a house, not an apartment. Olga lived in an apartment downtown, or so I'd been led to believe.

"This isn't your house, you don't live here."

Olga leaned forward in her chair. She nodded, tight-lipped. "You're right."

"Where are we? Why'd you have your guy steal me?"

Olga stretched her small hands on her thighs, pausing to consider. I surveyed the glass surface of the coffee table. There was nothing else there, no magazines, no coasters. The whole place was minimally furnished, like a show home.

"I had become somewhat concerned that you're being followed."

"You mean, by someone other than you?" I shot back. "What is this anyhow, since when does the World Health Organization have people followed?"

She shifted her shoulders in the most minimal shrug. "In point of fact we only started to follow you today. Other things brought to my attention that you're being followed."

I exploded. "What 'things'?"

"Right now I can't tell you. Sorry."

"Omigod, Olga, really? Then why say anything at all?"

She broke in: "I can tell you, however, that I haven't worked for the World Health Organization for several years. Since before your parents were convicted."

"Since they died to me, you mean" I said, rolling my eyes.

Olga fell silent, her eyes filled with pity. Softly she said, "Really, Roni? You're still telling yourself that story?"

I felt cold sweep through me, all the way to my fingertips. After a long time I spoke again, in a voice so parched it cracked. "It's easier this way."

ELEVEN

Finally, A Real Lead

At this point, obviously, I kind of have a confession to make. I may *inadvertently* have given you the impression that my parents died in the pandemic. That view might not be absolutely based in reality, but it's worked to keep me sane. The truth is painful in a very different way. They laundered money for foreign agents, for a government bent on destabilizing the USA. And the worst of it is, they didn't even know. They 'simply and merely' took their money and washed it, almost no questions asked, and found themselves being held responsible for more than they bargained for. Or maybe they knew all along, what they were getting into? The prosecution believed they did, but my parents have always denied it, pled ignorance and greed.

Who knows what they were thinking? So my version wasn't a total lie – I kept one part of the truth. The people I'd believed my parents to be, intelligent, responsible, upstanding citizens and all? Those people were *gone*. In their place were a couple of chumps – and that's the best-case scenario.

"You mother especially, she misses you a lot," Olga said, gently. "Couldn't you take her calls, at least?"

Tears brimmed in my eyes. "Is this why you stole me, to guilt me into visiting my lying, cheating, *fascist* mom?"

Olga winced. "Don't use that word."

"Why not? It's the truth."

"They have never been fascists."

I shot back, "They laundered money for fascists,

though. Didn't they? For literal Russian oligarchs, funneling money to propagandists. Fascist-enablers."

Olga let out a deep sigh. "It's not a word should be thrown around so easily. The fact is, your mom and dad screwed up. They didn't look closely enough into their clients' background, that's true. They're paying for that crime. But they're still your parents."

I began to laugh, bitterly. "And they're still your friends. Figures. You're another crim."

"I'm not a 'crim' Roni."

"You just admitted to abducting me," I said, wiping away a tear. "So yeah, I think so. And what else? You're CIA? I mean let's face it, that's crim-adjacent."

Olga pressed her lips into a hard line. "I'm not CIA."

"Did my parents make you my guardian after you moved to the CIA? Or before?"

"I said, *not* the CIA. And it was before."

I scoffed. "Great. Such judges of character, my parents."

"You're still upset. I get it."

"Oh, you think?"

She gave a grudging sigh as her eyes met mine – calm focus reflecting back my resentment.

"All right. We didn't ever really get onto the best footing did we? I should have gotten to know you better, Roni. Will you forgive me? I'd like to make amends, starting right now."

I took a deep breath, not sure where to go next.

"Drink your soda," Olga suggested. She picked up her Pepsi and sipped. "Everything's better when you're hydrated. Would you like a snack? Let's eat and drink and catch up, yes?"

I reached for my phone. "Let me just tell Kenzie and his moms where I am."

Olga gave a tiny shake of her head. "Not right now,

sorry dear." She reached into the pocket of the knitted cardigan she had on and withdrew a tiny SIM card. "Your phone. I've turned off Wi-Fi, too. No-one can know you're here."

A tremor ran through me then, a faint callback to what I'd experienced during my abduction. What if I had horribly misjudged my so-called 'guardian'?

Olga seemed to notice the shift in my mood because her tone became imploring and two shades warmer. "I get that you need the distraction, Roni. But you need to stop making your podcast."

I set down the can of Fanta. "You've been listening?"

In Olga's eyes I spotted a flicker of what I'm going to claim as *admiration*. Hey, I'll take whatever affirmation I can get from a parent substitute. "Did I listen to *What Happened to the Santiagos?*" She suppressed a smile. "I did."

"And?"

Olga pursed her lips before replying. "I'm not one for a cliché, but in this case I believe it's appropriate to call it a 'can of worms.'"

I didn't respond. If she truly believed that, then I could rule her out as my secret source: Olga couldn't be 'Abby.' *So what* if she'd heard the trailer? That wouldn't be a huge stretch, since she was my legal guardian. Even if she only called or texted once a month to check in with me, I could imagine that on the quiet, she might actually pay some attention to me, the way parents do.

So – no more mystery about why she'd had me followed. Olga was worried, for some reason. She was looking out for me. Maybe our parents had always known more about the Santiagos than I had. If the child trafficking connection was real, that might also explain the silence from teachers at D.C. International.

There are things people really do not like to talk to kids about.

"Roni, I asked you a question," I heard Olga say, interrupting my train of thought. "How much do you know?"

"I know that Maxim was probably trafficked," I admitted. Might as well tell Olga, since I'd been planning to tell the whole world in episode three. "But we can't figure out whether Masha was involved."

Olga's flat expression didn't give much away but I could tell she wasn't surprised. "All right," she said. "But what led you to the Atlas place in Georgetown? Was it just a coincidence?"

I faltered, momentarily confused. Olga seemed astonished that we'd tracked down the Atlas Studios, yet not that we'd linked Maxim to child traffickers. Again, I hesitated. It was all going to be in podcast anyway, so why not just spill?

I told her all about Kenzie's clever IP-tracking of the message on my podcast and how he'd traced it to the owners of a museum in Russia, which had led us to the Atlas Studios. At this time I didn't mention his theory of the true origin of the message, which was Mexico City.

All in good time. Even without the Mexico part, Olga really seemed impressed. "Some of his process doesn't sound strictly legal," she conceded, "but did your friend at least take the necessary precautions to cover his tracks?"

I nodded a few times despite having no idea what she was talking about. "Totally, he did."

Olga leaned back into the tub chair, one hand grasping her chin as she fell into a long, pensive silence. I waited, slurping my Fanta and running my eyes over the errand boy/kidnapper once again. This time, my attention lingered on his chin dimple. He was actually pretty hot, if I'm honest. Stockholm Syndrome is real. He swooped by, picked up my empty can of soda and vanished like a butler.

"All right," she announced, sitting up straight and making eye contact. "Here's what we're going to do."

I waited. Olga seemed to think some more about whatever it was and then continued. "I'm going to tell you a few things about your friend Maxim and his mother. You can't put any of this in the podcast or publish on the Internet, ever. Which is why you *need* to end the podcast. Ideally, delete the trailer."

"What? But the first episode is ready and it's so good."

She spoke over me. "I'm sorry, Roni, really I am. Hear me out, will you? By the time I'm finished I hope you'll want to help me. And if you want to help Maxim, you'll do as I ask."

I froze. "To help *Maxim*? You know where he is?"

Tersely, she nodded. "I might. That's why I need your help. But first, let's get something out in the open."

Kidnapper/butler showed up right then with a tray of sandwiches and more sodas.

"Peanut butter," he said, indicating the white-bread sandwiches on the left. "Or jelly," he added, pointing to the whole-wheat sandwiches on the right.

"PB *or* J?" I observed. "Why not live a little and mix it up?" But by the time I'd picked up a peanut butter sandwich he was gone. They probably teach the vanishing technique in butler school.

Olga finally moved onto her own confession, which was the long-overdue explanation for what she'd been doing since leaving the World Health Organization.

"Your parents and I met at college – you knew that, yes? We all studied computer science. They went into finance and set up their accountancy firm, I went into bioinformatics – examining the data in human genetic code. I'm an expert in big data. That, plus having worked for the World Health Organization led me to working for the United Nations. In the Office of Counter-Terrorism. Analyzing patterns in a different kind of data."

This was a long way from what I'd expected her to say. She acknowledged my surprise. "Not as glamorous as the CIA or FBI, perhaps. But important, nonetheless. Although as you can imagine, your folks didn't approve."

Glumly, I nodded. My parents had often expressed skepticism of the United Nations, calling it 'useless as a chocolate teapot.' The sad truth was, organizations that laid down international laws, for example against money laundering, were what gave them a business in the first place. I guess they'd managed to persuade themselves that those laws shouldn't exist, because they preferred to think of themselves as ordinary accountants who'd done nothing wrong. "Honestly, I'm surprised they let you be my legal guardian."

"I wasn't their first choice," Olga admitted, wryly. "But I *was* the only option the court would accept. Hey, let's put a pin in a discussion about your parents. Can we? I promise we'll talk a lot more about them. Unfortunately, right now we're in something of a dilemma. Your friend Maxim may be alive. For the first time since he and Masha went missing, we may have a lead on where he is."

"Omigod, you do? Where?"

"A place called Tapachula in Mexico. It's in Chiapas, have you been there?"

I shook my head. My father had some family in Mexico City, so we'd visited a few times, but nowhere else, not even Cancun. Now I was really confused. "Why's he in Chiapas?"

"We believe Maxim escaped to there from someplace else. And I'm not sure how or why he ended up in Tapachula, if it even is him."

"So were he and Masha deported?"

Olga took a breath, as though it pained her to say what followed. "They weren't officially deported, by which I mean that they had valid papers to remain in the USA. But someone extremely powerful wanted them deported, so that's what happened. They went to Cuba."

"Seriously? They sent a twelve-year old kid to *Gitmo*? That's even worse than being trafficked."

"No, not Guantanamo. It wasn't that type of 'deported.' 'Trafficking' is closer to the truth. Their abduction was strictly criminal, not political. People were bribed; we know this. Maxim is worth a great deal of money to certain parties. Which is why we need to find him, fast. If I've been able to track him to Tapachula, then so will others. His life will be in danger."

"Maxim is worth money? Why? Specifically him or any kid? Is this, like, some gross Epstein situation? How did you find him? And who else is looking?"

Olga made a damping-down gesture with one hand. "Whoa there, slow it down. I can't answer all your questions, Roni. Much of this is classified. I'll tell you what you need to know in order to help me. Deal?"

Of course, deal. *Information? Gimme.*

"At the UN Office of Counter-Terrorism we have access to many private databases. Twenty days ago, the name 'Maxim Santiago' showed up on one of these. It happened shortly before your podcast trailer dropped, which frankly made me suspicious. Roni, do you remember how you got the idea to investigate that mystery?" When I blanked her, Olga shrugged and continued. "It's probably a coincidence. They do happen. In my line of work you tend to suspect everything and everyone, but yes, there are occasionally actual coincidences. Anyway, Maxim Santiago's name came up in a database of volunteers working with a small charity in Mexico. There's very little information. No photograph. No biographical details. Just a name."

"A name, that's all? There must be hundreds of people called 'Maxim Santiago.'"

"One hundred and twenty-four. That's just in the United States. Another fifty-nine in Mexico. And that's not all. A few days later the same search came up blank for that database. The record was gone. At first I thought maybe he'd left…"

"But maybe he got the record of his name deleted? Or did it himself?"

Olga gave a couple of nods, looking impressed. "It's what someone who didn't want to be found would do."

"And makes you suspect that your guy in Tapachula is our Maxim?"

She smiled, wistfully and gave a heavy, resigned shrug. "Two parts hunch, one part hope. That's where you come in. Roni, would you recognize Maxim? He'd be eighteen now, he'd probably look somewhat different. You'd know him, wouldn't you? You and Marc Mackenzie."

"That's what this is about? You want me to go to Mexico with you to check out this random Maxim Santiago?" I laughed. "You didn't have to kidnap me to get me to agree to that, 'Auntie' Olga. All you had to do was ask."

TWELVE

SPYWARE

So many questions. What I could have used right then was a time-out, an hour or two to take stock, ideally with Kenzie.

Being 'kidnapped' and then discovering that my guardian was behind the whole scheme, was a bit of a shocker. It wasn't easy to go from seeing her as Dr. Olga Garcia, my parents' old college buddy, to seeing her as mysterious Olga Garcia, officer of the United Nations Counter-Intelligence Committee Executive Directorate.

Then there was the teeny fact that my guardian was having me followed. This was too much. It was as though the ground were shifting under my feet. Total disorientation.

One minute found myself believing that Maxim had been dragged along with his undercover agent mom as she left the country on a mission, or got captured, or her cover blown or whatever. One of those spy things, anyhow. Then along came the child trafficking clue. In this scenario they'd been lured to the airport, presumably, perhaps threatened? Then thrown out of the country by corrupt border guards acting on the orders of some shadowy, very powerful person or cabal.

I hadn't yet gotten to grips with what it could mean. The spectrum of possibilities was so grim, I shied away from the implications. Organ harvesting was at the most horrific end, obviously. If there was a way to help Maxim without ending up on the menu myself, it felt crucial to do what I could.

We hadn't spoken about it directly, but I was certain that Kenzie would agree. At this stage I should make something clear: I hadn't yet told Olga everything that me and Kenzie had found out. Partly because she hadn't asked, but also because in the precious few minutes I'd had to reflect, while Olga left me to go to the bathroom, I came to an important realization.

Olga was behaving as though she assumed Kenzie and I had been followed. According to her, that's why she put her own person on me, almost certainly before our trip to the Atlas Studios. Meanwhile, 'Abby,' Message-Sender of Mystery, had left us a breadcrumb trail. That trail led first to the Atlas Studios and then to the leaked 'Vault 7' CIA documents, to mentions of 'the unicorn project,' child trafficking and 'K-FDN.'

It didn't seem like Olga was 'Abby.' Whoever was feeding us hints, seemed to be encouraging us to investigate. Whereas Olga had made it crystal-clear that she wanted the podcast shut down.

And there was more, like Olga's minimalist approach to her professional life. We weren't close, but she was my legal guardian. Didn't I deserve at least to know what she did for a living? She'd tried to breeze over the fact that she worked for the United Nations in a *'didn't I mention it?'* kind of way. I didn't buy that. Certainly, I would have remembered a cool-sounding job in counter-terrorism. Olga had withheld that she no longer worked for the World Health Organization yet now she wanted my help, wanted me to travel to Mexico with her to identify someone who just might be my childhood friend, Maxim Santiago.

It was a bizarre approach to take, given that Olga was eager to talk me into travelling overseas with her. Even though my parents had chosen her to 'guard' me and the court-approved funds left for my education, until I was eighteen, the reality was that I barely knew the woman. Something didn't fit. Or rather, there was too much going on. The whole picture seemed too crowded. I kept returning to the same over-riding suspicion.

There had to be a simpler explanation.

Why couldn't I see it? I longed to talk to Kenzie, who as well as being an all-round great guy and best friend, was my preferred sounding-board, when it came to the podcast. Why wouldn't Olga let me have my phone? Who was she afraid might be following me?

I cracked my knuckles and wrung my hands. (Yes, really. Before you sneer, next time you're feeling stressed try going without your phone for ten minutes.) A quick check of the corridor told me Olga was still in the bathroom, so I kept riding the paranoia train.

What if our being followed wasn't the real problem? What if Olga wanted to prevent me calling anyone? What if she actually needed me to stay in a confused state?

I sensed myself being drawn toward what Olga wanted me to do. Firstly, it'd mean a trip, and who doesn't love an airplane ride and some foreign adventure? Secondly, Olga would be helping me since apparently, counter-terrorism was her thing. She'd be in charge. If things went south, it wouldn't be all my fault. I'd be able to sit back and enjoy the experience, instead of having this constant itch-you-can't-scratch.

Counter-terrorism. Child trafficking. How did I end up in a world where these terms weren't just things I read on the Internet? I'd listened to Olga speak about those things with evident sincerity, and even so I couldn't quite believe it. Kept thinking I'd wake up in a minute and it would have been a dream. Or she'd round the hallway with her butler and they'd laugh and admit the whole thing was a prank. Yeah, cool Auntie Olga who had me abducted for kicks. A story we'd tell for years to come. Right?

But no. I wasn't waking up and this was feeling all too real.

What did Olga mean about having me 'watched?' Had butler-boy been driving around the city, shadowing me? She'd claimed it only started the day we visited the Atlas Studios. I wondered what Kenzie would say. Maybe there was an electronic tracker somewhere on my person? Or *spyware on my phone*.

Once the thought had occurred to me, it lurked in the back of my mind, refusing to leave. Before I could process my suspicion, Olga returned to the living room. She'd changed out of what I assumed were her office clothes – brown slacks, white shirt, smart court shoes – and into pale gray joggers, a plaid shirt and white sneakers. Her straight brown hair was in a simple pony-tail and she'd switched contacts for a pair of glasses with tortoiseshell frames.

I immediately felt more comfortable. This was the Olga Garcia I remembered from visits to the office, where briefly during a contract years ago, she and my mom had shared an office. Scientist Olga, not Agent Olga.

She resumed her place in the tub chair and once again engaged me with that forceful gaze.

"Now Roni, here's the plan. You and I will swing by Marc Mackenzie's to pick up your passport. You'll pack. Then you and I will fly to Tapachula via Mexico City. I've arranged to visit your uncle Johny – it's best if we give an excuse for the trip. We'll go to check out this charity and see if their 'Maxim Santiago' is your friend. If he is, great, fantastic. If he isn't, well that's useful information, too. We'll be back in D.C. within four days."

"All that way for just four days? Are you actively *trying* to burn the planet? Can't we stay a little while longer? Take Kenzie too, see the sights?"

"If the planet's your concern, why would you add another carbon-burning passenger?" she replied, tartly.

I hesitated. *Would Olga actually put spyware on my phone?*

It'd explain how she knew to find me at the Atlas Studios. It could also explain how the steam-message got onto the restroom mirror – she'd discovered from my messages that we were headed to the Atlas place and planted the mirror-writing before we arrived. Or she'd had some minion do it. Butler Kidnapper, for example. Maybe I'd seen him there, but too briefly to recognize him later at Olga's house in the 'burbs. I've been known to overlook even a cute guy until the third time I spot them.

"Well? Are you in?"

My lips twisted into a tight smile. "Honestly?"

Olga blinked, waiting for me to answer.

But why surveil me?

I thought some more about what she could discover from my phone. Maybe Olga wasn't 'Abby,' was not feeding me any hints, but she *knew I'd received them.* She'd waited, watched me unravel the mystery. Now she was jumping in with an innocent-sounding trip to help her identify a teenager who'd be almost nineteen years old by now, a guy that Olga-of-the-counter-terrorism-office alleged was in danger of being trafficked by a terrorist organization. For money.

No. *Too much* of this didn't make sense.

"It's just… I have chores," I finished, weakly. "I can't just check out in the middle of the week."

"It's Friday tomorrow. We'd be back Monday. A long weekend, that's all I ask."

I sighed. "Can I think about it? I really need to talk to Kenzie and his moms."

Olga grabbed both my hands in hers, a gesture

fraught with such unexpected tension and at the same time, warmth, that I was caught off guard.

"It's all right, Roni. This must seem terribly sudden. Maybe even frightening."

I nodded. "Yeah, honestly, it is a little scary."

"Your phone has been hacked," she said, with absolute clarity. I stared into her eyes which were now wide open and signaling urgency above anything else. "I ran a check just now."

"Pegasus…?" I said, uncertainly.

The tension bent for a moment and she let out a startled chuckle, as if she found it adorable that I believed I understood *anything* about what was happening.

"*Pegasus*? No – it's… Never mind. There are other types of spyware, Roni. And your phone is definitely infected. You've been tracked since May 4th – does that ring any bells?"

In a dry throat, I swallowed. May 4th was the day I'd released the trailer for *What Happened to the Santiagos*. "Seriously, what?" I paused. "So *you* didn't hack my phone?"

"Me? No. is that what you've been worrying about?"

"Or send me the hints?"

"What hints?"

I paused to dissect her expression. She seemed genuinely baffled. Yet more confirmation that Olga was definitely not 'Abby.' "So you're *just* following me?"

"Not sure what you mean by 'just,'" Olga said, warily.

"You said it yourself – my phone is hacked. Kenzie figured it was. I thought maybe you did it."

She shook her head, her eyes wide. "No. If you've been hacked, that's someone else. We should probably talk about that. I'm just following you. Since the day you went to the Atlas Studios."

"Why then? Did something happen?"

And how did she know we'd be at the Atlas Studios?

"Bobbie called me. She was worried about you and her son. Upset because he'd spent two thousand dollars of cryptocurrency buying data. That cryptocurrency was his inheritance from Bobbie's first wife, Nadine, who didn't have much money but I guess got lucky with crypto-coin. It's worth quite a lot now, according to Bobbie."

"Wow. I had no idea."

"About a week ago, Bobbie shared that she's worried Kenzie might have broken the law by buying that data. So I thought it best to shadow you both, at least for a little while."

I sat back. "I'm stunned. Kenzie did *not* tell me he'd spent that much."

"Spent it on *stolen* data, no less. The data that led you to the Atlas Studios."

My mind had gone into overdrive by now.

"And you really didn't hack my phone? Cos if you did, Auntie, that might be a bit of an issue Whoever *did* hack it knows pretty much everything about my investigation."

"Yes, they do," replied Olga, her voice low and serious. "At least they know everything up until when Tobias put you in the van. Until he took out its SIM card, your phone would have been transmitting your every conversation, every location you visited while carrying the phone. They'd have been able to read every message you sent or received – up until Tobias removed the SIM card."

"Oh. My. God. Sidebar – your butler's name is Tobias?"

"Take this seriously, Roni. Someone else has all that information, right now."

"Well fine, who?"

"Who?" My question halted Olga in her tracks and she seemed to gather her patience before replying. "Two main possibilities, one bad, one terrible."

My eyes widened. "And…?"

"Bad would be CIA. Terrible would be Chekists."

"Why would CIA be bad? Aside from the obvious, I mean?"

With half-lidded eyes Olga admitted, "Because the Cheka has operatives everywhere. The CIA is a bureaucratic organization, paperwork has to be filed for everything. Someone, somewhere will leak it. Eventually, Chekists will know about you, too."

We stared at each other. I snapped my mouth shut and listened. Then she continued, "Since Tobias took out the SIM, everything we've shared here is private. What I said about Maxim Santiago, for example. Whoever is spying on you doesn't know what I told you. Roni, they *must not* find out. Do you understand?"

"Got it," I said, trying to brush it off.

Olga seemed ticked off by my nonchalance. "I'm being very serious now, Roni. There are dangerous people searching for him. A hunch led me to guess that this person in Tapachula might be our Maxim, but it won't take others long to connect the dots. *Much* less if they follow us. So we have to leave for Mexico, right away."

"Fine. But after I talk to Kenzie and his moms," I insisted. "I can't just leave the country. Can you give me until tomorrow morning?"

Olga's hand went to her temples this time, rubbing the right side of her face with her thumb for several seconds. She sighed, shaking her head. I could sense her disappointment. But legal guardian or no legal guardian, you have to respect boundaries. You don't jump onto an international flight with *anyone*, not until you've talked it over with someone you trust.

"Good." She nodded, then chucked my cheek with her knuckles. "You drive a hard bargain, *mija*. We'll figure it out. Your mother and father raised you well. Talk it over with Kenzie, Bobbie and Zara. Even though I've already told Bobbie I wanted to take you on a trip to see your uncle. Alright. Give me a few minutes to rebook the flights for tomorrow. I paid for full flexibility – unlimited changes to the booking until two hours before departure. Always a good idea when travelling with flighty teenagers."

"No, *you're* flighty," I grumbled, but not-so-secretly relieved.

She used her phone to make the changes, then put it down with a tired smile. "All done. I've forwarded the booking and login details so you can use your own phone to check in. I'll stay in a hotel somewhere nearby and pick you up early tomorrow morning."

But she didn't. By the next morning, Olga was dead.

THIRTEEN

Patria y Vida

Astounded, much? I was. And no, I'm not planning to gloss over Olga's death, but I figured a heads-up might be handy at this stage. After all, we don't want anyone getting too attached. This is a story about where my curiosity took me. I don't want people believing that Cool 'Auntie' Olga led me by the nose. Because no, not even a little bit. This is all on me.

In hindsight and especially because of what happened, I've come to think more kindly of Olga. She *was* cool, I know that now. Back then, I wasn't so sure. The day she had me abducted, it shouldn't surprise anyone that I found her to be cold, nerdy and problematic. As I slept in my own bed that night, or rather didn't sleep, I thought a lot about my guardian. Thought about why she had kept information from me and why she continued to do so. Thought about what kind of person she really was, beneath the mask.

Had my parents known the 'real' Olga? I couldn't be sure, ever. There'd always be this doubt now, whatever she tried to tell me. The uncertainty made me so anxious that around midnight I messaged Kenzie, hoping he was still awake. After a few minutes he messaged back.

    If you're so worried, don't go to Mexico
    with her.

    And what do I do the rest of my life?
    Avoid her?

You'll be an adult in six months. Then ignore?

Without Olga no access to trust fund until I'm 25, so no.

Did Olga ever not give you what you asked for? She was ok with you living with us.

True.

OK then stop stressing and go to sleep. Night.

I rolled onto my back and slid my phone under the pillow. Kenzie was right. Tomorrow morning I'd call the UN Office of Counter-Terrorism and check if Dr. Olga Garcia worked there. If that part was true, the rest of her story would surely make sense. My parents had trusted her. I *had* to believe they weren't the kind of idiots that wouldn't thoroughly check out a person they put in charge of their only child.

I flipped the pillow and hugged the cool side to my face and chest. A little more relaxed, I began to cast my mind over the rest of what Olga had told me before she'd finally taken me home. She'd offered me more sandwiches and I'd downed a second soda. I'd gradually calmed down enough to think more clearly. I'd even managed to begin quizzing Olga, which led to me figuring something out. Something super important.

"The second message we got was left for us in the restroom of the Atlas Studios – FIND UNICORNS. It's got to be code, yes? Olga – is Maxim a 'unicorn?'"

Her extended silence was perfect. Perfectly *guilty*. She wasn't going to help me? Okay, fine. Maybe I could guess some more on my own.

"Makes sense that he is," I continued, watching her reactions. "Someone wants to find Maxim, they think I might lead them to him if I keep investigating. They feed me hints and tips. All of which makes me think they don't know what *you* know, Olga."

She smiled, somewhat enigmatically. "Go on."

"Am I on the right track?"

"You're quite good at this, you should consider a career in intelligence or security."

"Unicorns are… rare. Is that it? Does Maxim have a rare blood type and they want his organs?"

Olga inhaled, noisily. "That's quite some imagination, Roni. But you're way off base."

"Ah – then you *do* know why they refer to him as a 'unicorn'?"

She blinked twice. Again with the mysterious silence. "We're not there yet, Roni. I promise I'll tell you everything – *if* we find Maxim. But please, understand that it's for your own protection that I don't tell you now."

In fact the only other thing I was able to glean from Olga before we waved goodbye outside Kenzie's house, was a major bit of intel about the organization at which this 'Maxim Santiago' was a volunteer. Even that was only on account of my general sleuthiness.

Before we left her safe house or whatever it was, Olga went to the bathroom, this time to pee, not to change her outfit. She left her phone on the table. I was able to get to it before the screen locked. After checking gently that the bathroom door was safely closed, I searched her message app for 'Maxim Santiago' and found one mention.

Maxim Santiago Patria y Vida.

Obviously as soon as I got the chance, which was later in my own bedroom, I'd searched the Internet for a charitable organization known as '*Patria y Vida.*' I checked in Tapachula and also the entire state of Chiapas, then all of Mexico. There wasn't one. No such organization existed. This was shortly before I'd gone to bed. But on the edge of dropping off to sleep, in that between-time when your brain is halfway to shutting down, it occurred to me to look a little harder.

My Internet search for *Patria y Vida* had been dominated by links to a popular song from Cuba. The words mean 'Homeland and Life.'

I hadn't entirely overlooked this, in case you think my first attempt was sloppy. La Chica Curiosa does her homework, 'kay? In fact, I'd listened to the song just before going to bed. It was a tough, melancholy reggaeton track, a protest song. A message from the generation of 2020 to those idealistic revolutionaries of 1959. The song was a lament over the failure of revolutionary dreams, which now lay in ruins, while the young and old of Cuba today struggle with hunger and poverty. Roughly translated it goes:

> *This is my way of telling you*
> *My people cry and I feel their voice*
> *You five nine, me double two*
> *Sixty years of locked dominoes*

I watched the video. It was impossible to ignore the betrayal and anger and sadness in the eyes of the three singers. Then I started reading about what happened when the song was released. One of the artists fled to the USA – he knew the Cuban government would recognize it as a protest. People in Cuba started taking to the streets in actual protest, singing that song. In the USA, out of solidarity Cuban-Americans did the same. The Cuban government shut down street protests, often with violence. From 2020 onwards the island was a pan on the boil. Their government held the lid down firmly. It didn't matter to them how badly they hurt their citizens.

So yeah, I listened to *Patria y Vida* a bunch of times. The lyrics must have been on my mind because as was about to sleep I thought about the line 'you five-nine, me double two.' That's how the song referred to 1959 and 2020. Not '59-20' but '59-22'. You had to know Spanish to hear it, though.

5922. There was something familiar about the number. I knew I'd seen it somewhere recently. But I couldn't recall *where*. I fell asleep trying to remember. Well, I was so exhausted, I slept through the alarm. When Kenzie's mom, Zara shook me awake there was a look of genuine alarm on her face, a harbinger of the horror that awaited.

"Have you heard from Olga?"

I shook my head, bewildered.

"Weren't you supposed to be catching a flight?"

I sat up, still groggy. Zara was pulling clothes from my cupboard and drawers, bustling about. "Put these on."

I reached for the phone, which was now on my nightstand.

Zara tsked. "Leave your phone. Hurry! You're supposed to check in at least two hours before! You have to get to the airport in fifteen minutes."

Only then did it occur to me that Olga *wasn't* lurking in the living room or kitchen, impatiently waiting for me.

"Wait – so didn't Olga call you either? Cos she was supposed to pick me up. Maybe it's fine. The flight's probably delayed."

Bobbie swept into the room then, phone in hand. "I've checked. The flight is not delayed."

Kenzie showed up at the door in his pjs. We looked at each other in turn, reaching a mutual understanding without any words.

"Olga gave me access to the booking," I said, hesitantly. "She said it's super-flexible."

"Then you should change it," Bobbie said. "Because you're not getting on that flight. Airport security is no joke these days."

Still reluctant, I picked up my phone. "Change it…? For when?"

"Doesn't matter," Bobbie said. "Why not the same time tomorrow? Olga can change it again if she decides she's ready after all. Then maybe you can catch a later flight today. First you need to talk to her, find out why she's late picking you up."

I yawned. "I'll call her."

I put the cell phone to my ear. It rang six times then went to a robot voicemail. Kenzie tried to say something reassuring to smooth things over with me, so did Zara. Bobbie, however, locked eyes with me and *instantly* got it. Perhaps Olga had shared more than I knew. Either way, Bobbie was under no illusions that this was normal. She knew that something was wrong. At that stage we had not even the faintest idea how wrong.

"Guess I'm not going to Mexico today," I concluded, pulling on a pair of jeans followed by a loose, striped cotton sweater.

"The reservation," Bobbie insisted.

I picked up my phone again, glaring. "On it." Clicking through to the flight reservation, I changed the booking for the following day. "Happy now?"

In a tone more conciliatory than her wife's, Zara said, "I'll drive you to Olga's hotel."

I hunted for my shoes, mumbling thanks. Then I had one of those odd feelings you sometimes get, call it a premonition. A vague sense of unease at the idea of leaving the house.

"Umm… would it be okay if I stayed?"

Zara frowned. "But shouldn't you come too? In case Olga's running late? Then you can leave together, right away."

"They're not getting on that flight," Bobbie said. She fixed her wife with an expression that was loaded with meaning.

I'm not sure if Zara understood whatever it was that Bobbie was trying to convey, but she nodded at once. "I'll go over there, find out why Olga's plans have changed. Roni, you eat some breakfast."

I didn't eat breakfast, we didn't get that flight, and me not going to the hotel turned out to be a pretty smart move.

FOURTEEN

CONNECTIONS

The night before, while driving me back to Kenzie's house, Olga and I had finally talked about the past. About Maxim Santiago and his mother, Masha.

"Do you remember how you met him?"

In the passenger seat I'd shaken my head, bemused. Not at the situation, which was less tense than it had been earlier that evening, even though our upcoming trip to Mexico already had me buzzing with trepidation. Her question seemed more like an ice-breaker, something she should have asked earlier in the process. But that was Olga – always business first, then fun.

"It was in the third grade. I guess we'd have been seven years old, seeing as how we both started at the same time at the D.C. International School."

"I remember. I recommended that school to them, in fact."

"That figures. Can't imagine they'd have gone for anything so 'globalist' on their own."

"They weren't like that back then," Olga reminded me.

"Anyhow, I started school aged seven. It was weird for me to have classes in French."

"I thought you were in the Spanish program?"

"After fourth grade I was. But when we applied to the school, the Spanish program was full. They got me private tuition in French a couple months before I started. Anyhow, in that first lesson a teacher asked me something in front of the class. I just froze, y'know?"

"You didn't understand?"

"Weirdly, I think I did. But I just couldn't get myself to say the words in French. So this other new kid, Maxim, watched me for a second. Then all of a sudden he takes my hand and whispers the answer to me in this *beautiful* French."

I paused, still remembering the feel of his hand. Warm and dry, his hand not much bigger than mine but with all the assurance of a grown-ups. The way my ear buzzed from his whispered French. How he observed me for a few long seconds, with those serious brown eyes, far too earnest for the age we were.

"Then in English he says, 'don't worry, they want us to be happy, they want us to like them.' And instantly, I felt calm. He was talking about our classmates. I had no clue, I assumed they were waiting for me to fall on my ass. That was pretty incredible insight for a seven-year old, don't you think?"

"Perhaps not for Maxim," Olga had replied, quietly.

Later I would remember how easily she had accepted this. I'd had years to get to know Maxim so for me it didn't seem like an odd comment. He really *had* seemed wiser than his years. But later, after everything that happened with Olga, I started thinking about what this little aside said about how well she knew Maxim. Pretty well, it seemed. So why did she need me to identify him?

Right after Olga had made the observation, however, I was too absorbed with telling the rest of the story she'd asked for, the story of how I met Maxim.

"After that I saw Maxim as more than an ally, but also a protector."

I wasn't being entirely honest with Olga. Truth is, I had a crush on Maxim, the first crush of my young life. It struck so early that I didn't wholly comprehend what was happening to me, only that I loved sitting beside him in class, loved to see him smile, loved even more the occasional reappearance of that oh-so-serious expression. Pure soulful concern. I recalled the warm, dry, comforting feel of my hand in his. It was as though, while we had that connection nothing bad could happen. It might seem like a small thing but I couldn't forget it, couldn't stop from wondering – would that ever happen again? And if it did, what would that even mean?

In the fourth grade a spot opened up in the Spanish program. I moved across and Maxim and I were no longer in the same class. Had I known from the start that we'd never be as close again, I might have been heartbroken. But what does any kid know about their future, at that age? My mom promised me that she'd arrange play dates. I believed her, but it didn't happen. Anyway, in the fourth grade they sat me next to Marc Mackenzie and I found a new friend.

Kenzie made me laugh a lot. We used to tease each other, write 'I love Miss B,' draw love-hearts in each other's notebooks and then try to attract our teacher's attention to it. We had an unspoken rule to use pencil so the victim could get to any graffiti with an eraser before 'Miss B' noticed, and a friendly agreement to issue a warning and a hint about where it might be written. Idiot that I am, I once wrote in ink. Don't even ask me why. Kenzie was incandescent. I still remember being shocked that he could be *so* angry with me for *so* long. And yet eventually, he did forgive me.

The vibe between me and Kenzie was a lot more fun than what I felt around Maxim. With Maxim, I'd be unable to stop myself trembling lightly whenever I saw him alone. I'd wonder if he'd come over to talk to me, or if he'd even noticed I was there. When I realized that he never seemed close with anyone, I was relieved.

Yeah – relieved to see him alone. I know how it seems, but it's the truth. My jealousy kept rearing up, even though I didn't understand it at the time.

"We didn't hang out much until the fifth grade," I continued. "That's when Maxim asked me and Kenzie to form a jazz trio with him."

Olga nodded, hands at ten and two on the wheel, eyes on the road ahead. She remembered our trio. "Your mom and dad were so excited to see you perform that song."

Sitting in her car, I'd been shocked into silence. How could I have forgotten that?

Yes, we'd performed for our parents, privately. It'd happened just once; a rehearsal, one week before Maxim and Masha disappeared. Maxim had agreed to Masha's request that we play *The Forgotten Village* once through at her house, before our parents took us home. Mr. Garibaldi had promised to let us perform in the next school palooza in front of all the community – usually Maxim's solo spot, but he'd not yet listened to us play. That must be why I didn't remember earlier, in the music room. We hadn't played it to anyone *there*. But at Masha's, we had. We were sounding okay by then, which was the only reason Maxim agreed to let the parents hear. Their faces when they heard us – wow.

"Olga, that's amazing. I'd forgotten. Thank you," I'd told her, touching her forearm. "Thank you for reminding me."

The next morning, as I waited for Zara to return from the hotel with Olga, I checked my backpack one last time and remembered my discussion with Olga the previous night.

I sent a message to Zara: **What's up? On your way back yet?**

Then I lay back on my rumpled bed, phone in hand. I must have dropped off to sleep again. I woke suddenly, confused to find myself in a bustling open-air Mexican market. Olga was next to me but when she opened her mouth and talked, no sounds came out.

Oh fine, fine, I told myself. *I'm dreaming.*

Dream-me wandered lazily through the aisles admiring mounds of dark green limes, mangos, pale yellow guanabanas, streaked, stubby bananas, apricots – a blaze of color. The air felt warm, heavy and moist. Nearby but out of sight, a tinny stereo played a *cumbia.* Olga materialized in front of me again with a triumphant grin, saying, *Ya chamaca, ya lo encontramos. Hey girl, we found him.* Her finger loomed before my face, an opal-studded ring prominent and matching the blue of her nail polish. My eyes followed this silent, pointing index digit to where fifteen yards away stood a tall, lean, tanned teenager wearing a blue and red tank-top and jean shorts. His light-brown hair was cut in a faux Mohican, shorn at the sides. His jaw was square and clean-shaven. His eyebrows were thick and prominent… then they faded, becoming light and thin. His eyes were blue, then green, then brown. I couldn't make out his face. Feature by feature, he became fuzzy and diffuse.

Because this is a dream, I reminded myself. I woke up. My phone was buzzing, ringing. Zara was calling.

"Stay there," she said. There was a peculiar, muted note to her voice. "I'll be right with you."

"What about Olga?"

"Stay there," she repeated and hung up.

My earlier premonition ought to have kicked in again but in the moment, I ignored Zara's strange tone. The warm, happy memory of locating Maxim in a Mexican market – even though I knew it was a dream –

had bled into my waking state. I retained a lingering image of Olga from the dream. She'd looked totally different. Confident as usual, yes, but also supremely relaxed and happy. Her fair hair had been loose and tumbled in waves around her shoulders, she had on these large, super-trendy sunglasses, jogging pants combined with heels and a crop-top. And on her fingers a collection of colorful rings and perfectly-manicured nails.

So no, I didn't fret. I just checked my bag one last time and waited. All the while humming a total earworm – the *cumbia* tune that'd been playing in the background of my dream. Later I remembered it well enough to use one of those apps to identify the song as *Procura* by Chichi Peralta. Which figures, because my own mind is definitely incapable of composing something so catchy. The clues of this bizarre premonition were there, if I'd been awake.

Zara rocked up a few minutes later. The instant I saw her face, I knew. If my mind had been shielding me from something terrible, the barrier finally came tumbling down.

"What's happened to Olga?"

"The paramedics are with her now…"

Zara put down her handbag and took both my hands. I felt my throat go dry, like coarse sandpaper as I tried to swallow. All the moisture in my face seemed to have evaporated. Even my eyes seemed to creak.

"I'm so sorry, Roni. Olga is dead. It seems likely she had a heart attack. Very sudden. Do you know if she'd been having cardiac problems?"

Of course I didn't know anything about her medical issues. I barely knew Olga Garcia. I'd experienced more connection with her in one brief dream than in all the times I'd hung out with her. But also, I wasn't *entirely* clueless. Olga's death wasn't natural, however it might seem.

FIFTEEN

MY MISERABLE TRUTH

The next hour, I barely remember. I was in shock, for sure. What I recall from the immediate aftermath of hearing that Olga was dead, is astonishment at hearing that Zara had done something completely *wild*.

At first it seemed like cool-wild, but by the end of that day this opinion turned around completely. What she'd done was wildly reckless, thoughtless and extremely dangerous. The *something* Zara had done was to retrieve Olga's cell phone from the hotel room.

Zara was the first on the scene, along with one of the hotel receptionists. They had gone together to the room, after Zara raised the alarm. Olga wasn't answering Zara's calls, nor the door, even though she hadn't checked out. The front desk guy at first wasn't happy to disturb a guest's room, but the panic in Zara's voice had eventually persuaded him. So together they walked in to find Olga's still-warm corpse, wide-eyed and mouth gasping for air. The receptionist called the ambulance. He'd stepped outside the room for just a moment, becoming impatient for the paramedics to arrive. That's when Zara got the brilliant idea to grab Olga's phone.

When the paramedics showed up they bagged Olga's possessions, ready to hand over to the cops, who showed up a little afterwards. No-one noticed that the phone was missing. My first thought when I heard all this was that Olga probably had another one – the work phone from the UN.

Oh yes and Zara managed to unlock the phone she took. She'd been left alone for a minute with Olga's dead body, so you can guess how.

Returning to her own house, Zara placed Olga's phone on the table. She explained how she'd grabbed it, unlocked it and then changed the screen lock. I was rapt with admiration. We all were. That's some top-drawer detective work. Zara, the sly minx – who'd have thought?

"I was worried that Olga might have some private information about Roni, in her phone," she admitted.

Kenzie flashed me an anxious look. Tears sprung to my eyes. *Zara was protecting me.* I wondered fleetingly if Olga's final will and testament mentioned a new guardian for me. Or if she even had a will. My mom and dad hadn't anticipated that Olga might die before I reached eighteen, so there was no backup guardian. Obviously, I was already thinking that I wanted Zara and Bobbie to adopt me. That Zara would do something so risky to protect me, made me certain that I was right to choose them. If they'd have me, that is.

I picked up the phone and began to scroll through Olga's texts and messages. It didn't take long to find something to make my bones shudder.

FIND UNICORNS.

Over my shoulder, I could sense Kenzie growing still.

Zara asked, "Who sent Olga that message? What does it mean?"

Kenzie and I glanced at each other. I nodded slightly as he prepared to reply; "We don't know who sent it. But someone left the same message for us in the restroom at the Atlas Studios."

Bobbie boggled. "I'm sorry – *what*?"

We explained the whole message-in-steam on the mirror in the Atlas Studios bathroom. Immediately, Bobbie and Zara transformed into a couple of cops doing an interrogation. When did we see it? Why did we go there? Who knew we'd been? Did anyone follow us? Were we sure? Hadn't we seen anyone come out of the restroom, before I'd gone in there? Roni, try to remember!

I answered with the truth as far as possible, reminding myself that I'd been planning to podcast the whole story. *Been planning* was the salient point, because now I wasn't so sure. Olga had insisted that I cancel the podcast. Now she was dead. It was plain to see that two and two were adding up to four. However, I hadn't yet figured out that it might be smartest to tell no-one else about our investigation. The shock of Olga's death was still settling on me, like snow, fear chilling me slowly from the outside.

"You think 'find unicorns' has something to do with child trafficking," Zara said, frowning as I finished talking. She sounded highly skeptical. "And that Masha might have been involved?"

"Olga told me Masha wasn't involved," I replied, stubborn as you like. "That should be good enough for us."

"But how well did Olga know Masha?" asked Bobbie. She looked at Kenzie and me in turn, as if we might know, which we didn't. Like I said, I hardly knew Olga. "Then why," Bobbie continued, "should it be good enough for us that Olga said she wasn't?"

"I think Olga knew Masha," I said, considering. "Just from the way she spoke about her. Like, she seemed super-confident, just threw it out there without any hesitation or doubt – 'Masha is not a child trafficker.' Or something close to that."

I began to remember the conversation more clearly. Olga had admitted to me that Maxim probably *was* being trafficked by someone and that it was for money. The only part she'd had difficulty believing was that

Masha was in on the scam. Not that I shared this with Bobbie and Zara, although I perhaps should have. I was in shock, not processing anything properly. So *much* shock that it wasn't until much later that evening, alone and trembling under the quilt, that I remembered '5922.'

It had turned into a long, exhausting day. The cops visited in the afternoon to interview me about Olga. I told them the truth, that I'd been abducted by Olga's butler 'Tobias.' If I'd had more presence of mind I might have lied and said that he picked me up after school for a scheduled meet with my legal guardian. But like an idiot, I told the truth.

Maybe it was just as well that I did, because Kenzie, Bobbie and Zara had been trying to contact me in those hours during which my SIM card had been removed. I'd left it out of the phone until I was safely back home. The cops already had the address of the house in the suburbs to where I'd been taken. They'd traced the address from Olga's other phone, the one that had remained with her body, presumably her work phone.

"The house is owned by the United Nations Office of Counter-Terrorism," one cop told us, sounding a little disappointed. "It's one of the places they house visiting officials."

The whole set-up appeared to be 'clean,' yet I could tell that like us, the cops were wary. Olga's death didn't seem natural to them, either. They'd sent for a toxicology report. It was obvious they expected it to come back with a verdict of poison.

"Can you think of any reason why someone might want to kill your guardian?"

"Maybe because of her job in counter-terrorism?"

"Hmm," the cop said. He didn't buy my alleged ignorance, either. But what could he do?

After they'd gone, Kenzie and I managed to get some alone time in my room. I announced I had a headache and beckoned him to follow me. His moms were reluctant to let us go but I only slightly had to play up my genuine stress. When I said I needed to lie down, I wasn't kidding.

At this point in the evening I swiftly brought Kenzie up to speed on what I'd discovered about *Patria y Vida* and '5922.' I was certain it was a clue to Maxim's whereabouts. Why else would Olga leave a cryptic, reggaeton-themed message about Maxim Santiago?

Kenzie looked doubtful. It could be that I didn't explain it well enough for him to follow. That's on me; I have a tendency to gloss over stuff.

"Olga sent that *Patria y Vida* message to a cell phone with a D.C. area code," I told him, by way of clarification. I showed him the message. Then in front of him, I tried calling the number from her phone. There was no reply.

"Well, that was dumb," Kenzie commented as I ended the call. "Olga's dead. Now whoever you just called will be able to find out that someone *other* than the cops has her phone."

He was right. I froze, horrified that I could be so stupid. At least I had the presence of mind to open Olga's phone, remove the SIM card and turn off Wi-Fi. I punched his arm, in frustration. "If you knew, why'd you let me do it?"

"Me? Stop *you*?" Kenzie scoffed. "Like that ever works. Anyway, it's done now. You should take out *your* SIM card, too."

I shook my head rapidly, not wanting him to be right. "Seriously? My SIM, in my phone?"

"Yeah, 'fraid so. Your phone was at the same place as Olga's last night. Better to be safe. Padi, do you want to tell me what's really going on? Cos I'm pretty sure you didn't tell my moms and the cops *everything*."

I tried to bluff. "Oh, you're 'pretty sure?'"

"Yep. We've been friends a long time. You think I can't tell when you're hiding something? Remove your SIM. Don't freak out – you can still use the phone for web stuff."

I did as he asked, cursing under my breath. I handed him the SIM card, which he crushed under an empty glass. For a moment I turned my back on him so he wouldn't see how red my cheeks had gone. I felt terrible about not sharing everything I knew. By then, the fear had well and truly slipped into my bloodstream. I couldn't think straight. I was making idiot mistakes, such as calling from Olga's phone. What if the next thing I did or said led to someone else getting killed, someone I really cared about? Because when it came to Olga, that was my miserable truth. Olga might have been my legal guardian, might have known all about me. But I didn't know *her*. Until yesterday I had no idea what she did for a living. I'd cared more about her in a dream than ever in waking life. Yet even so, this brush with death was close enough to paralyze me with fear.

What if Olga was murdered because she was searching for the Santiagos? Did that mean they'd be coming for me next, tying up all their loose ends? At that moment, I just wanted to forget all about it and to delete the trailer for *What Happened to the Santiagos?* But there was still '5922' and did I mention that I'm incurably curious? Which is why later, when I should have been sleeping, I jumped right back in.

5922

Before we get into what happened next, it's important to remember that my bag was *already packed* and I had a *totally flexible* reservation for two seats on a flight to Tapachula via Mexico City. Not that this is an excuse or anything, but I feel like it's a mitigating factor. Had it not been for that, things might have been very different. I'd have stayed in DC. To this day I'm almost certain that Olga's killers would have come after me.

Did I put myself in even more danger through the choices I made that day? Maybe. But let's not kid ourselves; that morning, approximately 24 hours since Olga Garcia was found dead from a recent heart attack, with a record of a call from Olga's phone made from Kenzie's house and my details in her other phone, I was already in danger.

I didn't get much sleep that night, on account of '5922.' The overwhelming stress of the previous day had sent me to bed early, quivering like a frightened kitten and with about as much fight in me. Yet after a few hours' sleep, a teeny tiny bomb went off in my subconscious. Around three in the morning, I woke up sharply, and not because of some hideous demon at the end of my bed or whatever. No – what woke me was a sudden, clear image of *where* I'd seen '5922.'

The image of '5922' came from a memory I'd been struggling to recall, ever since I read the lyrics of *Patria y Vida* after finding the message on Olga's phone: *Maxim Santiago Patria y Vida.*

At first I'd suspected '5922' was a clue to his

address, a street number or zip code or something. But when I woke in the middle of the night, the image seared into my brain was of a website listing charitable organizations registered in the state of Chiapas, Mexico. Not the most thrilling information, which is probably why it didn't make much impression. All the same, yay for the subconscious mind and its ability to retrieve trivia, even if the filing system can be somewhat erratic.

I grabbed my laptop, sat up in bed, turned it on and searched my browser history for '5922.' There it was, tucked away on a very boring list of charities and non-governmental organizations. The driest website you've ever seen, devoid even of photos, but the information I needed was there.

Friends of 5922 – charity focusing on support and legal advice for Cubans in Mexico wishing to emigrate to the USA. Tapachula, Chiapas.

This *had* to be the organization where Maxim Santiago was a volunteer. Olga had believed so, I was certain. '5922' had to be a clue to that song, *Patria y Vida*. For whatever reason, Olga knew about it. Maybe she was a fan of Cuban music, who knows? Either way – she'd used her personal cell to send a coded message about it: *Maxim Santiago Patria y Vida*. It was too bad that I didn't know *to whom* she had sent the message. For my sake, I had to hope it was to an ally, someone that wouldn't go straight to the cops when they discovered someone using Olga's personal phone *after* she'd been registered as dead.

Yes, in hindsight it sounds delusional to expect that such a person *wouldn't* go to the cops. But it was the middle of the night and I'd been under tons of stress. Not the best state to deal with the consequences of a thoughtless phone call. I chose to be optimistic, yes, I admit it.

I googled the street address of 'Friends of 5922' and committed it to memory. Not very difficult – it was 7a Avenida Sur 47b. Not by the time you read this, obviously, in case you bothered to look it up. After everything that happened, the organization was disbanded. But we'll get to that.

Their headquarters were located close to a hotel, the tiny, yet oh-so-environmentally-conscious Blue Dolphin, only thirty dollars a night. My finger hovered over the link 'Make a Reservation.' I could always cancel. I went ahead, booked three nights starting the following day.

A plan was already forming in my mind. I didn't yet know if I dared go through with it. Even *pretending* that I might – larping as an international spy on the lam – was thrilling. An incredible buzz, on a par to the feeling I'd gotten when reading that very first clue, the message from 'Abby' on my podcast: '*Remember The Forgotten Village?*"

Then, with my imagination still playing out a semi-fantasy in which I was Olga's sidekick and suddenly first in line for an assassination attempt, I deleted all references to Maxim Santiago from my phone. Every single one. Finally, around four am, I went back to sleep. It wasn't for long.

Around seven, Bobbie marched into my room in what felt like a replay of the previous morning but starring her not Zara, even though it was two hours earlier than yesterday. I shook myself awake and tried to focus in on what she was saying.

"Did you make a call from Olga's phone? The police want to know."

"The police?" I repeated, slow and stupid.

"The lead detective called Zara, just now. Olga was poisoned – they were right. Novichok. The police have Olga's work phone. The detective says you called it yesterday, from her personal phone. Is that right? Or was it Kenzie? Because Zara definitely didn't."

I grimaced. "Novichok? I've heard of that."

"Yeah," Bobbie said dismissively, her expression severe. "It's a nerve agent. The Cheka – the secret service of the Third Russian Empire – uses it. Don't change the subject – did you make that call?"

I tried to turn the grimace into a smile, but it probably ended up coming across more like a death mask. "Ye-es?"

Bobbie threw up her hands in dismay. "Honestly, Roni! Now you've incriminated Zara. They'll know *she* took the phone. Removing evidence from a crime scene is a crime!"

I rose to my feet and looked her in the eye. "No. Zara couldn't have known at the time that it was a crime scene. She only knew that my legal guardian was dead and that private information about me was on Olga's phone. That gave her the right to take the phone – to protect me."

The fear in Bobbie's expression seemed to subside. "You're right. Yeah. How could she have known Olga was killed? They've only just confirmed it was murder."

She managed a relieved smile, gave me a quick hug and turned to leave. But then, she added a *very* worrying coda. "Anyway, the police want to speak to you. They're coming here at eleven."

SEVENTEEN

Novichok

It's a good thing Bobbie wasn't facing me right then, because I'm pretty sure all the blood drained from my face. I went to my laptop and began to research Novichok. What I found made my straight hair begin to curl.

According to Wikipedia: Novichok (Russian: Новичóк, lit. 'newcomer, novice, newbie') is a group of nerve agents, some of which are binary chemical weapons. The agents were developed at the State Scientific Research Institute for Organic Chemistry and Technology by the Soviet Union and later by the Third Russian Empire. They'd been used in the assassinations and attempted assassinations of Russian dissidents abroad as well as foreign citizens. The government of the TRE routinely denied all allegations of approving any use of their exclusive nerve agent. But no-one believed a word of it. 'The Czar's Poison' was its nickname for a reason.

So that's who was coming after Olga and the 'unicorns' – the freaking Czar of the Russian Empire. *Great.* Thank you, life.

I couldn't be sure that my hunch was on point, of course. It might have been a coincidence – maybe they wanted Olga for a totally different reason, and not because of something to do with a possible Cuban-Russian spy involved with child trafficking and terrorist organizations. Even so, at the time it felt like hearing that Darth Vader was on my trail. I didn't want to wait to find out how effective was the assassin they'd send.

By the time Kenzie knocked on my door around

thirty minutes later, I'd already made my decision. I'd showered and dressed and was figuring how to get out of the house without anyone seeing. I didn't want to be there when the police arrived. If whoever was behind *this* could get to an agent of the United Nations Counter Terrorism Office, I had to assume it'd be a cinch to 'hit' me. After all, how hard could it be to infiltrate the cops? According to Olga, even the CIA would rattle with the sound of Chekists.

Kenzie, bless his heart, was still in his pjs when he confronted me.

"You're *what?*"

"I'm leaving. Cover for me, yeah? Say I'm in the bathroom with cramps. Or something."

He gawped. "Where will you go?"

"I'll use the ticket to Mexico. Remember? Bobbie told me to change the reservation for today. And I'm pretty, pretty glad she did." I sat on edge of my bed and pointed to my packed case. "All ready to go."

Kenzie was aghast. For a few seconds he simply couldn't talk. The abject horror in his eyes wouldn't budge. It was infectious. Watching him, I began to panic.

"If you blab, Kenzie, swear to God, I'll... I'll... that'll be it for us. *Forever.* Do you understand? I'm counting on you."

To my huge relief he began to relax, at least as far as his expression moving from horror to concern. "You're unbelievable. All this because the cops want to talk to you?"

"No, dummy, not because the cops want to talk to me. Because Chekists killed Olga. On account of her being on the trail of Maxim Santiago, the son of a Cuban-Russian spy, probably. Ay-kay-ay a 'unicorn' – whatever that is – and mixed up in child trafficking, on top of it all."

Kenzie quailed. "Jeez," he said after a pause. "Do you even know what you sound like?"

I glared. "I do. Like I need psychiatric help, and fast. And yet. This is where we are."

He looked thoughtful. "If anything, it's worse than that. If you're right…"

"Which I am."

Kenzie shrugged but didn't disagree. "If you're right, and if our leaked Vault 7 intel is reliable, then the child trafficking was either done *by* or *to* the benefit of a *terrorist* organization."

"Ex-actly. Anyone who could get to Olga could find out she was scheduled to fly to Tapachula. With *me*. I have to assume they know that much."

I thought he might protest but instead, he fell silent for a second, then, "They probably left both Olga's phones at the scene to make it seem like a natural death. That kind of attention to detail, it's…" He shuddered. "Brrr. Whoever it is, they're an expert. Scary."

Nodding, I pulled on a pair of sneakers and began to lace them. "Right now, I figure they know I'm here, that we didn't go to Mexico. Zara had access to Olga's fingerprint and so did they. That means we have to assume they've examined the phone."

Kenzie agreed. "Yeah. It's safest if we assume we're *not* dealing with incompetents. They got Olga good, *and* they left a phone to entrap whoever else she might have brought into the mystery."

A lump formed in my throat. They got Olga because of me. Because they hacked my phone and tracked my movements. Maybe they didn't track me all the way to Olga's safe house, but they got close enough. I couldn't bring myself to tell Kenzie. There are levels of idiocy you just don't want to admit.

I said, "If they're surveilling Olga and me, they'd

have seen that the flight was booked for yesterday. They'll assume we didn't go. That the booking expired and no-one's going to Tapachula. Which leaves the coast there clear – for them." Blinking, I whispered, "If that guy in Tapachula is our Maxim, he's in danger."

"Just a little. So *you* want to reach him before they do. Is that the plan?"

It was a relief to see how quickly Kenzie caught on to what I'd spent the small hours of the morning figuring out. I have zero problem with people being smarter than me – when you're as impatient as me it's way easier to deal with than the reverse.

"About that," Kenzie said. "I googled Tapachula. That's a city of three hundred thousand people. How're you or the Chekist going to find him?"

"Them? No clue. Me? I have his address."

"What? How?"

"Remember what I told you about Olga's *Patria y Vida* clue?" I did a hand-wavy thing. "It's in that vein. But y'know, tick-tock."

"Padi – no. You don't get to just leave."

"'Fraid so."

I had to, and soon. Before my nerves frayed and I chickened out. A flight to Tapachula, a few nights on my own in Mexico. How hard could it be? I was almost eighteen, for crying out loud. Old enough to enlist in the military. If I was old enough to be trained to kill human beings, I was old enough for a long weekend on my own in Mexico.

I picked up my case. "According to the cops, the phone I called was Olga's work phone. Which means guess what? Olga sent that *Patria y Vida* message about Maxim *to herself*. It's a clue to where Maxim is, because she couldn't risk typing the address. It was in code. So there's a good chance whoever killed her hasn't understood it. Especially if they're Chekists in the USA, illegals or whatnot."

"How so?"

"I dunno. A hunch. Illegals here are trained to be expert in US culture, not Cuban. This feels like a niche, Cuban thing. You have to know Spanish to hear the lyric, because the song is referring to nineteen fifty-nine and twenty-twenty but the lyrics says 'double-two'. Double two, twenty-two. Fifty-nine, twenty-two, not fifty-nine, twenty."

He shrugged. "That is 'niche.' Just the same, all the respect in the world but you're a Mexican-American, not *Cubana*. If you can figure out a 'really niche Cuban thing I'm pretty sure a trained Kremlin agent can, too."

"Maybe, maybe not. I feel like I got lucky. Maybe they won't?"

He gazed, eyes large and soulful. "Padi. Roni, think about it. Please. There's a lot riding on your 'maybe.'"

"My best chance is to beat them to it."

"Why?"

"Because once I've passed on Olga's warning to Maxim Santiago, there's no reason to harm me."

"*If* you get there first. *If* you don't make whoever they send. And *if* they don't just decide to off you for the heck of it. Those people are dangerous, Padi. You do *not* mess with Chekists."

I looked him straight in the eye. "I've thought about this all night long. Whichever way you slice this pie, I'm in danger until either Maxim gets the warning from me, or they get to him. And I don't want to stay here in D.C. waiting for someone to grab me off the street again. If you and your moms cover for me just a few days, I can *do* this, Marky Marc. The flights are booked, hotel is booked. I'm going."

Kenzie took a deep breath, releasing it slowly. "You are one dedicated podcaster."

I grinned. "Aren't I, though?"

"But if you think you're doing this alone, you don't know me very well. Kay? Your little speech about *'that'll be it for us. Forever.'* Turnabout is fair play. Unless you let me do this with you."

I tried to object but he put a finger to my lips and hissed. "Shh. No discussion. Give me five minutes to pack, then come find me. We'll go out my window, yours doesn't open all the way. In the meantime, change the reservation – put Olga's ticket in my name. M-C-K-E-N…"

"I know how to spell your version of 'Mackenzie'" I growled, pushing him out of my room. At the time, I had zero intention of allowing him to do something as plainly idiotic as to join me in something I deep down realized was almost suicidally dangerous. I knew what it felt like to be grabbed off the street. I knew how difficult it would be to live in fear of something like that happening again. Kenzie didn't. There was no good reason to drag a bestie into my own circle of hell. That's why I planned to ignore him and leave the house, the instant he closed my bedroom door.

But Kenzie was right. The window to my room *was* jammed.

EIGHTEEN

CAMBODIAN-OWNED DONUTS

We ended up leaving via Kenzie's bathroom window.

A lot had happened since my abduction-slash-discussion with Olga and I'd suppressed-slash-forgotten some of what we'd said. But waiting for Kenzie to pack, my thoughts began to clear. I remembered how convinced she'd been that I was being followed via spyware on my phone. She'd been so sure of it, she'd had Tobias remove the SIM card from my phone. I won't lie, at the time I didn't really believe Olga. A big mistake for me to put the SIM back in my phone. Thank goodness Kenzie had taken it out when he did.

I had to do better.

They killed Olga they killed Olga they killed her ran through my mind. Would I be next? The hairs on the back of my neck prickled. The skin on my forearms turned to gooseflesh. I felt something I'd never experienced before yet instantly recognized.

I was someone's prey.

It's a scary sensation, it washes over you in a wave. For a brief second I felt like it might be paralyzing me but with one single thought, that fear vanished. Then it was behind me, fading, like the fizz left after an electric shock.

The thought that saved me was this: *We can't let them follow us to the airport.*

Okay. I focused on my breath, in and out, until I felt my heartbeat slow. We couldn't leave through the front of the house, therefore Kenzie's bathroom window made sense. After that? I fought to recall any spy film or TV series I might have seen with relevant information, but came up with zero. What I needed was in there, had to be. Inconveniently, in that moment my mind was blank.

Kenzie arrived at his door, backpack slung over his shoulder.

"Aw, flip," I said, remembering. I had *one job*. "Forgot to change the booking to your name. No problem – we'll do it on the way. C'mon, we're going through your bathroom. Questions later."

If he was having second thoughts, I saw no signs. I mention this now, because later he definitely did. By then, it was too late.

We skirted red maples in the backyard and climbed over the fence, landing in the yard of the next door house. Dashing across that, we skipped over a wall at the back to another house on a neighboring street. A minute later we were strolling down that street, a little breathless but flushed with the confidence of an early win. Anyone surveilling the front of Kenzie's house would hopefully think we were still inside.

"We need a taxi," I told him, eyes scouring the road for an empty cab.

"On it. Why the devious exit?"

"Because Olga told me I've been followed for days."

Kenzie appeared to take this in his stride. "You were *already* being followed? You mean, even before you called Olga's phone from her other phone?"

"That's what she told me."

"Who's following you?"

"Unknown."

I didn't want to complicate things by telling him her theories. Clearly, it'd given Olga the jitters. Why else have me abducted just so we could talk? If she knew I was being followed, she had to ensure that whoever was tailing me didn't discover she'd reached out.

Evidently they'd done exactly that, or Olga would still be alive. *Aha*, you're probably thinking, *not necessarily. What if the person following you wasn't the same as the assassin who followed Olga?* And it's a great question. That's why you're probably smarter than I am, because at the time, it didn't occur to me.

On the way to the airport with Kenzie that morning, my plan to evade our tail was to switch taxis partway. I'd seen it in some film or TV series but I had no idea whether it was legit. Every time I thought about Olga, I felt pangs of distress mixed with twinges of exasperation. Would it have been too much trouble over the past two years for my legal guardian secretly to train me to handle myself in her world of counter-terrorism? Then I reminded myself that Olga hadn't succeeded in staying alive. So maybe she wouldn't have made the best trainer.

All we needed to do was fly to Mexico City, catch a connecting flight to Tapachula, grab a ride to the hotel, amble down to the offices of 'Friends of 5922' and ask for Maxim Santiago. If it was him, pass on a warning about the Cheka. If it wasn't, wish him well, reverse the order of all steps and return home.

No problemo. Even for a couple of seventeen-year-olds. So why were my teeth chattering on the inhale?

"We need two taxis," Kenzie remarked. "So we can change part-way. I know just the place, we can go through a side street and pick up another taxi on the other side. No way any car following us will be able to get around the block fast enough."

"Whoa, smart move!"

He continued, "And your phone has no SIM, so I'll

make the call. Better hand over the flight booking details, too. I'll make the changes."

I blinked with gratitude. Thank goodness one of us was thinking straight.

"Jeez. I've never seen Dulles International Airport so packed," he said when the second taxi dropped us outside the departures terminal.

"Tell me about it. Almost makes me miss the pandemic."

We headed for the security line. It was a monster. I was beginning to feel dizzy, partly hunger and partly nerves. The abduction and then Olga's death had made me lose my appetite for so long that it had now been over forty hours since I'd eaten more than a snack. Maybe it was the fact that I was finally taking steps to make sure that neither I nor Maxim, if it was Maxim, ended up dead like Olga. Or maybe my body was just craving protein, salt and fat. I scrolled through a list of food concessions in the neighboring departure lounge, practically drooling as I contemplated burgers and frosty milkshakes.

"Kenzie. We need a good excuse for why we're out, at least until the flight takes off." I checked the time on his phone. "That's two hours and thirty-two minutes. Else one of your moms might figure out that we've gone to the airport and get it into their heads to call someone and stop us leaving."

After a moment, Kenzie spat a few options. "We're at the zoo. No, the Smithsonian. No, our congresswoman is doing a meet-and-greet at the Capitol. No, wait, wait." A gleam entered his eye. "We won an invite to free donuts at the opening of a new Cambodian-owned donut place in Georgetown. It's from California. A *really* good one with the pink boxes and everything."

"Yeah, we should definitely go with the donuts. It's

whimsical enough to sound real. Also your moms know how obsessed you are with them, they might actually buy it."

We shuffled ahead in the security line.

He muttered, "I feel bad lying to them."

"Serious?" I fixed him with a stern glare. "If you feel bad now, telling them we're in a different part of D.C. scoffing deep-fried treats when we're *actually* at the airport waiting to leave the country, then how're you going to deal with telling them we're in a genuine foreign country waiting for a flight to a town on the border with Guatemala?"

Kenzie shook his head a little, as if he were trying to shake free some uncomfortable, persistent water in his ear. "I'll be fine."

"Yeah, totally seems like it."

"It's not all lies. There really is a new Cambodian-owned donut shop," he said in a small voice. "It looks so good."

I'd never doubted it. Kenzie knew every single donut shop in the city, their entire menu, and had ranked the various donuts. Also, he didn't like to lie. It'd be a lot easier for him to make the call if there were some truth mixed in. "Maybe we should eat at Dunkin'" I said. "Then you can talk honestly about eating donuts."

"I'm a horrible son," he lamented.

"But an amazing friend."

We reached the front of the security line and dropped our backpacks onto the conveyor belt. I checked the time. Two hours and six minutes before take-off. Once we were in the air it didn't really matter if they came after us. The image of Zara and Bobbie giving us thunder-stares if they caught up to us in Mexico, however, was definitely unnerving.

Would they threaten to ground us until we turned

eighteen? A definite possibility. Would they laugh in my face when I asked them to adopt me? It was getting more likely by the second. But then I thought about Olga, about how she'd died. My heart froze a little bit more each time I accepted it. If I'd *only* done what she'd wanted, gone straight to the airport that first night, she'd still be alive. I wouldn't have to sneak off to Mexico to finish what she started. Kenzie wouldn't have to lie to his moms.

Deep down I understood that it wasn't my responsibility or fault – Olga was a grown-ass woman, she made the decision to wait until the next day of her own free will. Yet I wasn't off the hook either. If not for me, she'd probably be alive. That was a cold fact, something I'd have to carry for the rest of my life. Which was why I had to find this Maxim Santiago candidate and warn him. I never, ever wanted to feel this guilt again.

NINETEEN

SEEING CHEKISTS EVERYWHERE

Bobbie and Zara did not take the news well. Kenzie's expression grew increasingly appalled as he listened through earbuds. I watched, taking bites from the chilled Gansito I'd bought at a bodega in the departure lounge of Mexico City airport, while we waited for the Tapachula flight. After a moment he pulled out one of his earbuds and jammed it into my left ear.

I objected, "Eww. Gross." Then I heard Zara on the verge of tears.

"I hope you never find out what it feels like to be put through this by a child."

Bobbie took over then, steely and calm, yet fierce and – honestly? A little scary.

"Here's what you're going to do. You're not going to Tapachula. You're going to rebook that return flight from Mexico City. If you're back home by this evening, we'll put this down to youthful misadventure. Understand this – you're causing real distress here."

"Moms…" pleaded Kenzie.

I interrupted. "Bobbie, I'm *not safe* in your house. Whoever killed Olga is following me. We made a call from her personal phone to her other phone, which I admit was really, really stupid, not *least* because it implicated Zara for removing Olga's phone from the scene, like we already talked about, but it's *done* now. Over! No take-backs allowed! Which means that Olga's killer will have tracked me to *your* house."

"But… but the police have Olga's other phone," Bobbie said, bewildered.

"The police can be infiltrated," I replied. I know it sounds extreme, but in that instant I was fully paranoid, seeing Chekists everywhere, even in the D.C. police.

"Doesn't even have to be the cops," Kenzie interjected. "Whoever killed Olga could have cloned *both* phones. The one *we* have and the one the cops have. The killer couldn't take either phone. It was meant to look like she died of natural causes, so why *wouldn't* her phones still be in the room? But they *could* take her phone data and set up another phone that'd *behave* like Olga's work phone. Call her work phone, you'd call the clone, too."

"And then they'd know you called from our house…" Bobbie murmured, dismayed.

"And then they'd know," agreed Kenzie. "I'm sorry, Mom."

Zara said, urgently, "But who is following you? And why?"

"Olga didn't say. She also told me I was being followed. We're not making this up. I had to leave, finish what she started. If I do that, then there's no point killing me. Right now though, I'm a target. I know too much."

Bobbie fumed, "Why didn't you mention any of this last night?"

"We didn't want you to worry," Kenzie said.

Zara sounded despondent. "What makes you so sure they'll stop?"

"Olga was searching for someone. She needed me to confirm their identity. Someone killed her, I think because they don't want that person found. I find who Olga was looking for, warn them, and it's over."

That was the theory, at least. It didn't seem to be going over all that well.

"This is far too dangerous! Let the police handle

it." Zara insisted. "They already know Olga was poisoned."

"Roni," Bobbie said, "You have absolutely no way of knowing whether this stops after you do whatever it is you think you're doing."

"Bobbie! I'm not," I said, clearly enunciating every syllable. "Safe in your house! And if you follow us, *you will lead* whoever was following me straight to us."

Silence. When Zara spoke again her voice was brimming with disappointment. "And when Olga told us that she was taking you to visit your uncle Johny, that was a lie?"

I sighed, relieved that the tension level seemed to be dialing down. "Yeah. I'm *sorry*. Listen, *none of this* was my idea. Olga needed my help and I wanted to help find my friend. C'mon, you know he was a big deal for me and Kenzie."

"Yeah, moms. This wasn't a huge issue, not until Olga got killed."

"Well, it really is now," Bobbie concluded, heavily.

I guess they felt cornered. Their maternal instincts were screaming at them to find us, help us. How must it feel to be told that this very action might lead to my death? And maybe Kenzie's too. A sickening realization, but also not my fault. None of this would have happened if I hadn't been curious, but that's life isn't it? Cans of worms don't usually advertise their contents.

"You're sure, absolutely *sure* that these people could follow you to our house?" Zara asked.

"I'm just a low-level hacker, *mami*," replied Kenzie. "And even I know that phones can be cloned. We have to assume that anyone who'd take on an agent from the Office of Counter-Terrorism will know what they're doing."

"Novichok," Bobbie said. The fire had gone out of

her voice, replaced with trepidation. "You know they call it the Czar's poison?"

"Uh-huh," we agreed, unhappily.

The extent of the danger seemed finally to strike Bobbie. "Is that who you think is after you? Chekists?"

"Mom, we don't know. But yeah, maybe."

"Oh dear!" Zara sounded distraught.

Bobbie became thoughtful. "And you're sure that you're not being followed now?"

"We were super-careful," Kenzie said.

Another long silence. Was Bobbie imagining either of us being abducted and tortured until we told Olga's killer everything we knew? I sure was.

Eventually, Bobbie said, "You've not exactly left us much choice, have you?"

Kenzie was on the verge of tears. "We didn't mean to cut you out!"

"Yeah, Bobbie, listen to your son. Better that only two of us are in danger, instead of all four."

"I know you're basically adults, but you're still our children!" Zara said, breaking into a sob. "*We* protect *you*, you don't protect us!"

"Ideally, maybe," I said, trying to sound reassuring. "But, y'know, it is what it is."

Bobbie broke in, curtly, "What can we do to help from here?"

She'd switched into her usual eminently practical mode and I loved her for it. Kenzie's moms had finally accepted that we were all in a no-win situation. Or rather that the only way out was to identify this Maxim Santiago candidate and pass on a warning that the Cheka were hunting him.

"Just root for us, moms," Kenzie urged. "This'll all be over in a couple days and we'll be home."

"We'll buy a burner phone and text you from it," I told them. "It'd be great to have you on standby if we need anything."

"Sure," Bobbie agreed. "Buy it as soon as you arrive in Tapachula, you hear? Text me the number immediately. And call us any time of day or night for anything, agreed?"

Zara chimed in, "Absolutely anything."

"Thank you moms," Kenzie said, "Thank you thank you thank you, I love you both, you're the greatest, the GOAT!"

"Yeah," I agreed. "Thank you. Seriously. You've no idea how much it means to know you have our backs."

What we'd all missed in the kerfuffle, however, was this: *Whoever killed Olga already knew where Maxim Santiago was.*

That's why they could afford to take Olga out. If they hadn't known his location, their best plan would have been to let her run all the way to Maxim, leading them straight to his door. I thought I was so clever deciphering the 5922 clue, but whoever killed Olga could have had hours, while she was a prisoner in her own hotel room. Enough time to clone data from her phones, discover the same message that I found – *Maxim Santiago Patria y Vida* – and arrive at the same conclusion as I had. All this *before* they poisoned her.

In fact – spoiler alert – Olga's killers knew where to find Maxim Santiago. They had known for at least twenty-four hours. I don't know if they figured it out the same way I did and you know what? It doesn't matter. What's important, what is *crucial*, is that while Kenzie and I were sneaking out of his house, checking over our shoulder the whole time, Olga's killers were already in Mexico.

But as it turned out, they didn't know about me – not yet. Which means that if someone really had been following me in D.C. – and Olga was certain of that – then it was *someone else*.

I'm telling you all this now, because it gets crazier from here. Kenzie and I were walking into a trap that no-one even knew existed. The mystery of 'the unicorn project' was about to lead us to someplace I hadn't even imagined existed.

TWENTY

BLUE DOLPHIN HOTEL

From the outside, the Blue Dolphin Hotel in Tapachula doesn't look like much. There's a doorway in a pastel blue house on a street where half the buildings' paintwork is peeling and every fifth window is cracked. Kenzie and I peered into the reception area, an entrance hall piled high with backpacks. A slender, white woman in her twenties stood behind an oak desk, eyes fixed on the flat screen of a computer, two fingers twisting a braid in her long, brown hair.

Kenzie and I stepped inside and heard her totting up a bill for two German boys, who were checking out. Beyond, the lobby was a true gem of an old house. It was like staying with an aged great-aunt or uncle who hadn't touched their centuries-old home since they were a kid in the 1950s. We shuffled from foot to foot, waiting our turn. Meantime, I took in the décor; ramshackle furniture, an easy chair, a rattan sofa with floral cushions, a glass-topped coffee table from the seventies casually strewn with battered copies of *National Geographic*, a hammock in one corner, improvised shelving stacked with old paperbacks and magazines, a record player beside a pile of faded vinyl. Crackly piano music played from a record on the turntable, crooned over by an old-timey voice. The album cover showed Agustin Lara, a middle-aged guy with sharp cheekbones and slicked-back graying hair.

The receptionist flashed a smile at the Germans as they shouldered backpacks and left. Then in English with a faint Ukrainian accent she addressed us. "You're in the Tacaná room. Breakfast is from seven to nine in the lounge, one hundred fifty pesos per person. All the usual Mexican dishes. We don't provide pastry but there's a bakery next door if you like to pick up something and take it here. The dipping pool is open from eight to ten at night, towels in the courtyard. There's a fridge there too, if you like to bring cold drinks or snacks. Hot snacks available from the bar from six to eleven. Are you vegan? We have a variety of non-dairy milks and vegan dishes. All waste should be placed in recycling boxes in the courtyard, please take care to sort according to the labels. All our energy comes from our biofuel generator and solar on the roof."

Kenzie picked up the breakfast menu. Normally all that Mexican food would have excited him. But under these circumstances it seemed surreal to think of enjoying anything.

The receptionist handed me a brass mortice key on a loop of string attached to a thumb-sized piece of smooth driftwood bearing the room's name.

"You made a reservation for just one person. Unfortunately we can't upgrade because all the rooms are taken. But there's a hammock."

"We'll be fine," I said.

Kenzie followed me through the double-glass doors into an open-air space dominated by a tiled staircase and lined with pot plants and hanging baskets brimming with bougainvillea, hibiscus and passion flower and morning glory, a riot of pink, purple and orange in the shady courtyard. Our room was on the ground floor, its only window facing directly onto the 'dipping pool', a deep concrete tank about two yards square filled with water dotted with flower petals and surrounded by more potted plants. Backing the pool was a high, stuccoed wall on which was painted a mural of a blue-gray dolphin arcing gracefully, its nose inches from the roll of foaming surf.

In the room Kenzie folded himself inside the hammock and peered at his phone. "Guess I should buy that burner and call my moms."

I turned on the AC and began to unpack, setting my phone to charge until Kenzie objected, sitting up in the hammock and placing both feet on the ceramic-tiled floor.

"Your phone's no good here. No SIM, remember? And WiFi's not safe. I'm guessing unlike me you don't have VPN access."

Annoyed, I put down my phone. "No, *you* don't have VPN access," I hissed.

"Never mind," he said, with a resigned shake of his head. "Hopefully, we shook off your stalker."

"Hopefully? We're counting on it."

Kenzie blinked, closed his eyes for a second, lay his phone screen down on his belly and set the hammock on a gentle side-to-side swing. I watched him for a second, amused, then checked through my backpack, trying to figure whether it was worth the trouble to unpack. My stuff was as easy to access there as in a drawer.

Eyes still closed, he wondered aloud, "What do we know about this charity our 'Maxim Santiago' works for?"

"Friends of 5922? They help Cubans who are trying to get to the USA. Allegedly."

"But we figured out that Maxim's mom might be a Russian spy based out of Cuba."

I nodded. "An 'illegal.' Based on what *you* found out about where the message '*Remember The Forgotten Village*' was posted from, yeah we did."

"Mexico City, bouncing off the Elena Atlas Museum in Siberia." Kenzie sounded thoughtful as the hammock gently swayed. "Then you found the mirror message in the bathroom of the Atlas Studios. Left by your stalker."

"Presumably," I reminded him.

"Fine, *presumably*. We're presuming a lot here, but on the other hand we need some kind of working theory."

"Fine, whatever. But you didn't trace anything to Tapachula, did you?"

Reluctantly, he agreed. He wriggled free of the hammock and headed for the bathroom. "Anyhow – how can you be sure this 5922 isn't some cover organization who'll hack your phone?" Then he disappeared behind the door and called out, "Okay if I hit the shower first?"

"What d'you mean, a 'cover organization?'"

The shower began to run as he responded, "Just don't connect your phone to the Wi-Fi."

"I won't. And explain 'cover organization'!"

He didn't reply. Kicking off my shoes, I lay down on the single bed. The tension began to seep from my muscles. But soon enough, the relief of having arrived safely to such a chill hotel wasn't enough to suppress the memories of Olga's death. I heard again, the anguish in Zara's voice and the fuming rage in Bobbie's. Kenzie's warning thundered within me. It wouldn't *even have occurred* to me not to connect to the Wi-Fi. Was I really so close to being in trouble without his help? A scary thought. I still didn't really understand what he meant, but figured it had something to do with our stalker being able to hack my phone.

It puzzled me, because at the time I thought Kenzie had agreed we'd most likely left Olga's killer behind in DC. We hadn't, in fact, because like I said, unknown to us they'd already hacked her phone and reckoned where she planned to go next. Kenzie had actually identified a new danger – the possibility that 'Friends of 5922' was a 'cover organization.' I was too tired to get why he suspected this. Yet a cold sensation in my guts warned me that he could be right.

This is why you shouldn't get involved in espionage. Honestly, I don't recommend it. You can't imagine the paranoia. Maybe a little, from reading this. But I don't want to bore anyone, so I'm leaving out *tons* about what it's like to be constantly on edge, sleep eluding you, fear always under the surface, never sure who you can trust, always trying to piece together misshapen fragments of information into something that might make sense. It's just exhausting. All you can do is to keep an eye on the prize and work through it all.

I picked up my phone and then remembered it was useless and put it down again. Very frustrating not to be able to use the Internet whenever you want to. I have no clue how people managed back in the day.

I changed into a clean shirt and shorts. Despite the AC, the clothes I'd put on that morning in D.C. were already sweaty. Outside, the temperature had crept up to ninety degrees and the air was heavy and damp. I closed the room's door behind me and wandered into the courtyard, admiring the flowers. This trip was no vacation, but it felt a little like the last one we'd taken to Costa Rica with Kenzie's moms. Adorable little family-run guest houses on virgin beaches, fiery sunsets and mountains of tropical fruit for breakfast. Then I remembered Olga was dead and this wasn't a vacation.

Steam began to rise from the base of the bathroom door. No sign of that shower ending.

"I'm going for a walk," I shouted. "The fifty-nine twenty-two place is two minutes away. I'll check it out and be right back." I waited for a reply from Kenzie but there wasn't one. Maybe he hadn't heard. I hesitated for another second. Then I picked up the notepad and pencil that had been left for us, on the dressing table.

Gone to 5922. See you there? Don't forget key.

The sooner I had eyes on the so-called 'Maxim Santiago,' the quicker this would be over. If he was volunteering today, perfect. Kenzie and I could have dinner and a swim tonight, maybe even a reunion with Maxim if he was *our* Maxim. Do a little sightseeing tomorrow and be fresh for the return flight the following day, arrive back one day earlier than expected and squiggle our way back into Bobbie's and Zara's good books.

I stepped out of the hotel and its fan-cooled air and slammed into a wall of heat in the street, like D.C. in mid-July. A woman was selling *aguas*, fruit juice mixed with sugar and water, out of a case on the sidewalk, so I bought a bottle of guava water and cracked open the lid, drank half the bottle down in one go. Passing an opening in a building I glimpsed rows of crusty white sticks of bread on a shelf and ducked inside – the bakery that the receptionist had mentioned. Next to the loaves were eight different types of sweet bread. I picked a white-encrusted *concha* and a minute later was tearing off pieces of soft, sugary bread and cramming them into my mouth.

I'd just finished eating and drinking when I arrived at the front door of the correct address for 'Friends of 5922.' It was an unmarked concrete and glass building, old and in crummy condition, the door wide open onto the street. Inside was a chaotic office, dented filing cabinets and a desk on which sat a laptop computer. There was no-one around. I was amazed that anyone would leave a laptop unguarded until I noticed that it was tethered by a sturdy-looking cable to a metal hook embedded firmly in the nearby brick wall. The only other item on the desk was a bell, the kind shops use for customers to ring for attention.

I waited another few seconds, wondering if I should go back to get Kenzie. He should be out of the shower and dressed by now, unless he was being a total diva about his hair or something. On a whim I dinged the bell. There was a moment's silence then a scrambling noise as someone seemed to practically hurl themselves down some stairs behind a door towards the back of the office.

And then *he* was there.

Thinner, taller, the meticulous faux-Mohican of childhood evolved into a mop of unruly, shoulder-length, wavy light-brown hair. His shoulders were broader and his upper arms toned (so shoot me for noticing), he had on tatty khaki shorts and a grungy blue-and-red tank top featuring the Cuban flag. It was him, unmistakably. Maxim Santiago, all grown up, lanky and earnest, tall and tanned and honestly? Kind of hot. I shied away, slack-jawed, trying to think of something cool to say and failing, wishing that in all my vague imaginings of our meeting I'd bothered to dream up what I might say.

It took Maxim even longer to recognize me but as I stood there in dumb silence, eventually he did.

"Padi?" he said, almost a whisper. He took a step forward, incredulity giving way to dawning elation. "Veronica Padilla? Omigod, it's you. It's really you!" For a minute he seemed as thunderstruck as me, unsure whether to take another step closer, to hug or bump elbows, pump fists or what.

"Yay!" It was the best I could manage in the moment. "Surprise!"

TWENTY-ONE

STUCK IN A MOMENT

After an awkward minute, Maxim Santiago asked permission to hug me. I couldn't get over his easy-going humor. Where was the super-serious boy who'd driven Kenzie and I like a monomaniac sensei during rehearsals of *The Forgotten Village*?

Maxim was beaming so widely that I thought his cheeks might crack. It was impossible not to mirror that smile. "What's going on? Are you on vacation here?"

"*Do* people come on vacation here?"

"Oh, yeah. It's a tremendous spot to visit Chiapas and Guatemala. And off the main tourist trail so no *yumas*."

"*Yumas?*"

"Foreigners. It's Cuban. I work with a Cuban charity, guess I'm picking up their slang."

Later I realized he'd used this to tell me that he wasn't Cuban. Weirdly, I couldn't remember ever asking where his folks were from, back when we were kids. I'd definitely made the connection now. Maxim had given me a chance to ask about his work, so I did.

"There are big problems in Cuba right now. Maybe you heard about it? A lot of people are trying to leave. If you have money for the ticket you can claim you're going on vacation to Central America. Then you travel to Mexico. Here in Tapachula you can apply to enter the USA legally. And we help people to do that. There are lot of Cubans here. Also from Haiti. Really horrible problems in those countries, so people need to get to safety."

I looked at him in sheer admiration. It seemed such a responsible, communitarian thing to do, made me feel kind of silly with my podcast and everything. And totally at odds with him being the target of Olga's killer.

"Wow. Honestly, I'm impressed."

He gave an aw-shucks laugh. "Don't be, it's pure self-interest."

I didn't see how that could be true. Self-effacing nonsense, I told myself.

"So what happened to you, Padi?"

It was on the tip of my tongue to tell him about the podcast, but I stopped myself. Suddenly having found Maxim Santiago, the whole idea of a pod about his 'disappearance' *might* seem a teeny bit obsessive. With Maxim acting like he thought our meeting was a coincidence, I was suddenly shy about confessing how much effort I'd put in, searching for him.

"Oh, pish. Stayed on at D.C. Inter. Grew up a little, I guess. Stupidly, I managed to become a kind-of orphan during the pandemic."

"What's a kind-of orphan?" he said, instantly picking up on my evasion.

I let out a slow sigh. "They didn't die. They're both doing eight years for money laundering. I'm a prison-orphan."

Maxim let out a startled laugh. When he noticed my flinty expression he stopped short. "How are they doing? In prison, I mean? I can't imagine your parents doing hard time."

"I don't talk to them. They're dead to me."

"That's cold," he remarked. "My mother actually is dead. But at least I have a good memory of her."

He eyed me with sudden curiosity that I had no interest in satisfying. Instead, I thought about Russian illegals and wondered if Masha had died in action or been executed by her paymasters. If they *were* her paymasters, that is.

"How about you? You just disappeared. No-one knew where you went or why. What happened to you, Maxim Santiago?"

Maxim shrugged the whole thing off. "Oh – a lot. Remind me to tell you sometime. But I want to hear more about you! And Kenzie. How's Kenz? Are you both still at D.C. Inter? Are you guys friends? Do you still play jazz?"

And on it went. He peppered me with questions, all the while locking the building behind us and escorting me down the street until we arrived at an ice cream parlor on the corner. The front of the 5922 office was just about visible so we made sure to take a table facing it and watching for Kenzie.

The waiter set down a tray holding two sundae dishes of ice cream and wooden spoons.

With a bashful grin, in English he said, "One mango sorbet, one mamey."

Maxim dug into the pale-orange mamey ice cream, enthralled by my babblings. Later when I recalled our meeting I'd remember how every now and then the spell would break, he'd peer down the street with a calculating look, then straight back to being a rapt audience. At the time I only noticed the smiles and encouragement.

He marveled at the news that I'd basically been adopted by Kenzie's moms. "So Kenz is like, your brother now?"

"I guess so." Shrugging, I added, "It's something of a situationship."

"He feel the same way?" Maxim asked, teasing. When I took too long to think it over he moved back to the topic of my parents, asking me a question that not one single other person had ever asked. "Do you have a strong memory of the last time you were happy with them?"

It was such an unexpected approach – although why would it be? – that I got startled. Maxim didn't react to my discomfort. He just waited it out, calmly spooning ice cream into his mouth.

"I don't… like to think about it. Ultra-secrecy is in the nature of white-collar crime. So everything seemed to be fine, great, until one day it wasn't. In a way, that was the worst part. Knowing that they lied to me, so convincingly. That they didn't give me any reason to suspect. That my happy family life crumbled to dust one day, two years ago." I tried to smile but instead my eyes filled with tears. When I lifted my hand to wipe them away he grabbed my fingers.

He shook his head, very slightly. "It's okay."

I didn't want to talk about them. I never wanted to talk about them. Yet that afternoon on the sidewalk outside the ice cream parlor, I found myself fantasizing aloud that something I could have done might have changed the course of their action.

"If they'd given me some clue about what they were doing, who knows. If there had been anything I could say."

He listened without making any comment, tilting his head for a moment as if weighing my words. When I was done and tears were rolling down my cheeks, he gave a few sympathetic nods. I picked up a napkin and dabbed at my face.

"They'd have done it either way," he concluded, with a hard edge to his tone. "Even if you'd begged."

"You haven't heard me beg, though. Irresistible."

He smiled gently, precisely as much as I needed to see. "People do what they want to do, then they justify it."

"Not always. You made Kenzie and me practice our

piece *way* more than we wanted."

"Nope," he replied, curtly. Then he added, "No," this time tenderly. "You can hurt someone against their will, definitely. Having them take action, that's different. You can persuade someone to take an action, but the seed of desire has to be there from the beginning."

I watched him with growing unease. There was something so throwaway about his delivery. It felt like he'd known these things for a long time. When had he learned this, I wondered?

"What about your mother?" I asked. "Do you remember the last time you and Masha were happy?"

"Oh, yes." Our eyes met, his attention firm and steady. "We had breakfast. Shakshuka, that day. Eggs in a spicy tomato sauce, it's really good. Masha tested me on my homework. Then it was time for class. I hugged her. I remember the sensation of my arms around her shoulders, the weight of her head on my shoulder. I'd grown taller than her so that was new for me." He paused for a long time. "Sometimes I think part of me is stuck in that moment."

We talked some more and I basically skimmed my entire life story from the minute we last saw each other to today, with one major hole around my podcast. We said nothing more about his mom being 'gone' because all he seemed interested in was me, my life, me, me and me.

I know, I see it now, how he carefully told me almost nothing, which I took as a trade for my own silence about my parents, but obviously at the time it was hugely flattering to have all that attention on me, the boring one who hadn't disappeared. I had *missed* Maxim. Until that afternoon in Tapachula, I didn't realize how much.

Maxim's reaction seemed to be the perfect balance

of sympathy, compassion and support. I put it down to his volunteer work with refugees – so many of them have PTSD. I wondered if maybe he got some training in radical empathy, or something?

Spoiler – he didn't. Something else was going on. Be patient, we'll get to it.

TWENTY-TWO

WHAT HAPPENED TO THE SANTIAGOS

Kenzie showed up a few minutes later. It was one of those cringey situations, where you see someone from a long way off and then feel obliged to share goofy grins as you get closer. I started to stand up, but Maxim ordered Cokes so we had to wait for those. He didn't so much as shift in his chair. That was the first time I really *saw* our old friend again – the same absolute confidence, calm and without a shred of arrogance.

Writing about it now, I can see how it *sounds* arrogant, but Maxim had his ways. He behaved like the natural order of things was that he'd stay there, waiting for Kenzie to come to him, getting the waiter to prepare the table with a third chair, napkins, a menu, ensuring that by the time Kenzie arrived he'd feel like the guest of honor. Only when Kenzie was a few yards away did Maxim get to his feet, opening his arms for a bro-hug.

"*Asere, mi Kenzo*, how's it going?" Maxim clapped Kenzie's back, grinning. More Cuban slang. "You got thin!"

"Hey, Max. And you got tall."

"So how come you're here, the two of you? Where are your moms?"

Kenzie and I exchanged nervous glances, which Maxim noticed. Despite this he waited patiently for one of us to answer.

"They're in DC. We came looking for you," Kenzie admitted, eventually.

I sucked in air between gritted teeth. I hadn't

expected him to come right out with it.

Maxim scratched his temple. "Oh. Wow. I guess I should have seen that coming. I mean, like Padi said, who comes to Tapachula?"

Now it was Kenzie's turn to be surprised by me. "You didn't tell him?"

"We had some catching up to do," I mumbled. Dammit. What were we supposed to say now? We'd put all the effort into thinking of what to say to Bobbie and Zara, never planned what we'd say to Maxim.

Kenzie faced Maxim and said, "Someone's trying to find you, man. Someone apart from us, that is."

I jumped in. "It started out as a kind of game. I have this podcast, y'know the kind of thing, an unsolved mystery. We wanted to figure out where you went."

Maxim fell silent. The color drained from his face and he became very still, alert and intently focused on me in a way that was pretty unnerving. "Where I *went*?"

Kenzie nodded. "Yeah. Like, what happened to you? And your mom. You just disappeared, man. Vanished."

"Like smoke."

This would have been a natural opening for Maxim to tell us where he'd been all these years. But he'd successfully dodged my attempt to raise the topic, twenty minutes before. Now he said nothing. His attention moved slowly from me to Kenzie and then back, scrutinizing our faces for several seconds. Then slowly, he exhaled. "I see."

Kenzie and I locked eyes once again. The sudden shift in mood was very weird. And yet, as he fell into another pensive silence, I suddenly saw *our* Maxim through my twelve-year-old eyes. He was exactly, exactly the same as back then. Thoughtful, weighing everything before he spoke.

"Oh. My. God, Maxim! You haven't changed, I mean not even a little bit." I pinched up a fold of skin on my forearm. "Hey, I got goosebumps! You were such a weirdly *cool* little kid."

Kenzie cracked a grin. "S'true. We were totally in awe of you."

Maxim relaxed a little. "That's not true. The opposite. I loved you guys. Would have done anything for you. You have no idea how badly I missed you." Abruptly, he stopped.

Astonished, I realized that he was choking up.

"So where'd you go?" Kenzie asked.

Whatever emotional moment had gripped Maxim, he quickly moved on. "Cuba," he said, swallowing. "Yeah. Back to Cuba."

This was confusing, since he'd all but explained that he wasn't Cuban. I asked him to clarify.

"I was born in Cuba. But in this kind of closed community. We didn't speak Spanish. My mom, Masha, she was Russian."

I said, "Closed community? You mean, like a cult?"

"Uh huh, you could call it that."

Maxim sat down again and picked up his spoon, scraping up some of the melted ice cream in the bottom of the dish. Kenzie sat down too, and a waiter came over to take his order.

"You being in a cult... we didn't even think of that," I admitted. "We had some ideas, but that wasn't one of them."

Maxim smiled. "What were the other theories?"

"Oh, y'know. You were deported by ICE. Or your mom was arrested as a spy. And other stuff."

"Like what?"

"Just, silliness." I shrugged and made dramatic gestures, hoping to distract. Olga had told me what happened at the border, but she'd left out the part about Maxim going back to a cult. My thoughts went briefly to what she'd said about the border guards being bribed by someone powerful. The cult leader?

We were sitting in a very normal ice cream parlor in a very normal provincial Mexican town enjoying a mid-afternoon treat while most people rested during the siesta hours. Suddenly the notion that Maxim could have been trafficked as a child seemed ridiculous, far-fetched. No way was I about to make him think I was a fantasist who'd fall for something like that. Even if at the back of my mind I was already wondering about this cult. Cults might be involved in child trafficking, too.

"You believed that my mom was arrested as a spy?" he said, chewing it over. "Who did she spy for, in this scenario?"

"Russia. We thought maybe she was an 'illegal.' You know what they are? Deep, under-cover spies."

He nodded, slowly. "Under-cover Russian spy? My mother? With names like 'Masha' and 'Maxim?' More likely 'Liz' and 'Phil' wouldn't you think? Something less likely to give the game away?"

I paled. "Oh. Yeah. Didn't think of that."

"What kind of cult?" Kenzie asked. "Where was it?"

I was relieved to push past the embarrassing bit of our past, where I'd ever suggested that a Russian spy would go under-cover as a Russian. "Was it some kind of utopian thing? Do they have that in communist countries?"

"It was no place you know," Maxim answered, somewhat dismissively. "A boring, stupid cult, like all of them. They're all toxic, absolute crank. Every last one. I got out of there as soon as I could."

Kenzie said, "When was that?"

"I lived in Havana for a bit," Maxim said, spreading his hands on the cool marble of the round table. "Trying to escape to the USA. Tried a few times. It's not so easy."

"How did you manage?" Kenzie asked. "Was Masha with you?"

"Masha? No, she passed a few years ago."

There was untold pain in the quiet of his reply. "I lived on the streets. Not the easiest year of my life. But in Havana it's possible to get money and other kinds of help from *yumas*. Eventually, I left. And that's why I stayed here in Mexico, to help others get out."

I reached out and grasped his hand. Maxim made it all sound so routine, but what he must have been through!

"So that's what happened to the Santiagos?"

He winked. "Yeah. That's what happened."

And it actually *was* the truth. With major, astonishing chunks left out.

TWENTY-THREE

CRAWLING WITH SPIES

Our extremely normal afternoon couldn't continue indefinitely. At some point we were going to have to tell Maxim about Olga and warn him that Chekists were onto him. But we must be idiots, because we put off the evil hour, bumbling along like we had no care in the world. And Kenzie told Maxim how he'd spent the intervening years.

Meantime, my thoughts wandered. I began to review everything that happened with Olga. Was it possible that Kenzie and I had misinterpreted events? Could it be I was fooling myself by seeing Chekists everywhere?

Let me just say it now – I wasn't. You wouldn't be reading about any of this if the entire story fizzled out one sweltering afternoon over ice cream. But for some reason that I don't understand, the minute we saw Maxim in front of us, obviously safe and working for a charity, once we heard the plausible – if unusual – story behind his and Masha's untimely disappearance from our lives all those years ago, it became difficult to accept that Olga's killer could actually be on their way to Tapachula to kill Maxim, or whatever.

We were not, however, alone on this mission, something we'd momentarily forgotten. As promised, Kenzie called his moms from the burner he'd bought just before meeting us. He told them we'd found Maxim, that he was fine and we were all safe. And actually, it was Bobbie and Zara who reminded us of the danger. I saw him grow quiet as their conversation continued. He ended the call sounding queasy.

Maxim noticed. "Bad news?"

Kenzie swallowed and nodded. He glared at me as if to say 'you do it!'

Maxim picked up on that also. His attention flicked across to me. "Something up?"

"Well, here's the thing, "I began. I puffed out a breath. "Yeah. So what's going on…" I tried again, this time introing with a glassy smile. "This may sound weird, but…" I fired a 'help me' look at Kenzie but he replied only with brisk shake of his head. Apparently it was all on me.

Maxim gave a chuckle. "What's going on? Are you pregnant? Did you run away together?"

The tension-bubble burst. We both denied it, speaking fast and over each other.

"Me? What? By him?" "God, no! It's not, we're not…"

His grin widened. "Ahh. *Chicos!* Still so *easy*. Like that time we – "

"Someone's hunting for you," I interrupted, breaking across Maxim's attempt at mischief. "Someone dangerous. Maybe connected with your cult? I don't know."

The grin vanished. That's when I knew this was real. A normal reaction would have been to assume we were still joking around, and keep laughing. But Maxim stopped at once. He didn't seem surprised but rather, afraid.

He exhaled rapidly. "Go on."

"My guardian, Olga…" I stopped. For the first time it struck me that it wasn't a coincidence that Olga, too, had a name that was common in Russian. "Do you *know* her?"

Maxim shot me an intense glare. "Olga Garcia, from DC? Of course. She's my aunt."

I was confused. "Sure, I mean, I call her 'Auntie

Olga' but she's not my aunt."

"No, she is actually my aunt, my mother's sister."

Kenzie and I gasped. A detail that Olga had kept from me and also his moms.

Maxim pressed me. "Well? What *about* Olga?"

"She was searching for you. She wasn't sure you were here. How come, by the way? If she's your aunt, I mean."

A little uncomfortable now, Maxim ordered another soda. "I was planning to get around to sending a message. As I told you, things haven't been easy."

But his story was beginning to sound off. If he had an aunt in the USA, why had it been difficult to leave Cuba? She could have sponsored him to come to the US. Why had he been 'forced' to live on the streets in Havana? And why, after he'd escaped Cuba, had he stayed in Tapachula?

"Olga saw your name on the list of volunteers at Friends of Fifty-Nine Twenty-Two. She and I were on our way here to find you. But two days ago she died, poisoned, by Novichok."

Maxim listened in silence until I'd finished. Then he sucked on the paper straw until the Coke in his glass was almost gone. He poured more from the bottle, watching the ice cubes swirl.

"Max," Kenzie asked in a low voice. "Was your mom a spy? Were you trafficked?"

Somehow in this new and suddenly stark reality it was so much easier to say these things aloud. Maxim brought a palm to his forehead and wiped away the beads of sweat.

"I wouldn't say 'spy.' Agent of the cult, yes. *Ex*-agent. It's the kind of cult that doesn't make it easy to leave. Masha and I escaped once, years ago. When I was little, we went to live in the USA. But they made us go back. I told you about that."

"Back to the cult?"

He scrutinized us in turn, giving each an even nod. "Back to Cuba. Yes. After a few years Masha died. And later I escaped, this time alone."

"Do you know who's tracking you?"

He looked weary. "I can handle them."

"Get a load of this guy!" I scoffed. "Olga was a trained agent of the United Nations Office for Counter-Terrorism and *she* couldn't handle them."

Unfazed, Maxim drained his glass and rose to his feet. "And I'm just a kid, is that what you're trying to say?" He pulled a wallet from the back pocket of his jean shorts and took out a few fifty and twenty peso notes, planting them on the bill under the Coke bottle. "Thanks for the warning, Padi. I appreciate it. You took a lot of trouble to reach me, I think. Did you come just for that?"

It was hard to know how to respond. Maxim's reaction had moved so far and so fast from what I'd expected. I couldn't keep up. His initial fear at hearing that Olga had been killed by Novichok, was gone.

"We're booked in the hotel for three nights," Kenzie replied. Either he hadn't picked up on Maxim's huge tone-shift or else it didn't worry him.

Maxim took that in, nodding. "What do you want to do while you're here? The volcano's pretty, though it's really too hot to go hiking. Or there's a beach not far away."

"We lay it on you that some Cheka hitter is hunting you down," Kenzie said, taken aback. Maxim was acting very oddly and finally, Kenzie was taking notice. "And you suggest a trip to the beach?"

"Weather's kind of hot and all." Maxim shrugged. "You got a better suggestion?"

There was so much I wanted to ask. Kenzie too; I saw it in his eyes. Yet Maxim's effortless confidence had once again asserted itself. It seemed so natural than to just go along. As though we were back in that rehearsal room playing *The Forgotten Village*.

I said, "Just so we're on the same page here – you're not worried about the Chekists? And we can just plan an evening at the beach?"

Maxim was breezy-peasy. "I'll have to borrow a car but yeah, basically."

It would have been easy to simply let it go, but I forced myself to stay on point. "When I first told you about Olga you seemed scared."

"Yeah," Kenzie said. "Aren't you upset about her, seeing as how she's your aunt?"

"Olga and my mom weren't close. Yes, when you said she was killed, at first it was a bit of a shock. But a lot has happened to me since we were kids. I know everyone in this town. Including the Chekist." He watched our eyes widen. "That's right. Mexico is crawling with them. There's even one in Tapachula, hangs out in a bar with other eurotrashy types."

I flashed Kenzie a triumphant look. "See? What'd I tell you? Didn't I say this country is crawling with Russian spies?"

"I don't think you said 'crawling.'"

"There aren't many Mexican illegals," Maxim continued, almost to himself. "It's possible they'd send a Cuban. That could be a challenge. But any new Russian arriving in Tapachula is gonna stick out like a candy apple in a first-grader's hand. I'll see them coming. So don't worry, and thanks for the warning, I appreciate it. Now, where are you staying? You should go and pack for the beach."

We ambled back to the hotel (it was impossible in that heat to do anything fast) and led Maxim to our room. He promptly dropped himself into the hammock, seemed to lose himself in contemplation of the ceiling, casual as you like, holding a cell phone to his ear as he waited for a call to connect. When he spoke it was in languid, Cuban-accented Spanish, which he most definitely had not had back in the day. It sounded like he was asking a buddy to loan him a car for the evening.

Kenzie went into the bathroom. A second later I heard his exclamation. He stepped out again, facing me. "Someone's been inside the room."

Maxim ended his call. Kenzie returned to the bathroom. When he re-emerged he was holding a towel. "I left this hanging to dry on the rail. It was on the floor."

Normally I'd have challenged him but in that moment I noticed that the drawer in the bedside table was slightly open. I'd placed a packet of Chiclets and my allergy meds in there. I knew for sure that I'd closed it. I always close drawers in hotels, in case bugs or spiders sneak inside.

"Yeah, I definitely closed this drawer."

Kenzie thought for a second. "We just got here, so it can't be the maid."

"Then it's happening? They've already found us?" A void seemed to be opening up inside me, and from it emerged a creeping sense of terror. Kenzie and Maxim both looked scared. For a moment we were all three paralyzed, no clue what to do or say.

Maxim scanned the room, suddenly alert. His eyes landed on two glasses on the dresser, both containing a small amount of water. "Those yours?"

I froze. Had we drunk water from the bottle provided?

Maxim took my silence as a 'no.' He swung his legs out of the hammock and planted both feet on the floor. "Two half-filled glasses is a classic Cheka calling-card. If they're not yours then... whoever was here was counting on me coming to your room with you, but gave up waiting. This is a message to *me*, letting me know they're in town and watching me. Chekists enjoy showing confidence. Too much, actually."

I turned to Maxim, raising my chin. "You said you could handle it."

He replied, uneasily, "I can." More decisively he added, "We're leaving. Bring everything. You can't come back here."

I picked up my canvas backpack, which I hadn't yet unpacked. Kenzie did the same with his.

"Ready."

Maxim paced softly across the room, motioned us to be silent, then listened carefully at the door. After a few seconds he motioned us to get in line behind him as he prepared to open it.

"Stay close. Move quickly, move quietly. And if I tell you to run, run."

TWENTY-FOUR

HIDEOUT

This was close to my worst-case scenario. I didn't enjoy thinking about downsides of anything, but on the flight over I had forced myself to run through a few. Thank the deity for that.

If oftentimes I don't like to dwell on the downside, it's not because I'm ignoring that bad things happen but because there's stuff I don't like to remember. My parents laundering money for oligarchs, for one. Also, my tendency to obsess over things I can't control.

Sneaking out of our hotel room never to return gave me horrible flashbacks to fearful scenarios I'd had about this whole trip, something I'd worked to suppress. Most ended with me and Kenzie tied up and screaming while our fingernails got ripped out. I could just about envisage that. Anything nastier, I blocked.

We were in Maxim's hands now. And despite our fun afternoon of reminiscing, we had to trust a guy who admitted he'd:

✓   Been brought up in a cult
✓   Escaped from a cult
✓   Lived on the streets of Havana
✓   Escaped Cuba, possibly illegally
✓   Knew the Russian spy in Tapachula (How could he know them? A serious question that I should have asked earlier.)

Maxim's life was a million miles from the one Kenzie and I had lived. Realistically, what could we know about how he'd react in any given circumstance? What if he was offered the chance to trade us for his freedom or something else?

As we prowled the streets of Tapachula behind Maxim, I insisted, "Kenz and I should leave."

Kenzie agreed. "We came here to warn you. Which we've done."

"We're going to the airport. Right now."

Maxim seemed mildly irritated. "Clever. I'll bet the Chekists didn't think of that. Good thing they won't be waiting for you at the airport. Why do you *think* they left the half-empty glasses of water? They're flushing you out, hoping I'll follow along."

Kenzie scoffed. "*Bullshit* they left any kind of 'sign.'"

Maxim stopped short, pivoted. "You don't believe me?"

I jumped in. "How come you know so much about the Cheka, if your mom really wasn't a spy?"

"That cult I was born into? It belongs to a Russian oligarch whose relationship with the Czar is, well, let's just call it 'volatile.'"

I stared. It was so awful, it just might be true. "'Belongs to a Russian oligarch?' Great, just what we were missing." I recalled Olga's words to me – she'd warned me that whoever had Maxim and Masha taken back to Cuba was powerful enough to influence US border agents.

Maxim turned right at the next junction. We were two streets away and parallel to where we'd started at the hotel and still headed downtown. He kept looking this way and that, checking doorways as we approached, eyes scanning the low roofs.

Kenzie tore his eyes away from his phone. "How about the bus station? Maybe we can change our flight, go from Tuxtla Gutierrez."

Maxim nodded. "That's good. But you need to do better. Any predictable move, they've already thought of."

I asked, "What's *your* plan?"

"Borrow a car, head for the beach. I know a place where we can hide out for a few days."

"A car?" I stopped walking. "The one you called your friend about?"

"We're all good. She's driving it to a different location."

Maxim made another turn, now heading out of town. I jogged to keep up with his long strides, trying to think of when he'd had a chance to call his friend a second time, to change the meeting point. It was odd, because I couldn't recall seeing him use the phone again. Then I promptly forgot this niggling detail.

The street we'd reached was busier than the last, a row of laundries all open to the street, their prices featured on sidewalk billboards. Cars were parked down both sides of the road as people dropped off and picked up bags of laundry. Maxim picked up his pace and darted into the 'Bubbles' laundry. We followed, ignored by the two guys working there, one folding shirts and another emptying a machine. It was roasting hot despite two giant fans on overdrive. Maxim swerved around piles of bagged laundry and then, on a whim appeared to change his mind, doubled back and grabbed a grubby Panama hat that sat atop a pile of laundry. He placed it on his head and then, when he'd checked that we were keeping up, made for the back door, emerging onto the street behind, a quiet, residential street. He stopped in front of a dirty, white Toyota Corolla.

"Yesss!" Maxim beamed at the car, pulling the front of the hat down a tad. It suited him. He went for the rear door. It was unlocked. "Get in. Lie down until I say the coast is clear."

We tossed our backpacks onto the floor of the car and did as he asked. Inside, unbelievably hot. Maxim dropped into the driver seat, reached into the glove box and withdrew a key, the kind you have to put in the ignition and turn.

"You wanna maybe crack a window?" I grumbled. "It's a sauna back here."

His head just inches from mine on the bench seat, Kenzie whispered into my ear, "He could be taking us anywhere. We've been with him the whole time, right? He never heard back on his phone about where to find the car."

I pulled my head back enough to look at Kenzie, mouthing, "You noticed that, too? Think it's a set up?"

Grimly, he nodded. "Car's probably been here all along."

I silently cursed. The car rode along at a leisurely pace as Maxim drove through the small town, turning a few more times until finally we reached some kind of freeway.

"You can sit up now," Maxim announced.

We were coasting along a long, straight highway passing farms on either side. Maxim rolled down his window and warm air moved briskly through the car, the wind-drag so loud there was no point trying to be heard over it. After a moment it was less furnace-like and he closed the window.

"We can't risk stopping for gas," Maxim explained. "So no AC. And no more open window, either. Uses too much power."

Kenzie eyed me, ominously. This time, Maxim caught the look. I thought I saw a flash of disappointment in his eyes before he chuckled, dryly.

"You don't trust me. That's too bad. Can't risk letting the Chekist find us. Listen, I don't know how you found me but then we haven't really talked about that, have we? Pretty sure you'd tell them everything in five minutes. And then, when they were absolutely certain that no amount of pain would persuade you to give up one more detail, they'd kill you. Bobbie and Zara would never hear from you again. No-one would find your bodies."

This sounded so deranged that after a second or two, Kenzie let out a roar of pure frustration.

"You're *full* of it!"

"What, you think the Mexican government cares if Chekists take out a US citizen on their soil? They're either afraid of the Czar or they're on the take."

Kenzie fired back, "How do we know *you're* not working for the Russians?"

Maxim dropped into a lower gear and hung a left into a narrow road that I guessed ran parallel to the beach. He sighed, the sound loaded with regret. "You shouldn't have come." After a brief silence he added, "Right now you don't have a lot of choice. We'll get to where we're headed in around thirty minutes. Then we can all relax a little. Not too much. And you can ask me anything. *Anything*. For now, watch out for any car that seems to be following. Anyone that approaches quickly and then sits behind us, that's someone we need to worry about. Can you do that?"

Without saying a word I turned my attention to the road behind us and thought about Olga. His literal aunt! I remembered how I'd felt when she'd cornered me into going along with her scheme. Exactly like this — I'd felt coerced. Was Maxim's entire family this manipulative?

No-one followed us, so far as Kenzie and I could tell. Gently steaming like three tamales in corn husks, we drove through miles of banana plantations with bunches of fruit protected inside blue plastic bags. We passed a little hamlet of thatched huts and finally turned off the highway into a long, unfinished driveway of black, volcanic gravel.

The car came to a stop in front of what looked to be a deserted hacienda. The faded yellow trim of its white stuccoed walls had seen better days, the wooden columns that supported the roof and created a shaded corridor along the front of the property could have used a lick of varnish. Ceramic pots lined the corridor, each one filled with a plant that'd been burnt to a crisp by the sun. The place had to be deserted – what kind of person allows any living thing to die from thirst?

Our sweat-soaked clothes stuck to us as we stepped out of the car. An iguana over a foot long lazily crossed our path, with an icy stare as if to say 'get the heck out of my house.' Kenzie cooed at it – he loves iguanas. But he knew better than to get closer. Look but don't touch.

I glared at Maxim. "A car, a house. I'm guessing you have the keys, too? How does someone like you come up with all this at the drop of a hat?"

He paused. "What are you insinuating?"

Kenzie said, "Dude, don't be a dick. You know what she's asking. How come you were able to set all this up? You made one call and so far as we heard, you didn't ask about no house. You're connected, right? I mean, just admit it. We should know how deep the crap flows if you expect us to wade in."

Maxim ignored us, wandering along the corridor until he reached the fourth plant pot. Kenzie and I were muttering about the pathetic hiding places his friends used, when he pushed the pot against the outer wall and stood on it, then poked two fingers into a small hole under the tiled roof. He pulled out the keys with a grin. "No spider! That makes three times in a row."

"You don't like spiders?" I didn't remember that about him, but then again D.C. isn't as bad as Cuba or Mexico for critters. "I didn't know. Me either."

He strolled back to where we were waiting before the main door, a huge, weighty and ancient piece of timber. A minute later he was turning the heavy iron key in its rusty old lock.

"Don't be fooled by the exterior," Maxim commented. Then he pushed open the door to reveal a lush green lawn surrounded by a quadrangle, an old stone fountain in the center. Six orange and lime trees were heavily-laden with bright and dark green fruits and provided plenty of shade. The paintwork on the interior facades was immaculate, bright white, deep ochre yellow and cobalt blue. Six mahogany doors studded the walls and with only a brief pause to relish our shocked reaction, Maxim led us for the nearest.

"It's a *narco* house," Kenzie said, in a tone of wonder. "That's it, isn't it? Hence the crummy exterior, the nowhere address."

Maxim held the door open for us, motioning us inside. "Not exactly. If Don Jose Alberto Carillo knew I was here he'd probably have me skinned, or at least part of one leg, to punish me for *ser presumido*."

"My dude," said Kenzie, "you better be joking."

Maxim grinned. "Of course. Beto would never hurt me. C'mon in, *su casa es tu casa*."

We followed him into the cool interior, a long sitting room with high white walls and long timbers holding up the tiled roof. Dotted around were an assortment of antique wooden chairs, small occasional tables and bench sofas. The walls were bare, but faint rectangular marks suggested that paintings had once hung there.

"Beto put all the good stuff in storage. I come here to water the plants and generally care-take. Best of all, no-one but him knows I'm here." Maxim took my hand, then Kenzie's. His eyes were clear and earnest. "We need to be somewhere other than town."

Once again, my own doubts surged. They'd lurked close to the surface ever since I found out about Olga's murder. If I'd thought quitting would get me out of danger, believe me, I'd have quit. "I was worried we'd lead them to you," I murmured.

"Well, you almost did," Maxim acknowledged. "Any idea how they knew you'd be in Tapachula?"

"We think they cloned Olga's phone," Kenzie said. "But she would have booked a different hotel. So how'd they find our room?"

Maxim swept his right hand in a gesture indicating the whole room. "Tradecraft. They're spies, remember?"

Kenzie pressed both lips together tightly. His cheeks flushed with anger.

"Where's your 'Don Carillo' now?" I interrupted. "Does he ever visit?"

Maxim hesitated before replying, "He's in prison, so no, he won't be dropping by. I made the effort to make some useful friends. Figured they'd be useful, given that I'm on the lam and not entirely law-abiding, myself."

My eyes widened. "So you weren't entirely kidding, Carillo is a *narco*?"

"*Obvio*. Beto's doing three for tax evasion, living like a prince in a Mexican prison while the Drug Enforcement Agency try to get something on him. Anything that'll let them drag him out and into a max security hell-hole in the USA."

It was difficult not to sound scornful but I tried. "And you say this man is your friend?"

"Unlike some, I don't shun people just because they're in prison." The playful glance Maxim threw my way at this point was perfectly timed.

"Do *narcos* even have friends?" Kenzie groaned. "This is a nightmare. My moms are gonna *kill* me if they find out I'm staying at a *narco* house."

.

TWENTY-FIVE

NARCO HOUSE

Well, we'd found out what happened to the Santiagos. We'd completed Olga's mission, too; located Maxim in Tapachula, Mexico, tracked him down and warned him that the Cheka were after him. When we finally sat down and admitted all of this to Maxim, he was unabashed. On the other hand, he did seem to appreciate the heads up.

We still knew almost nothing about Maxim, his plans for the future or even where he lived. By now, I knew my podcast was toast. Unfortunately, my curiosity wasn't satisfied. That's always been my problem. The Maxim Santiago we'd found in Tapachula that day wasn't the answer to a question – he was a whole other mystery to be solved.

We'd been hanging out with him since mid-afternoon. It was now six in the evening and we'd ended up in the deserted hacienda of a *narcotraficante*. There could be no doubt that Maxim was our childhood buddy, unchanged in many ways. Yet he'd obviously experienced wild stuff, things we could probably not even imagine. Looking at him, especially into his eyes, made me uncomfortable in a way I could barely articulate. I wanted to talk to Kenzie about how he made me feel, I was desperate to do that, or even to a wall, if there was no-one else to listen. But we couldn't seem to shake off Maxim.

Was it intentional? I found myself wishing he'd at least take a moment to go to the bathroom, so I could be alone with Kenzie to get some of this off my chest. Maxim didn't though; he just got on with his garden watering, superficially ignoring us but always staying within earshot. Then I had a brainwave. I picked handfuls of limes from the tree and took them to the kitchen, searching through the drawers for a knife, a jug and some sugar. Then I set about making *agua de limón*. I chilled the water with bowl of cubes from the ice-maker, poured three tall glasses and set them on the table. Maxim wound up the water hose and stepped back into the living room. He gulped down a whole glassful. I refilled it, immediately.

"There's a freezer," he said, gasping at the chill of his drink. "All kinds of food there, tortillas, steaks, chicken, shrimp, ice cream. We can walk to the beach from here and get coconuts. Oranges and limes in the garden. Enough for weeks."

Kenzie appeared incredulous. I shook my head very slightly and topped up all three glasses. We all took a couple of minutes to rehydrate, downing glass after glass. Maxim's bladder held out longer than mine or Kenzie's. I found myself alone with Maxim before I had a chance to say anything to Kenzie.

"Marc can't stay here much longer," I commented to Maxim as Kenzie headed for the bathroom. "You must know that. So why're you making out we can stay here for weeks?"

"Why can't he stay? Because of his moms?"

"*Obvio.*"

Maxim grinned and switched into Spanish. "Bobbie and Zara, hey? They used to throw pretty awesome parties, do you remember? Especially Halloween."

"They still throw great parties." I paused for a second, then continued. "And they're my family, now."

A look of empathy crossed his face. He took my hand and squeezed. "I'm sorry. It sucks about your mom and dad, but maybe don't rule out reconciling?" Then he returned to the subject. "Kenzie's moms know you're both in Tapachula, yes? Do they know why?"

I confirmed that they knew everything.

Maxim closed his eyes briefly, then breathed in and slowly released the breath, as if he were doing a de-stress exercise. "That's dangerous. Kenzie should call them and tell them to leave the house, right away. Go somewhere they won't be found."

"They want to come here."

"Bad idea, very bad. That would get us all killed."

I paused, frozen by the words *'get us all killed.'* Two days ago people didn't say things like that to me. Yet already it had become something I could hear, absorb and move on from. Then I snapped out of it and asked, "Why?"

Kenzie had wandered back into the living room. Maxim stood up. "Hold that thought." He held up one finger and headed for the bathroom.

Finally alone with Kenzie, I swiftly related what Maxim had told me. "He's not telling us the whole story," I concluded. "The more I think about it, the less it adds up."

"I don't like the way he looks at you," Kenzie pronounced, heavily, "and I don't buy his story about helping Cuban refugees, either."

I was stunned and silent. As Kenzie watched me react something seemed to fall away from him, a wall he'd been keeping between us. There was a helpless sorrow in his eyes. I didn't know how to respond. Before we could say another word, Maxim returned.

"So. Is this where you ask me what I'm really doing in Tapachula?" Maxim asked, with disarming simplicity.

"You read our minds," Kenzie replied, with just a hint of a sneer.

Maxim gave a humorless smile. "No need – you're both kind of obvious."

"The charity you're volunteering with checks out," I

said. "And Olga found your name on a database of registered volunteers."

Maxim slapped the table. "Wow. I guessed something way more sinister but yeah, of course. The register of volunteers. It's always the simple things that trip you up."

Kenzie pressed him. "But you do work with Friends of 5922?"

"Yeah, I do."

I said, "What about this *narco*?"

"Beto Carillo?" Maxim placed his forearms on the table and let his face fall into his palms. "*Ay mi madre.* If only I'd known you were coming. This is really bad timing."

"Do you work for Carillo? Apart from tending his lawn, I mean."

Reluctantly, Maxim pulled away his hands. "Now and again he does *me* a favor, so now and again I do *him* a favor."

"You're friends with a *narco* who's in prison? I guess you're going to tell us he's innocent?" Kenzie said.

"Oh-ho no, he did the deed. But he's not a big player. Hasn't had anyone killed. And he hasn't killed anyone." Maxim held his index finger and thumb slightly apart. "He's like, a narco junior. A rich kid who partied with *narcos* and discovered he really liked the lifestyle. Guys like him often move product for the cartel. Squeaky clean backgrounds, move in 'nice' circles. No-one looks at them twice. But yeah, Carillo is twenty-six years old and already a *preso* so…" He shrugged. "Maybe this life isn't for him after all."

"And you run drugs for him?"

"Me? No, I have *nothing* to do with any of that. Carillo helps people to leave Cuba. His family is from Havana, he donates to the charity where I work, has a *lot* of contacts in Cuba. Maybe if you answer some of *my* questions, I'll tell you what you want to know."

"Oh yeah?" I said. "And what's that?"

A slow grin spread across Maxim's tanned face. "You first."

TWENTY-SIX

K-FDN

That's how I ended up telling Maxim everything about the podcast. I'd have told him sooner, but I was embarrassed, afraid it'd seem like I'd been thinking about him all these years. From the first moment I saw him in that grimy office of 'Friends of 5922,' all grown-up, hints of muscled arms, tanned, long hair and those same, solemn eyes, I felt something stir in my stomach. Then came the twinges of guilt, the questioning of my own past and my motives for doing the podcast in the first place.

At the time I had no coherent opinion on the matter. This is all me reminiscing a while later and realizing what was going on. Every so often I'd get a tiny insight into what was happening inside me but I'd push it down. In the moment there was so much more to focus on, such as evading Chekists.

"If there even is a Chekist," Kenzie said, moodily. "Two half-filled glasses – he really thinks we buy that?"

The lemonade was working its way through us and ten minutes later Maxim left the room again. He'd barely reacted to anything we'd told him about our podcast investigation. Not about the podcast comment *'Remember The Forgotten Village?,'* nor the weird mirror-message FIND UNICORNS, nor about the file we'd found in 'Vault 7,' the leaked document on Wikileaks that mentioned 'K-FDN."

Obviously, I'd asked him directly – did he send the message *'Remember The Forgotten Village?'* Obviously, he denied it. Denied it without expressing much interest, either, which was kind of strange. I still got chills thinking about the first time I saw the message, the way it transported me instantly to a time in my life I thought was long gone. But for Maxim, hearing this seemed like just one more data point. Nothing I told him triggered a response more dramatic than mild chin-stroking, apart from his brief initial reaction to the news that Olga had been poisoned by Novichok.

Maxim stayed in the bathroom so long this time, I began to wonder if he'd gone away to think it all over, or to research something on his phone. Would Wi-Fi even work, since the *narco* house was effectively mothballed?

I responded to Kenzie. "You really think he invented that thing about Chekists? Listen – Olga told me someone was after Maxim. Then she died from Novichok: the Czar's poison. You traced that message on my podcast from Mexico via Siberia: Russians. Maxim, Olga, Masha – all Russian names."

"I'm not saying no Russians are involved. But haven't you noticed that since we met him we've ended up doing exactly what Maxim wants? He tells us Chekists are after us and we simply drop everything and follow him to the middle of nowhere."

"You were the first to notice someone had been in our room."

"Yeah. But *he* made it about Chekists."

I actually thought the two-half-filled glasses thing had the ring of truth. Even so, there was a prickling sensation at the back of my neck. Why would a Chekist leave a sign for Maxim? How did they know he'd come back to the hotel room with us? And why would they assume he'd instantly send us to the airport?

Kenzie agreed it was odd. We came up with, and debated, only one other possible explanation. Could Maxim have sent someone ahead to set it all up?

"He had no way of knowing we'd be paying him a

visit," I pointed out. "So he couldn't have set anything up before I found him."

"Right. Also, we didn't see him touch his phone the whole time we were at the ice cream place. Or on the walk back to the hotel."

"Then he must be telling the truth," I concluded. "And to be honest there's no reason for him to bring us out here if he just wants to talk."

"It's not like we were avoiding him," agreed Kenzie. "He could have talked to us in town. But now he seems set on staying, which is a problem for us. If we're not on that flight in two days my moms are going to do something. Either fly over here or call the cops."

I thought for a few seconds. "We need a plan to get into the airport without being noticed. Could we maybe go in disguise?" I flipped a thumb in the direction of the bedrooms. "*Narco* guy's wardrobe might be interesting."

Kenzie's eyes lit up. "I love that for us. Shotgun the fur coat."

From across the room, where he'd been standing in total silence for who knows how long, Maxim chimed in. "Padi should dress like a boy, too. Put up your hair in a beanie or a baseball cap, wear Beto's clothes. They'll be paying close attention to any girl-boy couple." He took a few steps into the room and added, "If you're really going to do this, be sure to change your shoes, too. That's the most common mistake people make, not changing their shoes."

I turned to face him. "Then you'll help us?"

"If that's what you want. But first – I promised to answer your question."

Annoyingly, Maxim was right, not that I was prepared to admit it. "Well, not exactly. What you actually said was that you *knew* what *I* wanted to ask."

Maxim beckoned us over to a wide sofa, which

faced directly two doors that opened onto the patio outside and its fountain. This side of the house was in shade now and the ceiling fan kept the temperature comfortable. I sat next to him and Kenzie took an easy chair nearby.

"So what is it?" I leaned forward slightly. "What do I want to ask you?"

He nodded, and then spoke casually, as though what he was telling us were something of scant consequence, "You want to know what is a 'unicorn.'" Watching my response, Maxim ran fingers deep into his hair, rubbing one side of his head as he pondered.

"Well, obviously. Also, what does Cheka want with you?"

"We're guessing the two things are connected," added Kenzie.

Maxim seemed to have concluded his considerations. "That's fair. And I'll tell you. But first we should eat. You like shrimp?"

While he busied himself with making dinner, Kenzie and I headed for the master bedroom to check out possible outfits for our airport disguises. Now that we'd gotten Maxim to agree a plan that ended up with us taking a flight back to DC, we were both calmer. But we still weren't thinking straight.

Thinking back, there were all kinds of flaws in our plan. For example, how would we get through airport security in disguise? Poisoners don't need to feed you a poison – they can put in on your clothes, your luggage, anything that they can trick you into touching. One wrong move would be all it took and we could wake up to find ourselves cabled-tied to a chair, about to be tortured until we spilled the beans. And what happened when I revealed myself at Border Control? Could we really expect that the officers of the Cuban state, an ally of the Czar's, wouldn't just hand me over to

Chekists?

Those things should have been on my mind, if I'd been concentrating. I was distracted, however, hungry and looking forward to Maxim's promise of shrimp in a spicy sauce, excited by the prospect of finally learning the answer to what had turned out to be the podcast's ultimate question.

Who or what are 'unicorns'?

Narcojunior's wardrobe was a hoot. Fancy Hawaiian shirts, designer polos, Levis, Italian suits, shirts and shoes, plus probably every Nike sneaker that Louis Vuitton ever designed. We tossed some combos onto the ginormous bed and returned to the kitchen. The aroma of frying shrimp and smoked paprika had reached the corridor outside and we arrived to find Maxim plating out the spice and oil-drenched seafood. Into the center of the table he dropped a plastic bowl, for any shells we couldn't chew. He took a seat, grabbed a fork and made an enthusiastic start on the heap of shrimp on his plate.

Maxim waited until we'd both dug in before he began to speak. "So – your question. Let's start at the end. K-FDN. You say you don't know what it is. But by now you know should enough to figure it out."

We both stared. We'd found the term 'K-FDN' in the same Vault 7 leaked CIA file that mentioned 'the unicorn project.' But the redactions in the document made it difficult to understand the context. What extra information had we discovered since then? I couldn't think of anything.

"Dude, we haven't done any searching since we got here," Kenzie said, bemused.

"Not true. You talked to *me*. I told you a lot."

Kenzie asked, "Is it something to do with Carillo? Is it his gang's call sign?"

Maxim's easy grin surfaced and this time it irked

me. He could have simply told us, but he always did prefer to play games.

I took a shot. "K-FDN is something to do with the 'unicorns.' And you admitted that you were – in some form at least – trafficked. Is K-FDN where the 'unicorns' are kept?"

Maxim clicked his fingers and made a popping sound with his mouth. "Close. What else did I tell you?"

"That you were raised in a cult," I said, slowly. "A cult owned by a Russian oligarch."

"You got it. General Anatoly Petrovich Krylov is the owner of the cult, the Krylov Foundation. K-FDN. That document is talking about the Krylov, the camp where I lived. And yeah, the kids there are referred to by customers as 'unicorns.' Now you know half of it. Can you figure out the rest? What do you think 'unicorns' could mean?"

"They're rare," I said, recalling my last conversation with Olga. She'd told me that my theory – that kids with rare blood types were being trafficked for organ transplants – was wrong. Yet she hadn't offered a better explanation. I could think of other grisly scenarios, but none that made as much sense. "Is Krylov trafficking kids with some kind of rare characteristic? That's beyond evil."

"Krylov is evil," Maxim agreed. "But he's also a drunk. Incompetent. That place is nothing like as tight as it used to be. It's not impossible to escape the camp. I did it. Others have, too."

I put down my fork. In the last minute or two, Maxim's demeanor had changed. He'd gone from playful to proud. This *meant* something to him. He was personally invested. It suddenly struck me exactly how.

"You... you're helping those kids to escape. That's it, isn't it? That's why you're here, working with Friends of 5922? That's why you stayed here, in Mexico, when you could have gone back to DC."

Like a proud uncle or something, Maxim beamed. "Yes," he said, quietly. "You got it. I hoped you would. I needed you to see it for yourself."

TWENTY-SEVEN

THE MIND GAME

"I was coming up to my sixteenth birthday. Sixteen is a big deal at K-Foundation. That's when they'd bring in the customers to view the merchandise. And no, it wasn't sexual, although Anatoly Petrovich is easily capable of selling someone as a sex slave. He was just another Yeltsin lickspittle who got rich from privatizing a Soviet resource."

We made him sidebar an explanation for this, since we hadn't heard of 'Yeltsin.'

"Boris Yeltsin, the first President of the Russian Federation after the collapse of the Soviet empire. The first and only democratically elected president they ever had. After him came Vladislav Vladimirovich Ilyin. No free election, just a 'temporary' appointment. Then a coup. Then the rise of the Third Russian Empire. And Ilyin's great 'Mind Game,' running psyops on not only the citizens of his own empire but all his enemies, too."

I'd occasionally heard people refer to Ilyin's 'Mind Game' but asked Maxim what specifically, he meant by 'psyops.'

"Psychological operations, in other words, mind games. The Nazis were the first to get really good at it, but their empire got hammered into the ground. Meanwhile the Soviets had the Cheka perfect the techniques."

"Oh, you mean propaganda?"

"I mean, propaganda on steroids. Until people will argue until they're purple in the face that both things are true, there is no pandemic because it's a hoax, and that the same pandemic was caused by a Chinese plot."

Kenzie chimed in, "Or that climate change is a hoax, but also you should totally prepare for a climate-related apocalypse."

"Yeah," agreed Maxim. "If you can control what a population believes or doesn't, you can control how they vote and what their politicians do. You can weaken an enemy long before you decide to attack militarily. You can divide the people, make half of them not want to defend themselves because all war is bad, even make them welcome your soldiers, make their allies buy your crummy excuses for why you needed to invade so no-one comes to your help. 'Game' is a euphemism, obviously, it's war by other means. 'Mind Game' is the war you fight so that you don't actually need to fight. Pure Sun Tzu – *The supreme art of war is to subdue the enemy without fighting.* And Ilyin is a master of that kind of war. Has to be, because militarily, his country cannot match up to its much richer enemies."

I said nothing, instead thinking with a rush of shame about what had been done with the money my parents had laundered and wondered – had they known they were probably foot soldiers in Ilyin's great mind game?

Curiosity wafted over his face for a second or two, then Maxim continued.

"Ilyin was the head of the Cheka during the time of Yeltsin. Chekist since he was seventeen years old. He and his Chekist buddies didn't like that their elite organization was suddenly relegated from global mind-hackery to state secret police. Meanwhile, all those hicks and fat, lazy generals that Yeltsin put in control of the nation's assets, which was literally everything, got rich. *Very* rich."

I'd heard enough to last a lifetime about the

Russian oligarchs, so we pushed him to move it along.

"One of those guys, Krylov was put in charge of a project so secret, it was totally off-book. A project run directly out of the General Secretary's office in Soviet times, and then from the office of the president of the Russian Federation. When Ilyin took over it was officially buried. But of course, what actually happened is that someone was bribed to keep quiet."

"It can't have been all that secret," I commented. "Or else we'd not have found any reference to it in the leaked CIA documents."

Maxim nodded. "Eventually, it leaked. Before then there were probably rumors. But the secrecy is for a good reason. Because Krylov is a child trafficker. No other way to put it. And the K-Foundation is a prison camp. A prison into which you're born. Like me. Like my mom. Like my brother."

"You said it was a cult," I pointed out.

"K-Foundation uses the same techniques cults use. Brainwashing. Lies about the outside world. Withholding information that might help you to get free. Physical abuse. Emotional abuse. It's systemic. A machine for churning out the end product."

"Meaning 'unicorns'?" It was frustrating that Maxim was still avoiding telling us exactly what he meant by that word. I hoped this might prompt an explanation but all he did was nod and move right on.

"I was different than other kids in the K-Foundation. Even though I was born there, I'd lived some of my life in the normal world. Masha escaped with me, took me to the USA when I was a little kid. I grew up in hiding, didn't even know about the cult. When we were finally caught, well, you can imagine. It was a huge shock." Maxim paused.

I wondered how the word 'shock' could possibly carry all the weight of being ripped away from a normal family home and forced to live once again inside the cult he'd described. Kenzie was quiet, too. It felt like we had nothing to offer a person who'd been through something like that.

"It took them years to track us down, but they were patient. Persistent. Czar Ilyin had a particular interest in us. My brother and I were part of a long experiment. They *really* needed us both alive."

Kenzie interrupted, "What kind of experiment?"

"I guess you could call it a genetic, social and psychological experiment. Ilyin must have known that if the experiment succeeded, he would have a new and huge advantage over his enemies in the 'Mind Game.'"

"What was the experiment?" I asked, impatient.

"We'll get to it," Maxim said.

"Seems kind of a roundabout way to go about it, Max," Kenzie admitted. "Can't you just tell us straight out?"

Maxim replied, evenly. "I could. But you probably wouldn't believe me."

Grumbling, I said, "Whatever. But this better be good."

Maxim's eyes flashed with disbelief. "Good? We're talking about breeding children to sell. There's no way anything about that is good."

One look at his expression and we both sobered up.

He continued, "Once they recaptured me and Masha, they kept me at the camp, trained me along with the other kids. Threatened me that if I ever told anyone about life in the outside world they'd kill us. First my mother, then me."

There was a hollow silence. Maxim shut his eyes, briefly. Other than that, I saw no sign that he'd lost control. But it was obvious, absolutely obvious what had happened.

I whispered it anyway. "You... you mentioned that your mom passed."

Dry-eyed, Maxim nodded.

"Because...?"

He blinked again, his voice suddenly dropping, his expression unreadable. "Yes. They killed her. Also, the one person I told about living in the US. He was an adult, but I think they'd have killed even a kid. After that, I didn't take any risks. I knew then that I was on my own. I could trust no-one. Not even my little brother."

"What were they training you for?" whispered Kenzie.

I half-expected Maxim to side-step it the way he had so many of our questions so far, but this time he gave a simple reply. "You'd call it 'spying.' We called it 'tradecraft.'"

Kenzie scoffed. "Child spies?"

"Not 'child,'" Maxim said, calmly. "We were sold when we were sixteen. 'Promised' would be a better word. We didn't leave the camp until we were eighteen. But from the time we turned sixteen, the customers could meet us, interview us, see our test results. They could bid for us."

"They auctioned you?" I said, horrified. "Like slaves?"

He let out a laugh, but I heard pain in that scorn.

"Why not? That's what 'unicorns' are."

The redacted Vault 7 file made more sense to me, now. In the memo that mentioned 'K-FDN' was a list of 'interested parties.' One of these was the Mossad – Israeli intelligence. From that, I'd guessed it was a list of secret service organizations.

"So they trained you from childhood to be spies and then sold you to secret services?"

"That's right. But only to countries allied to Russia.

They wouldn't sell to the West. Not even in Yeltsin's time. A handful of agents defected, like Olga. Chekists hunted them down, eventually. Even Olga, it seems, although she lasted longer than most."

I gasped. "Olga? She was a 'unicorn?'"

"Yes, Olga was one of us." Maxim said, no hint of bitterness or accusation. "We all dreamed of freedom, of escaping to a democratic country. Ilyin knew how dangerous that could be for him. He promised us all – escape to the West and you'll be looking over your shoulder for the rest of your life."

"But then…" I puzzled, "Does that mean Olga's killing had nothing to do with her searching for you?"

Maxim appeared resigned to never knowing. "Could be. Or could be that they found her because of it. Either way, Olga had been hiding from Chekists for a long time."

My curiosity was spiking, despite the tension of being in hiding with someone I'd just learned the Russian Czar was highly motivated to capture. How could spies trained from childhood possibly make such a difference? There had to be more to these 'unicorns."

"Anyway, when I get to be almost sixteen, I get to hearing that a particular customer is interested in buying me." Maxim grimaced. "It's not a country I'm eager to live in. I start thinking about escape. There was a rumor circulating that it could be done, that it actually *had* been done. That there was something like an 'underground railroad' for any kid who could make it to the nearest city."

He was talking about something like the secret network that escaped slaves used to reach safety, away from the slave-owning states of America, which featured in a popular TV series.

"If that was true, no-one was talking. None of the adults who guarded us, at least. Then I hear that my baby brother Sacha, of all people, is planning to run. He was a kid. *Twelve*. I thought of me at twelve and... I couldn't believe it. That kid either had a lot of guts, or else he was stupid. Either way, I decided to join him. To cut a long story way too short, we broke out, along with a few others. Most got caught, had to go back. Three of us made it out, but we got split up along the way. The camp is in a pretty remote part of Cuba, surrounded by cloud forest. We had to travel long distance however we could, all the way to Havana. Anyhow, Sacha made it out of Cuba. I got stuck on the island, so did Atlanta."

Maxim let out a long sigh. The gravity of the memories finally seemed to be piling in on him.

"I finally made it out, onto a boat to Mexico. I got funneled through Tapachula, like most Cubans who want to wind up in the US. But I couldn't stop thinking of Atlanta. A good kid, they deserved better. I decided to wait. Tapachula is like a river eddy – most anyone who leaves Cuba the way I did washes up there. If they're lucky. There is another option, which is to find some rich *yuma* or European to promise to marry you. Atlanta was only fourteen when we ran, so obviously that wasn't an option. And I decided to wait."

Finally, there was a break in the cool, yet deadly serious expression on his face, and he allowed himself a grin. "Atlanta got here a few months ago. That's when I knew. I could free the others from the K-Foundation, rescue them. All I needed was a team of three – me, Atlanta, and one other."

"That's why you're still here?" I asked.

Maxim nodded. "Like I said, Krylov's not what he was. He enjoyed the oligarch life, enjoyed living it up with the Westerners, getting invitations to their parties in Aspen, Martha's Vineyard and all that. Inviting them back to his yacht off Panama, or his villa in the

Caymans. Now, all of that is gone. Krylov is sanctioned up the yin-yang, couldn't even get an invitation to his own yacht if he offered to serve as crew. Has to live his life waiting. On the end of a phone to Ilyin, stuck in that shithole prison camp he built for us. From where escape is possible. That's what we discovered."

He raised his eyes first to me then to Kenzie. In Maxim's gaze was the burning fire of hope.

TWENTY-EIGHT

A WALK ON THE BEACH

Their name was Atlanta Camaguey and they showed up while we were at the beach. It was a five-minute walk through a coconut grove, all the way to the water's edge. Maxim's *narco* pal owned a lot of land around the hacienda and although it was no longer guarded 24/7, it provided a buffer from anyone on the lookout for two missing *gringos*. Maxim was certain his connection to Carillo was a secret, making it unlikely that anyone would search for him near the *hacienda*. Moreover, he didn't seem worried that Atlanta might be followed.

"When it comes to 'dry cleaning,' Atlanta is the greatest, can lose any tail," he assured us, then cracked a hint of a grin. "Tradecraft. The secret is to plan the route and take your time." As if struck by some niggling afterthought, his eyes narrowed and he began to speak again, then stopped. Whatever concern I'd glimpsed, he wasn't ready to share.

Atlanta rocked up more or less on schedule, approaching from the north, strolling on the stretch of flat, wet sand. They were a little taller than me and looked young, for sixteen. They had on turquoise neoprene shorts and a matching tank top. Hanging from their neck was a mini dive tank, the length of my forearm and about as thick. Their short, dark-brown Afro hair was shorn from nape to the base of their neck, but high and unruly on top. When they saw us they waved frantically, but didn't call out.

Maxim waved back. "Oh-ho, doing the last part of the cleaning run underwater. Very clever," he said, practically purring his appreciation.

"So she escaped with you?" Kenzie asked, a little too bluntly. "Must have been pretty young."

Maxim turned to him with heavy-lidded eyes. "*They* escaped with me. Non-binary. Don't call Atlanta a girl. The K-Foundation kids are like family to me. Biologically we're all cousins at least, probably."

I said, "But you're not close with your actual brother?"

Maxim didn't answer.

I'd grown curious about this 'Sacha' guy, Maxim's little brother. Maxim has said almost nothing about him but while he took a dip in the ocean he left Kenzie and me alone for around five minutes. In that time we put two and two together and came up with some data points. Kenzie guessed that Sacha was most likely a half-brother, because otherwise, surely Masha would have taken both boys to the USA when they escaped the K-Foundation the first time, when Maxim was a little kid.

"They could have different moms," I agreed. "Pretty heartbreaking if not. Think about poor Masha, having to take only one of them."

Either way, we concluded that the boys hadn't grown up together, which might explain why Maxim seemed uninterested in finding his brother, now they'd both escaped Cuba. By contrast, it was obvious at once that he and Atlanta were close. Atlanta grinned at me over Maxim's shoulder as the two shared a warm hug. They were instantly likeable, friendly and hugged me and Kenzie, too.

"Were you followed?" Maxim asked them.

Atlanta nodded. "Yep. The usual two guys." Maxim and Atlanta shared a thoughtful look, but neither said anything else about Atlanta's pursuit.

Maxim nodded towards me and Kenzie. "Their

flight leaves day after tomorrow. We're working on a plan to get them to the airport without being spotted."

Anxiety flashed across Atlanta's face. "Day after tomorrow? Let's hope they don't send the drone this way until then."

"I figured we'd have today and part of tomorrow," Maxim agreed. "After that we'll have to stay indoors." He turned to me. "Enjoy the ocean while you can."

I pointed one finger straight up. "Because of 'the drone?' For real?"

"Oh sure," Atlanta said. "They've already started in Tapachula."

"Aren't there laws about invading people's privacy?"

Maxim and Atlanta shared another look, as if to say 'aww, cute.' "Here? Not so you'd notice. Drone, camera and state-of-the-art facial recognition. If they know what you look like – and I'm guessing you're on social media, so they probably do – then you'll lead them to me. That's their hope."

I paused, stung by his sardonic tone and tacit accusation. Kenzie and I were both on social media, of course. Why hadn't we thought of that, deleted our accounts before we left the USA?

To my surprise, Atlanta came to our defense. "It's not their fault – this is all new to them."

Maxim seemed to swallow whatever bitterness was brewing within him. Again, the two 'unicorns' fell into a pensive silence. I had the weirdest sensation that both were suppressing their conversation. It was as though they were cutting their conversation short because we were there.

On an impulse I grabbed Kenzie's hand. He glanced at me in surprise but didn't pull away. "Looks like you two could use some alone-time," I said. "Kenzie, let's take a little walk."

Maxim looked taken aback but he didn't object.

Atlanta's reaction was closer to alarm. I almost expected them to outright challenge us, that's how irked they seemed. But, nothing.

"Be back for sunset," Maxim called after us. "This is the best place to watch it."

Kenzie and I wandered off. The surface of the sea had already turned golden as the sun dropped, and the sky was turning shades of peach and rose. We walked in silence awhile, stopping to pick up an occasional, undamaged sea shell. I felt super-relaxed in his presence, remembering the dozens of times we'd done exactly this, usually on a Chilean beach near to where Zara's family lived or in Florida, to where Bobbie's parents had retired. So chilled out that a bunch of niggling questions I'd been itching to discuss with Kenzie now faded into irrelevance.

"This is kind of cool," Kenzie began and then abruptly, mused aloud, "You think Atlanta's and Maxim are together?"

"You big dope, mind your business!" But on my mind was Kenzie's earlier comment to me – '*I don't like the way he looks at you.*' Could this be jealousy?

Kenzie didn't want to drop the topic just yet. "I can't imagine the Maxim we knew back then being interested in girls. Or boys, or enbies. He just didn't seem, I dunno, into that sort of thing."

"Bruh, we were twelve."

"I guess." He didn't sound convinced.

I decided to just be direct. "Is it because you 'don't like the way' Maxim 'looks at me?'"

"Not at all," he replied, shaking his head. "The way he looks at you isn't… I mean, you'd have noticed, wouldn't you? If he looked at you *that* way?" Now Kenzie seemed to be appealing for back-up.

I felt a blush begin. Maxim absolutely had looked at me that way, once, when were little kids. And yet even then I'd sensed it was an act. Why, I still hadn't figured out. "I'm not so sure. Remember when Danni Kinziger liked me? I didn't know. Or Marlon Juniper. Super, super oblivious."

"I don't think Maxim looked at you like *that*," Kenzie said, suddenly firm and kind of serious. "It's more like the way a cat looks at you."

Now I was mystified. "Cats look at you all 'pet me, feed me.'"

"A cat in the wild, I mean. In the wild, a cat only has three questions about any living thing it meets. *'Can I eat you? Can I schtup you? Do I need to fight you?'* When it's sure the answer to all three is 'no' then it relaxes and comes closer. Because then, well, maybe you can be friends."

"Not just a cat. Any predator behaves like that."

Kenzie nodded. "Correct. You didn't see it? Probably because you weren't watching him closely enough. But I was."

I forced a laugh. "You're imagining things. He was super happy to see me when we first met. You didn't see *that*."

"Huh. I wonder." Kenzie gave a brief shake of his head. "I get a really strange vibe from Maxim. Like, he's so much the guy we knew, but older. The way he always got us motivated to join in with his projects. The way he likes to take care of us, feed us – remember those fried egg sandwiches with ketchup that he'd have his mom make for us? Now, here, there's something new, different. Something I don't recognize."

Kenzie was right. But back then I had no clue. Even now, I don't understand why I didn't sense it, too.

We returned as the sun was about to hit the horizon. Maxim and Atlanta were sitting beside each other on the beach blanket. From a distance it came over pretty romantic. But as we got closer I saw that their hips and thighs were close, yet not quite touching.

Maxim sprang to his feet. "Can I speak to Padi, real quick?"

Kenzie raised an eyebrow, then nodded. "Sure. Why not."

Maxim led me back towards the tree line, still facing the sunset. The hairs on my arms stood on end as I waited for him to speak. I couldn't get what Kenzie had said out of my head. When we were out of earshot of the others, Maxim broke his silence, all the while regarding me as though I were the only other human being on the beach.

"Why did you come here, Padi?"

I thought it over for a few seconds. "Because Olga wanted to warn you."

"Olga." He reflected on this. "Your guardian, yes? Were you close with her?"

"Not really."

"But did Olga know things from your life, your past? Things you might have told her, or your parents?"

I frowned. "I guess. My parents chose her to be my guardian, so it seems likely they talked to her about me."

He was quiet again, pensive. "That last evening after you saw her, do you remember anything special?"

By now I was mystified. What could he be talking about? "Like what?"

"Were you looking forward to going to Mexico with Olga?"

"I mean, sure. It felt exciting."

"What about it felt 'exciting?'"

"The trip. A trip with Olga. I'd just found out that she was a kind of secret agent, which I thought sounded cool. Also Mexico."

Seeing you again, maybe. That last part, I did not say aloud. With startling clarity, I remembered dreaming about him that night. *Yes*, I thought. *Truly I am Pathetic.*

"I see," he said, evenly. "So – what happened? You hung out with Olga, she persuaded you to go to Mexico. Then?"

"She dropped me at Kenzie's. And that's the last time I saw her. She went to the hotel. Sometime that night she was poisoned."

"Let's stick with you. Olga dropped you off, she went to her hotel, it got late, you fell asleep. By the morning Olga was dead. Your trip should have been canceled, surely? Yet later that day you decided to go to Mexico anyway. Is that what you remember?"

It felt like I'd been checkmated. He blinked. I nodded. "Yeah, that's what I remember."

Very softly, he replied. "All right."

Only, it wasn't all right. Just a minute ago I had *insisted* that my main reason for being excited to go to Mexico was because of taking a trip with Olga. But that wasn't the reason. I was finally beginning to remember why. After what Kenzie had said to me on our beach walk, I very much did not want to tell Maxim.

TWENTY-NINE

ATLANTA AND JAGUAR

Atlanta was the first to suggest adding me to their team of two. I guessed at once that Maxim put them up to it. Kenzie and I had wanted to light a bonfire on the beach so that we could linger into the night, but Maxim said no. "No fires. No night lights. Including torches. When their drone gets here – and it will get here, eventually – we need to go dark."

"Then we'd better head back before the forest path gets too dark," Atlanta said with a smirk. Their voice took on a teasing edge as they said pointedly to Maxim, "We wouldn't want you to step on another tarantula."

Maxim and Atlanta shared a chuckle. It set off a twinge of jealousy because I didn't remember ever being able to tease him that way. When we were kids, he hadn't liked it at all.

We made our way back to the hacienda. The window shutters had been closed all day to keep the place cool, but instead of opening them up at night, Maxim left them shuttered. In the living room he lit four hand-held gas lamps and two wax candles, each as tall as the Easter candle.

While Maxim was fixing the lighting situation, Atlanta took me aside and suggested that I might be able to 'help.' It took me a moment to figure out that they were referring to Maxim's mission to rescue the K-Foundation kids. I was flabbergasted, didn't bother to reply. Instead I tried to conceive of a world where that might be a do-able thing.

"Listen," I began. "I'm not like Olga. I'm just… I'm ordinary. Even if I could help, which I can't,

Kenzie and I would legit be grounded for the rest of my adult life if we're not on that return flight to DC."

Atlanta didn't seem even a little bit abashed. "Remind me when that is, again?"

"We arrived today. Tonight, plus two more sleeps. Then we leave."

"So you've got two more days here?"

"That's right. Two days hanging out at Hacienda Narcojunior."

Atlanta let out a startled laugh. "Good one! Well, you should talk to Jaguar. I really think you can help."

"Who's 'Jaguar'?"

Atlanta looked skeptical but answered anyway. "Maxim. Y'know, Santiago."

"He's 'Jaguar,' now? Oh great, cos we were running low on nicknames."

Again they laughed. "Did you and Kenzie have another name for him, when you were kids?"

"Other than 'Max'? Nooo. He wouldn't have liked it. Even though he's the one who started to call me 'Padi' and Kenz, 'Kenzie.' 'Kenzie,' obvs because 'Marc' is too close to 'Max.'"

They smirked, knowingly. "Huh. He took the 'M' name for himself?"

I stalled. This hadn't occurred to me before. "We tried calling him 'Santi' but it didn't take."

"That's no surprise."

"Really? Why?"

Atlanta winced, as if I'd touched upon a troubling memory. "Our surnames aren't real. They're the towns our birth mothers were from. Those of us who had two mothers, that is."

"How can you have two mothers?"

Atlanta's expression was flat, unreadable. "One for the egg, one for the birth."

I thought about these words for a few seconds,

then understood. "Surrogate mothers?"

They gave a single nod.

"Then... Masha wasn't his birth mother?"

The mood turned suddenly somber. Atlanta didn't seem eager to continue this line of discussion.

"Masha was fourteen when Jaguar was born. Birth mothers had to be over eighteen."

I was lost for words. Fourteen? And yet she was still expected to donate an egg? It was obvious that something sick went on at the K-Foundation.

Atlanta changed the topic. "It's weird to think you knew Maxim before I did. What was he like?"

I paused to consider. "Like now, only smaller. Ridiculously talented. Like you wanted to hate him but somehow he was so..."

Perking up, they waited for me to complete to find the right word.

"*Honest*," I replied, after a moment. "*Direct*. Maxim seemed to exist in this bubble of his own... perfection. Like he didn't need anyone. At all. Until he did. Then..."

"Then he shone a light on you," Atlanta said. "Made you feel like you were the key to everything."

I nodded, impressed. Atlanta had phrased it perfectly.

They looked pensive, then gently smiled. "Jaguar's good at making a person understand how important they are. He doesn't like to waste his, ah, energy."

For a second it seemed like Atlanta had wanted to use a different word than 'energy.' Later, I would figure out the word they were holding back on.

"He doesn't do 'casual' friendship. You're either all-in, or he's a stranger. Oftentimes that made Jaguar's life difficult, at the camp. When we were kids. He went through..." Again, Atlanta picked their words very carefully. "... through some difficult times."

Their voice faded away. In their eyes I saw they'd checked out of the present and into a memory. I got the feeling it wasn't a good one. Then, rising to their feet Atlanta gave another friendly smile and said goodnight. Picking up one of the four gas lamps, they headed down the corridor towards the bedroom they'd picked out.

Meantime, Maxim and Kenzie had settled into the living room with a tray of cold sodas and a plate of leftovers from dinner. All we needed was a screen, a Playstation and Zelda and we'd be twelve years old again hanging out at Maxim and Masha's. At the thought of his mother I felt a stab of pity, imagining the intense grief her death must have caused.

No – I corrected myself – Masha's *murder*.

Atlanta had to be delusional if they thought Kenzie and I were going anywhere near the K-Foundation. I must have smirked as I thought this, because Maxim asked me what was up. Kenzie seemed curious, too, so I thought, *the heck with it.*

"So, I hear your alias is 'Jaguar.' That seems chill."

"My Krylov camp name. We all had one." Maxim broke off.

Kenzie did a double-take. "Jaguar?"

I continued, "You don't like to talk about it?"

Maxim shook his head, tight-lipped for a few seconds. Then; "Not really."

"Anyhow, listen. Atlanta – is that *their* nickname, by the way?" At this, Maxim rolled his eyes so I didn't push it. "They told me they think we could help. With your mission." I left it at that, waiting for him and Kenzie to crack up, laughing. They didn't.

"I need a team of three," Maxim answered. "Me and Atlanta know the terrain pretty well. We have a network in Cuba that's ready to help with getting into the country. We know the camp's security. It has to be a small team because we have to reserve maximum space in the chopper for the kids we evacuate."

I interrupted. "Excuse me, 'chopper'?"

"The helicopter."

"We know what 'chopper' means," Kenzie said. "It's just – Max, is this for real?"

Maxim was contemplative for all of two seconds then basically ignored the question and continued. "We have a way into the camp, we have a way out. We need one person, one special person." Then he fixed me with a look I can only describe as 'calculating.' "Maybe it *could* be you, Padi."

"What about me?" Kenzie fired back. "I'm pretty good at hacking."

I glared at him. "Whoa – you sure changed your tune! Now you want to volunteer for a suicide mission to yet another foreign country, one that would be a lot more forbidden to us than this one?"

This was no time to be volunteering for anything that entailed going to Cuba or climbing into a helicopter. It was a time for making excuses and finding a way to spend two days without being hunted down by international Chekists when we made a dash for the airport.

On the other hand, Maxim grinned from ear-to-ear, enjoying Kenzie's response.

"I could help with a stunt like that," Kenzie continued. "The hacking part, I mean. The chopper, not so much. How long do you need to plan?"

"Atlanta seemed to think it'd have to be in the next two days," I replied. Hopefully this would shut the whole thing down.

To my relief, Maxim seemed to concur. "Two days?" He pressed fingers of both hands to his temples, obviously frustrated. "More like, two weeks. To run scenarios properly."

I relaxed. "Then what d'you have in mind? Should we come back in a month or so, after things cool down with the Chekists?" Kenzie and I were off the hook, because there was no way on God's green earth that Kenzie's moms would allow that.

"Yes," agreed Maxim. "Later. But while you guys are here we could run a couple tests, see if you'd be able to help." He shrugged, "In case I'm wrong."

"Wrong about *what*?"

Kenzie chimed in, "What tests?"

Maxim sounded cagey. "I need to see how you respond in certain situations."

"For instance?"

Now cautious, he said, "I could show you tomorrow morning."

"I don't get it," Kenzie said. "What kind of tests?"

Without breaking eye contact with me, Maxim answered him. "Why don't you stick around and watch?"

A smarter person than me would have laughed the whole thing off, grabbed a lamp and headed for bed, waited out the two days and then headed straight for the airport in disguise. Most people, probably. Sneaking into an airport in disguise to avoid international agents of the Czar is, I would guess, more excitement than most regular people will ever experience. If I'd stopped to think it over, maybe I'd have taken that path and satisfied my curiosity. But no. I wasn't that sensible, or else you wouldn't be reading about any of this.

All I could think about were these 'tests.' What kind of test could possibly confirm I'd be able to help in a mission that involved going to Cuba and extracting some kids from a secret prison camp?

I *had* to know. I opened my mouth. "Is it dangerous?"

"The test? Not if you don't want it to be."

"Obviously she doesn't want it to be, dumbass."

Maxim shrugged. He turned to Kenzie. "Do *you*? Want to try something dangerous, I mean?"

"Is the thing you need me to do on the mission dangerous?"

Maxim thought for a second. "It could be."

"Stop tap-dancing, Max," said Kenzie. "*Is* it or isn't it?"

"A little. Unless things go badly wrong. Then, maybe a lot."

"So the answer is yes, it's dangerous. You clear on that, Padi?"

It was already too late, though. I was hopelessly intrigued. How much harm could it be to just *try* the test? "Can we do a *slightly* dangerous test?"

Maxim nodded. "Sure. Can you drive?"

"Like, a car? I don't have my license yet but yeah, basically."

He smiled, brightly. "Ever try blindfold driving?"

THIRTY

BLINDFOLD DRIVING

Do not attempt blindfold driving. Take it from one who's tried – it is a Bad Bad Thing on a par with 'car chicken."

At six thirty the following morning, Atlanta and I drove out in the little Toyota Corolla. They wrapped a cotton bandana around my head so that no chink of light could get through, tight enough that I couldn't open my eyes beneath it. I started the car very slowly, with Atlanta navigating as I steered towards the start of the long driveway leading from the public road to the hacienda. Beneath the tires, gravel crunched. After the first minute I began to notice all the information you usually ignore.

Eyes-wide-open is a giant distraction. When you're blindfold driving, vibrations enter your body from all parts of the car. The steering wheel obviously, but also the gas pedal and brake, the seat beneath you, the glass in the window. Each tiny piece of data conveys something useful. Not that I turned into Daredevil or anything, but I began to build up a kind of sense-map of the road. Palm fronds slapping the windows, the lighter gravel at the edges of the drive, the weight of the vehicle. All that data vanished once we hit the public road.

The road wasn't in the best condition. Its surface was a mixture of smooth asphalt with potholes that appeared too suddenly for me to do anything other than to slam the nose of the car into their crater. Atlanta's instructions kept coming, she stayed surprisingly calm even though I was screwing it up. But when we finally arrived at the highway that ran to the main beach, I began to hear other cars swooshing past. Heart thudding, instinctively I slowed down.

"Don't slow down," I heard Atlanta say. "This is a test of trust. Lean left. Lean right. Straight ahead."

"I'm doing thirty. That's plenty fast enough to kill us."

"Steady. It's roomy. My hand is right by the wheel. Nearest car is a hundred yards ahead and doing fifty. Speed up."

But I couldn't persuade my foot to budge. *This would be a really stupid way to die.*

"Trust me," Atlanta urged. "Remember in Star Wars? *Use the Force, Luke!*"

"*You* use the Force!" I snarled, and finally managed to pump down on the gas.

The burst of speed pushed me back into the seat. As the car leaped forward, blind to the world and lost in that darkness I imagined myself plunging into the abyss. Fear gripped me by the throat, pressed down on my chest like an anvil. For almost a full minute I couldn't breathe. Then I sucked in a deep gulp of air.

"Roni, why not just trust me, and try?"

The question seemed to come from both Atlanta and somewhere inside me. So I actually tried. Imagined myself as Luke flying in the trench, closed my eyes, cut off from the world and let go.

Maybe I'll die. Maybe it'll be quick.

For what felt like a split second, I disengaged. Then something incredibly weird happened. I sensed it. The *actual* Force. A surge of power through my arms and into the muscles of my right leg. You can be skeptical but that's the best way I can describe it.

"Omigod."

I began yelling, so much that I stopped listening out for Atlanta's patient instructions. It was like flying, plunging into pitch black, a magic carpet ride in the deepest night sky devoid of stars. Suddenly my limbs were moving without any conscious thought from me. A total out-of-body experience. I heard rubber screeching on tarmac as the car sped up – forty, fifty, sixty miles per hour. The wind-drag roaring as our little car whizzed along, swerving to overtake objects I couldn't see, dropping back into the right lane.

Atlanta's voice seemed to come from far away. "Oh wow. You're doing it!"

That's when I understood that I'd lost myself. In all of this, I was *nowhere*. Me, Roni Padilla, was a mere observer, locked away in some dark room wearing headphones that pumped sound effects into my ears. Like it wasn't real. Like I was a character in a video game, being played by myself.

That's when I lost control.

Atlanta grabbed the wheel. She screamed "BRAKE! BRAKE!" The car swerved left then right, the rear corner of the car knocked some hard obstacle, wobbled and we careered into a skid. Tires squealed, burning rubber.

"Pump! Pump the brake, on and off!"

Smooth asphalt beneath the wheels gave way as we slid into the shoulder, a rough cambered surface. Twigs snapped, dry leaves crackled. Finally, we rolled to a stop. I flung myself back into the seat, gasping for air, heart hammering against ribs, both hands fumbling to untie the blindfold. After a second I felt Atlanta's fingers push mine out of the way.

"Go. Just let me do it."

I blinked rapidly, adjusting to the dazzling brightness of the morning. Cars drove by and the Toyota trembled very slightly in their wake.

"How'd you feel?"

I placed a hand on my chest and managed to say,

"Relieved."

Atlanta gave a guarded smile. "I mean, when you were driving? Did you feel good?"

Swallowing, I found myself nodding. "Strange. But…"

"Exciting, huh? Quite the rush."

I forced a weak nod.

We swapped seats and Atlanta u-turned towards the hacienda. They turned on the radio and began singing along with some *reggaeton* hit. Judging by their sunny mood, I guessed that I'd passed the test. We didn't talk more on the way back, which suited me. My thoughts drifted, tumbling over each other as I tried to get my head around what just happened. As we swung into the hacienda's driveway, one over-riding impression emerged.

For at least twenty seconds I had genuinely checked out of my own body. It'd felt like watching myself become a puppet. The question was – who'd been in control? I was beginning to feel queasy. *I'd been someone's puppet.* I knew it, even if my brain struggled to accept it was possible. When I thought about who could have been controlling me, it became obvious: Atlanta.

It was like watching a gauzy image on a screen come into sharp relief, every pixel crystallizing into dazzling clarity. At first, it was just an intuition but as I followed it through, I became more convinced. Both Olga and Maxim had insisted it was nothing to do with their blood type or organs. Their rarity was something far more extraordinary.

"Unicorns' were rare because of their *unique abilities*. My guess? Some kind of psi power.

In my head it sounded bizarre, yet when I lined everything up, it was the only theory that made sense. Atlanta was a 'unicorn' – so rare that global intelligence agencies lined up to bid for Atlanta and other K-

Foundation kids. Spies trained from birth seemed somehow implausible. Why would they all come from one isolated camp in Cuba?

Then, I remembered the long silences shared by Atlanta and Maxim, how little we'd seen them talk, and yet they seemed to understand each other. I thought about how Atlanta had somehow known to leave a getaway car for Maxim outside the Bubbles Laundry, even though we hadn't seen him make a call or text them. About how they'd known to show up precisely when they were needed.

And finally, creeping at the edge of my conscious mind was the memory I was afraid to confront, the true reason I'd decided to search for Maxim, even after Olga was dead; my dream that night, of finding Maxim.

We drove back to the hacienda in silence until, as Atlanta was parking, I dared to come straight out with it. "Based on what you just saw me do, would you actually risk anyone's life?"

Atlanta tried to hide their initial, stern reaction by fidgeting with the lock. When they eventually replied, it sounded defiant. "You act like we have a lot of choice."

It was no kind of answer and we both knew it.

"Over in that camp," Atlanta continued, with evident difficulty, "are people we – that *I* – care about. People we won't leave to become slaves."

Atlanta's eyes met mine. They were on the edge of tears.

"Ohhh. This is… personal?"

Atlanta nodded very slightly. "So you get it?"

We returned to the hacienda. Back in the living room I asked Maxim directly. "Well, that was quite some 'test.'"

"Be happy," he replied, mildly, as if what had

happened wasn't basically one of the most traumatic things I'd ever experienced. "You passed."

"Is that what 'unicorns' are? Kids with psi powers?"

He watched me for a second or two, then gave a dry chuckle. "You could call it that. But it's more. A lot of regular people have psi powers, latent, untapped. One in a billion might accidentally unleash their powers. Or more likely, never understand that they have them, never learn how to harness them. Unicorns are different than the normal population. With us it's not latent. We grow up around other kids with the same abilities. We get *training*."

Kenzie sat up so abruptly that he knocked over an empty soda can. "That's why the secret agencies recruit you as spies?"

Maxim nodded. "That's why."

Kenzie shook his head in wonder. "Are you trying to tell me you're like the X-Men in Professor Xavier's school!"

Maxim and Atlanta exchanged a derisive look, then he replied, "Sure… if Professor Xavier was a clueless flunky who got promoted because of his ability to kiss ass and the school was more like Guantanamo."

"Is it really that awful?" I interjected. I don't know why it was so hard to believe that anyone would treat kids that badly but yeah, I was naïve.

"You tell me." A twisted smile hovered around Maxim's lips. "They have softball and the food can be edible, although there's never enough. That's the good side. Doesn't compare with Masha's cooking and D.C. Inter, though. Then there's beatings and solitary confinement in a dark concrete cell. I did weeks in the hole after my first escape attempt."

"But, your powers? Can't you like, mind control the guards?"

"In Krylov's camp? No. They can block our powers."

I stepped over to him, watching his expression turn from concern to curiosity. I placed both palms on Maxim's cheeks and turned him gently to face us both. He allowed the contact, our first since that initial hug, even seemed to enjoy it.

"Maxim! You honestly have psi powers? Hand to God, swear on your mother's grave and all?"

"I do," he replied, solemnly. "Hand to God, swear on Masha's grave. And all."

Kenzie murmured, "Hot damn!"

Maxim cracked a half-smile. "So – we good, now? Will you hear me and Atlanta out?"

THIRTY-ONE

INCLINED

"Fly a helicopter?" I stalled. "You cannot be serious."

For once, Maxim didn't respond with that easy grin of his. He seemed genuinely to care about my shocked reaction. His tone became soothing. It gave me flashbacks to that rehearsal room, me and Kenzie yelling at Maxim that we couldn't possibly play *The Forgotten Village*, not us, not mere beginners, that he was an idiot for thinking we could.

"Padi, listen to me. You drove a car blindfolded, doing sixty on the highway. You overtook two cars. And you kept it up for twenty-three seconds. Believe me, compared to that, what we're asking is simple."

(It wasn't. I'll just put that out now.)

Kenzie weighed in. "Where are you getting a helo from, anyway?"

"Beto Carillo knows people."

"Carillo? What is it with that guy, how come he's doing you all these favors? Is Carillo a unicorn, too?"

Maxim blinked, calmly. "You think he'd be in a Mexican prison if he was?"

It was an intriguing comment; we should have paid it more attention. But like a lot of things that were said and done in the heat of the moment, it simply zipped by.

"Fine." I nodded. "Let's circle back to the whole issue of whether I can even fly a helicopter, which absolutely, I *cannot*. You say Carillo's people are somehow getting ahold of one. Then can't they also provide a pilot?"

"What makes you think they'd be able to do that? Carillo's contact in Cuba is a scrap merchant. The chopper is old Soviet stock, sold off by some corrupt Russian general or other. There'll be a manual we can consult. They'll supply it fueled and in working order. That's the best deal anyone's going to get. There are no private flying schools in Cuba. Anyway," Maxim continued, "I'll be flying it. Ninety-nine-point-nine percent of the time, at least."

Kenzie couldn't contain his scorn. "Oh, now *you're* going to fly a Soviet military helicopter?"

"You think I can't? Plenty of private flying schools in Mexico."

"Training on Soviet military helos?"

Patiently, Maxim explained that he'd learned to fly a similar craft and racked up many hours on the simulator for the actual chopper he'd be flying. The one he'd be flying was currently parked in a scrap yard outside Bayamo, a small town near Santiago de Cuba.

"Sandra, one of Carillo's team, will give us a lift in a Cessna to Holguin, Cuba. She's headed south anyway."

"So we'd be hitching a ride on a drug plane?" I exclaimed.

"Relax, Sandra is picking up the product afterward, in Colombia. You won't be going anywhere near it. In Holguin we'll get a taxi to Bayamo. Pick up the chopper. Then we head for the K-Foundation. Me and Atlanta break into the camp, extract the kids. You wait in the chopper, guarding it. Ready to lift off if anyone approaches. And the second we're all aboard, I take over. All you need to do, Padi, is to let yourself be inclined, like before."

It was the first time I would hear this word, or any of the words they used to describe their powers.

"Inclined?"

"Yes," said Atlanta. "A 'unicorn,' if we're using that word, can temporarily 'incline' a person to perform motor actions."

"But only if they're willing," added Maxim. "It's inclination, not forced."

"And that's what happened to me?" I said, awestruck as the truth dawned.

Atlanta nodded. "For twenty-three seconds."

"Oh! After you told me 'use the Force, Luke.'"

Kenzie snorted. "Atlanta said *what?*"

Maxim, however, was determined to keep us on-topic. "Padi, you'd only be there as backup. I'd be inclining you."

I said, "But won't you be escaping from the camp or whatever?"

"I'll be inclining you," he repeated, more firmly. "Like I was today."

"You can do mind control from a distance?" Kenzie sounded as shocked as I felt.

Once again, Maxim brushed off his question. His energy and focus was all directed, I noticed, towards persuading me. "That's why I figure we'd need a week to drill this whole thing. Run a few scenarios. Atlanta and I have been working on getting in and out of the prison – we've set up a similar security system in the woods round back of the hacienda."

"What kind of system?" Kenzie said. "How're you going to take it down? Maybe I can help."

The mention of 'security,' seemed to pique Kenzie's interest. But I was already backtracking.

I told myself that it was a shame there was a bunch of psi-powered kids imprisoned in Cuba, even worse that they faced a life of getting sold into slavery. Truth was, there are probably millions of people in all kinds of horrible circumstances, all over the world. Between here and DC, easily thousands. Like any decent person,

I did what I could to help. I'd done my fair share in raising money for activist causes and charities. It had crossed my mind to someday study law so I could maybe play some part in protecting human rights or the environment. Climbing into a helicopter and sneaking into a foreign country for some light-covert military operation, however, was in a whole different realm of existence. Put plainly, I'm not the military type.

"You don't want to help," Maxim concluded, crestfallen.

"It's a *lot*, Maxim. Way too much," I replied, gently. There was so much disappointment in his eyes, I could hardly bear to face him. "You'll get your third person, I'm sure. An actual telepath."

He was quiet for a long moment. "Yeah. Maybe. I just thought – what with you being a latent. Not as rare as a telepath but still, you're one in a few thousand. I got my hopes up. But it's true, this isn't your fight. You shouldn't risk your future. You neither, Kenzie."

An oppressive weight seemed to float up off my shoulders, chest, everything. The excitement and energy Atlanta and I had brought into the room after the blindfold driving stunt, it just vanished in a puff of regret. I was bone-weary and my eyelids suddenly ready to drop. I made some feeble excuse and headed for a nap.

As I left I heard Atlanta remark, "Jaguar, you can't just drop it now. What about Coati? And the others?"

Maxim's reply sounded doubtful. "Maybe if Padi and Kenz knew more about what it's like to live in a regime like Ilyin's. I dunno. If they knew what it is to exist in captivity, where everyone's afraid. Where children can be bred, bought and sold by the state."

They'd spoken *just* loud enough to have intended it for my ears and Kenzie's. Coati, which they pronounced 'co-ah-tee,' I guessed was the name of Atlanta's boy or girlfriend. After hearing their comments I couldn't sleep. Too much had been said, too much had happened. Maxim and Atlanta had blown up my simplistic model of reality with as much ceremony as the opening of a supermarket.

Psi powers are real.

Even if I'd wanted to doubt it, the truth of it had gotten into my bones, muscles, ligaments and nerves. For twenty-three seconds I'd been 'inclined,' my body controlled by another person, via my own mind. I still remembered how it felt. *Inclined* seemed too timid a word for it. *Puppeteered* would be better. And yet I'd been the one to cut it off, even before I understood what was happening. The instant my will rebelled, the strings had been severed. Perhaps Maxim was telling the truth about inclination being voluntary?

I began to think of ways the ability could be used. In Maxim's hands, his team of three could include a second pilot, one who'd had zero training. Where were the limits? How many minds could he 'incline' at the same time? What other types of mind control could he and the unicorns do?

Ask Me Anything

One hour later I still hadn't managed to sleep. When I laid down my head I felt the rhythmic rush of blood. Within me I sensed a shifting of tectonic plates. I couldn't tell whether these forces were threatening to tear me apart or remake me in some new, improved form. Did caterpillars feel like this inside their chrysalis? Would they resist the changes, if they knew how?

As it grew later, I came slowly to the realization that I *badly* wanted to go home. Coming here had been a giant mistake. I'd hoped to warn Maxim ahead of time that he was being hunted, but in the end we'd pretty much led those forces to him. If not for his telepathic powers, his foresight and experience as well as Atlanta's help, by now the Chekist would have him. Even here we might not be safe for long. He had described how the K-Foundation 'graduates,' the 'unicorns,' ended up in all kinds of international secret services. That *had* to include the Chekist.

Did it take a psi to catch a psi?

Once I began seriously to contemplate going home, however, I was filled with a different kind of fear. A low, creeping dread of what might be waiting for us at the airport. Even in disguise I knew I'd be walking into that concourse convinced that whoever was searching for us would spot me at once. Anxiety would be pouring off me like steam from a swamp. How would it happen, I wondered? Would some uniformed stranger approach us, present some official-looking id, pull us into an office and from there into the bowels of the airport?

It'd happened to the Santiagos, after all. It could happen to Kenzie and me, too.

The alternative was even scarier. This fear fizzed through me until all my skin seemed to buzz. The unknown. An abyss of total uncertainty. Flying to Cuba was the easy part. But then came the sheer crankery: stealing a military helicopter, flying it to the middle of Cuba, sneaking into a secret camp and rescuing a bunch of children.

My mind could scarcely contain the plan, let alone agree to go along. It was so off-the-scale *reckless* that I couldn't believe Maxim and Atlanta were even proposing it. Then I reminded myself, that's what I'd believed when Maxim told me and Kenzie that we could ever perform *The Forgotten Village*. The Maxim I remembered didn't propose things he couldn't deliver. Was it possible that this mission actually was in his wheelhouse?

I sat up. *Something* was giving Maxim the confidence to want to include me and Kenzie. Wasn't that at least worth investigating? Later in the day, I finally worked up to asking him.

It was around ten at night by then. The living room was dark apart from the TV. I flashed back to that last night at the Santiagos' house, me and Maxim playing video games in the dark, my final glimpse of his boyish features lit by the screen, flickers of gold and red. Now we were here, in an isolated spot somewhere in Chiapas, and there he was again, face glowing like a bluish ghost as he slumped on the couch. When he saw me approach, he paused the game.

"Hey."

"Hey." I sat diagonally opposite him in an easy chair. He turned to me with some curiosity, albeit apparently pleased to see me. "I have questions."

He pulled himself out of his relaxed slouch and leaned towards me, resting one hand on the arm of the couch. "Yeah. I imagine you do. What we're asking… It's hard, I know."

I took a shaky breath. "Yeah. It sounds impossible."

Gently, he shook his head. "It really isn't. If I didn't know you could do this I wouldn't ask."

"Max, I don't think I even believe that *you* could fly a Russian military helicopter, let alone me."

"Is that all?" He seemed relieved. "I can prove it to you."

Laughing, I shook my head. "Sure you can. But no, that's not all."

"What else, then?" His eyes were on mine, intense and earnest. "Tell me, Padi."

I heaved my shoulders up and down. "Where to start?"

"Wherever," he said, softly. "Go ahead. Ask me anything."

"All righty, I will. Why did you stay so long in Cuba? Why not ask Olga to sponsor you to come to the USA?"

He sighed, deeply. "I hadn't seen Olga since I was twelve. No address or phone number for her, no easy way to get that information in Cuba. I had to make other plans."

I found this a little hard to believe. Couldn't he have simply called the WHO in DC?

"Pretty soon all I cared about was planning a rescue. It took me some time to understand how our telepathy works around mundanes. In the camp our powers were tested once in a while, in a lab. But they didn't share any findings with us. In Havana, I spent a lot of time repeating a lot of those studies. That's when I discovered that some mundanes…"

I interrupted. "Is that what you think of us? 'Mundanes?' Like we're mindless drones?"

He blinked. "Not mindless. Not drones. But the fact is, we have capabilities that most people don't have."

"You think you're *better*?"

Maxim didn't shrink from the accusation. "Better at using telepathy, yes. You wouldn't get angry with someone who points out they're more athletic, or better at taking exams, would you?"

"If they decided that made them more valuable than other people, yes, I would."

"Society decides what it values, Padi. Not me, not you. When I escaped the camp and saw the outside world, from what I could see, society values *money*. And uses money to reward the best athletes, the best computer programmers, the best entertainers."

"That's what you think?" I said, appalled. "It also rewards the best con artists, the best criminals, the best lying politicians. Money isn't a value. I don't exactly understand what money is, to be honest. But *values* are things like honesty, charity, equality. Money has nothing to do with any of those.

"I agree," he said, making an effort to pacify me. "That's why I said 'from what I *could* see.' I didn't like what I saw. When I was a kid, living in D.C. I didn't notice things like inequality. I loved our school, I loved our music, I loved sports. I didn't understand that so many people don't get to enjoy those things the way we did. Growing up in the camp, we had none of those things. They weren't considered relevant. We studied almost nothing apart from languages and tradecraft."

With a hint of accusation, I said, "Then you and Atlanta *did* train as spies?"

"I never denied it. We weren't trained to enjoy our lives. Only to do our duty as elite intelligence agents.

And K-Foundation telepaths *are* elite. Regular intel agents have to do difficult things like sex work, sometimes even assassinations. But not the 'unicorns.' We were trained to make people give up their secrets, with barely any effort from us. And that's all. We didn't even have to share our controllers' ideology, like most of their regular agents. Or do it for the money. The people that controlled us had the key to our invisible chain."

"I don't understand, what 'chain?'"

"Our telepathic powers can be blocked with a drug. Krylov controls the drug, he controls the trade in unicorns. No-one buys a two-way telepath without also buying a lifetime subscription to morphorium. It's a drug that blocks our powers. Once you're on the market, they mix it with something addictive, so we can't refuse it."

"Can't the telepath just refuse to take it?"

Maxim gave a sad shake of his head. "Not easily. Once a controller puts down money for us when we turn sixteen, that's when they begin to turn us into addicts. By the time we leave the Krylov we'd do anything for our controllers, so long as they keep supplying the juice. When the controller gives us the drug we need, they also give a shot of morphorium, to stop us hacking their mind." He stopped, watching for my reaction. "Is this the kind of thing you wanted to know?"

"I guess." I thought for a moment. "Won't the kids you rescue be addicted, in that case?"

He flinched. I'd touched a nerve. "Some of them. Potentially, anyone older than sixteen."

"Can you find the addictive drug on the streets?"

"Maybe. It'd take time and be complicated, I'd have to bring in a supplier, assuming I could find one we could trust. Much better to dry them out."

"'Dry them out'? That sounds dangerous." This was a lot to take in and not at all what I'd expected. It was one thing to free people but was Maxim really ready to accept responsibility for their health?

He asked, "Does knowing this make you more or less eager to help us?"

I paused to think. "It helps me to understand, maybe?"

"That's good. It's important. But remember – we can't force anyone to leave. Some of them might refuse."

The addicts, I thought. A desperate situation. "It's horrible, what happened to you. Is that why you left before you turned sixteen, so you wouldn't get addicted?"

"That's part of it," he agreed. "And it's still happening to all those other kids. It'll never stop."

"That's why you want to rescue them?"

"Yes. First the kids in the camp. Then the rest of us. In a bunch of organizations around the world. I want to free them all."

My throat felt dry. I could see a dark place this might be headed. "And then what? You all work for world peace?"

He seemed surprised. "Why not?"

"You'd be the savior of all the people like you in the world. With the power to do… I don't even *know* what. Do you? Know your limits, I mean."

He grew wary. "What are you saying?"

"Do you really think I should believe you'd be working for world peace?"

Maxim paused. "You're right. Probably not. But I'm not freaking Magneto, either. I don't want to start a movement. I just want my people to be free."

"Magneto?"

"Telepath. Like me. A two-dub – two-double-u, a

two-way telepath. You know the guy, the bad guy from X-Men. The superpower supremacist."

This wasn't all that helpful, since I wasn't into Marvel Cinematic Universe, but I got the gist. Maxim sounded like he thought I was joking. But I very much wasn't. It had *sucked* to be inclined-slash-puppeteered. I felt sick at the idea of trying it again only this time, risking my life inside a humungous helicopter. *No way* was it okay to unleash something so gross on my fellow 'latents."

He watched me, closely. "What are you thinking?"

"Oh, you can't read my mind?"

"No. Even if you were a telepath, it has to be consensual. Every two-dub can block, send and read. Latents can receive a broadcast from one of us, but it's not mutual. With them it goes just one-way. With a two-dub, it's two-way."

"Then why do the controllers need to dose 'two-dubs' with morphorium?"

"Because we have other powers that work on anything with a nervous system. Oh, the controllers make sure they're well out of range before their two-dubs are field-ready."

I didn't know what to believe. But I was sure of one thing – an international trade in drug-addicted slaves could not be dismantled. Not by us, anyway. Even if we were grown-ass adults with jobs and cars and money, it'd be difficult. Maxim's vision wasn't merely 'ambitious.' It was an impossible dream.

THIRTY-THREE

Flight Demo

It was around eleven at night. We should have been resting but after Maxim's revelations I had no sign of sleep. He strolled back from the kitchen carrying two plates with deep-fried tortilla chips – totopos – and freshly-mashed guacamole. He handed me the snack, dipped a totopo in the guac and popped the whole thing in his mouth, crunching.

I selected a totopo. "So, you spent your year in the wilderness figuring how to help your friends escape?"

"Huh? Wilderness?"

"A metaphor. Your year in Havana? Living on the streets and all?"

"Oh, it was *dank*." He took a handful of totopos and between crunches, told me the lore. "Just reaching Havana was huge. I'd lived inside the camp for five years. I knew next to nothing about how to survive in a place like Cuba. It's not like DC, it's basically a police state. Most of my energy went into staying under the radar and finding some other way off the island. After time I found different ways. But by then I'd also started to think about rescuing the others. At first I assumed I'd rescue them from inside Cuba. I got the idea to use a helicopter, found one big enough to carry all the kids. That was in Bayamo. Well, I made friends with the daughter of the man who runs the scrapyard. He's an uncle of Beto Carillo."

It was finally starting to make sense. "Are you saying that you came to Mexico because of the narco-junior?"

He nodded, covered his mouth while he crunched

for a minute, then continued. "Through Beto's uncle I found out about Friends of 5922. That's when I realized – I could use their route to draw anyone that managed to escape from the camp, to Tapachula. I could wait for them there, far from anyone who wanted to catch me and send me back to Krylov. And I had to leave. Cuba wasn't safe for me. I had *no-one*. After my brother ran off and I got separated from Atlanta, I was alone."

I wondered if Maxim was angry about that. There was definitely an edge to his voice each time he spoke about his younger brother.

"You used this, what did you call it, before? The 'secret railroad?'"

"Underground railroad," he corrected.

"You used that to bring other 'unicorns' to Tapachula?"

"Yes. And not 'unicorns,' please. That's the buyers' word. Call us 'telepaths' or 'two-dubs.'"

"If you promise to call us 'normies' instead of 'mundanes.'"

"How about 'non-telepath,' instead of 'normies'? I'm as normal as you are."

"Sure, whatever," I conceded. "So before, you said about Atlanta being the first to make it to Tapachula?"

"Atlanta tested the route. It worked." He paused. I could see him in real time editing the information he was feeding me. "You don't want to do it, do you?" he breathed. "You're afraid. Of getting caught. Of getting hurt. Of what you'd be getting into."

I grimaced. "And you say you can't read my mind."

"I'm only saying what you've already told me. I'm actually not surprised. You were cautious back then, too. But we prepared, didn't we? *The Forgotten Village.* We rehearsed the heck out of it. And we killed. *Would* have killed, anyhow."

Maxim smiled. I couldn't help but smile back.

"We did. Too bad you left. You're right, that performance would have been legendary. Who knows, we might have kept on being musicians."

"Can you imagine?" He sounded wistful. "Everything changed for me in that camp. I was still a human being, eating, sleeping, basic biological functions. Other than that, I might as well have been taken to a base on the moon, might as well be an alien. Maybe I am. No-one knows where our powers came from. Some think aliens introduced them into humans, thousands of years ago."

I eye-rolled. "Please. Miss me with that crap."

Maxim chuckled. "Well, who really knows? All I'm asking is that you try. I'd be happy to prove to you that I can fly a chopper, if that's the problem. It wouldn't be the full 'beast-mode,' obviously. That bad boy is still in Cuba. But Carillo's personal helicopter is in an airfield not too far away. I'd be happy to give you a demo.

"You promise?"

"Sure. Get some sleep. We'll go out early then grab some breakfast on the way home."

It seemed like a fair compromise so I did as he suggested. At least I tried – falling asleep after the bombshells he'd dropped wasn't easy. Eventually I managed and dreamt all night. All I remembered after I awoke was an incoherent jumble, vivid images of tall palm trees, waterfalls in the lush rainforest, of jumping from a helicopter, of running through the woods, riding a motorbike behind sand dunes, the thick blue line of the ocean, eating sandwiches, stealing sandwiches, stealing untended wallets, dancing, a lot of dancing. Mixed in here and there was a fair-haired boy who observed me through sorrowful eyes. The story of Maxim and his brother's escape was evidently compelling enough to invade my dreams.

In the morning Maxim shook me awake and waited outside the door while I dressed. Atlanta was waiting in the car. We left Kenzie sleeping. It was five-thirty. By six the car was rolling into the empty parking lot next to an airfield in the middle of a banana plantation. Two Cessnas were parked there and a small helicopter. A guy I presumed ran the airfield showed up five minutes later. He led us to the helicopter and handed over the keys. A minute later we were strapping ourselves into the pilot and co-pilot seats and Maxim was pulling an audio headset into place.

Still half-asleep I watched him go through some safety checks. He talked me through it but I'll confess now, I took none of it in. I was too busy being amazed. He didn't stall, pause, didn't need to stop to recall anything. It was as though he were talking me through the basic steps of making a sandwich – the stuff of second nature. Then he started the engine and above us the rotor blade began to whirl.

"Hard to believe, but the trickiest part of flying a chopper is hovering in place."

"Oka-ay," I said, with a building sense of dread. "Didn't you say that's what you need me to do?"

He pulled at a lever. (Yes, it has a name, do *you* know what it's called? I didn't either, not then. Let's stick with where I was at the time.) The helicopter began to lift into the air.

"It took nineteen lessons before I could hover and land in the right spot. I had to learn all about the physics of it," he shouted above the clatter of the rotor. "The good news is that you don't need to know any of that. All you need to do is to let me incline you. And what I know how to do, your muscles will know how to do. Just let your conscious mind stay out of the way and you'll be fine."

We rose straight up, twenty, thirty, fifty feet into the air. As the ground receded I gripped the sides of the seat and screwed shut my eyes. He flew the craft in a giant circle around the airfield, then back the way we came, hovered over a spot for twenty seconds and then landed, like a feather coming to rest.

Okay, he knows how to fly a helicopter. At least, a small one.

Atlanta had watched from below, sitting on the hood of the car. When we stepped out of the helicopter they slid off and approached, beaming. "*Todo bien?*"

"*Todo bien,*" Maxim confirmed. Atlanta's Spanish was flawless, yet I'd noticed that they flipped to English and occasionally Russian when they spoke between themselves. Maxim claimed to speak six languages fluently. I guessed that included English, Russian, Spanish and French, the first foreign language I'd ever heard him speak. I wondered what the other two were.

True to his word, on the drive back to Hacienda Narcojunior we stopped at a roadside stall and picked up *tacos al pastor* and fresh pineapple juice. We arrived at the house and set the table for breakfast. Kenzie emerged from his room, recently showered and dressed in clean clothes. If he was upset that we'd gone out without him he didn't show it. Maybe he hadn't noticed.

The flight demo seemed to have boosted Maxim's morale. He passed around the platter of tacos, smiling and oozing confidence. I ate in almost-silence. He'd made it more difficult for me to wriggle out of helping with the rescue. I knew it, he knew it. Yet I still wanted to forget about the whole thing.

"Were you and Atlanta friends, back in the K-Foundation?" asked Kenzie.

Maxim and Atlanta didn't seem surprised to hear a question about their past. "Not like now," Atlanta replied, carefully. "But yeah, we knew each other."

"Atlanta and Coati were friends with my baby brother," Maxim added.

It sounded a lot like a reference to Atlanta and Coati as a couple. There was another silence. It wasn't difficult to figure out what was going on.

I decided to say something. "You might try being less blatant when you *think* at each other in front of us."

Both lowered their eyes. Still telepathing to each other, probably.

A little bitterly, Kenzie said, "This is how it's going to be?"

Maxim rolled his eyes. "Kenzie, Padi, I know it must be hard. But you should know that I was never friends with anyone the way I was with you guys. With you I was happy, but I was never happy in that camp. It's not easy to trust anyone when you're... When you go through what we went through."

I watched Atlanta. They said nothing, yet it seemed to me that they didn't agree. I made a note to ask about the background to this incident, but I may as well admit up front that over the next few days it slipped my mind. And then it was too late.

Kenzie finished a taco and licked his fingers. "I get it. You're a friend for good times but not bad."

It wasn't meant as an accusation, at least I don't think so but I saw Atlanta frown, as if they suspected it might be.

Maxim took a big bite and chewed, thoughtfully. "It's more that I have these, like, friendship slots. Only certain people can fill those 'positions,' I guess I could say. You and Padi were unique for me. We were a team. I never had that ever again. I missed you. I still miss what we had."

It was kind of an intense moment, a little awkward. I glanced away, to Kenzie's phone on the table. With my phone out of action since it was hacked, his was our only link to the outside world. I'd previously set a search alert for 'Krylov Foundation Cuba.' A notification flashed onto its screen. I watched as Kenzie seemed to blank out for a couple of seconds. Then he picked up the phone, gasping.

"Guys, get a load of this headline… 'Czar Ilyin of the Third Russian Empire to visit bio-research facility in Santiago de Cuba.'"

HACKERY

The story was published on Granma, official news service of the Cuban communist party. For an article about an alleged bio-research institute, it was light on details about the nature of the work being done there, or the purpose of the Czar's visit. It mentioned General Anatoly Petrovich Krylov, who would also be 'welcoming the Czar' to Cuba. The article claimed that Krylov had 'retired' to Cuba after 'long service' as a 'specialist military trainer' in Russia. The general had been awarded a medal in Moscow by Czar Ilyin, twelve years ago. By my calculations, he would have retired aged around forty, which seemed too young.

Maxim and Atlanta agreed it was sus. We worked on verifying the details. There actually was a bio-research facility in Santiago de Cuba in a fancy new campus on the tree-lined Avenida de las Americas. It belonged to the university and was close enough to a swanky five-star hotel that the elites who worked at the facility could throw back daiquiris and hang out by the pool during their lunch hour

"Cuba's a poor country," said Maxim. He sounded skeptical. "A place like that just for research? And in Santiago, which happens to be the nearest city to the Krylov camp? Major anomaly. I smell Ilyin."

We checked on the institute's own website and found a tepid announcement about Ilyin's visit. Even so, Maxim remained suspicious. "Ilyin has never been to Santiago de Cuba. Not even when this 'bioresearch' place was inaugurated."

I asked, "Has Ilyin ever visited the Krylov

Foundation?"

"Ilyin doesn't even know where it is. Yeltsin gave it to Krylov when the unicorn project was still based in Siberia. The location is super, top secret. Otherwise, by now one of the other oligarchs would have stolen it. That's how it works with those people. See something you like, ask Ilyin to throw the owner into prison and hand it over. It's survival of the biggest kiss-ass. Krylov was smart enough to keep a low profile. Even the two-dubs who live in the camp don't know it's inside Cuba. They don't even learn Spanish. And the guards – we call them 'sentinels' – they're recruited from inside the camp."

"We did wonder why you and Masha didn't speak fluent Spanish."

"Since we escaped once, obviously Masha knew the camp's location, at least approximately. That's why they killed her and the *one* person I told."

"Dangerous secret," Kenzie remarked.

Maxim fixed him with a tough stare. "*Valuable* secret. Priceless; unicorns are worth millions and most goes to Krylov. At least, it did. Now, well, looks like the Eye of Sauron finally found him."

"All slavery is a license to print money," Atlanta added, bitterly. She and Maxim were convinced that there was zero chance Ilyin's first visit to Santiago, the closest he'd ever been to the Krylov Foundation, was a coincidence.

Maxim picked up his phone and began to type. I was beginning to feel a bit cowardly for being reluctant to help. It wasn't only that I doubted we could succeed. Being inclined had seriously creeped me out.

"Maybe we can find out something on the dark web?" suggested Kenzie.

Maxim put down his phone. He'd brushed off Kenzie's previous questions. Now his attention was at one-hundred percent. From experience, I knew this was like having all spotlights in the theatre suddenly trained on you; dazzling, overwhelming.

"Tell me more." Kenzie seemed bewildered. "Well… if the camp's location is such a big secret, Chekists are sure to be interested. They'll be talking to each other, so there will be phone records. Maybe we can get the numbers of some of these guys and call one. Y'know, trick them into admitting something."

Maxim's hopeful expression drained away. He turned to Atlanta and cracked up. "*Oigan a mi tío!*" Listen to this guy!

Atlanta smirked. "These guys aren't in the phone book, Kenzie. And even if they were, they wouldn't give that kind of information to some stranger over the phone."

"Not knowingly, perhaps. But hackers have all kinds of data. Russian bureaucrats get paid so little that they'll often sell databases over the dark web. Not big-deal secrets obviously, that'd be too risky. Just stuff that to them is just random, meaningless data. Like phone numbers and contact lists."

We still didn't follow but Kenzie was hitting his stride.

"Everyone keeps contact info on their phones, right? Sometimes you don't just put in a name but also something about who that person is, so that when they call you, it's not embarrassing that you don't remember them. Like Tommy Princeton, or Julia Dentist. Well, we can search these databases for contacts listed together with K-Foundation or Krylov or K-FDN. A detail that an agent might add to a contact's name to jog their memory."

Atlanta sounded dismissive. "Kremlin agents wouldn't be that dumb."

Kenzie scoffed. "You want to bet? People do the

dumbest things."

"That's clever," Maxim agreed. "It might work. But that just gives you the names."

"And their phone numbers," Kenzie pointed out. "Then you or Atlanta call them. I assume you speak Russian?"

"Of course."

Kenzie continued. "Then you need to pretend to be some Kremlin functionary. Calling to check up on the operation because you're writing some dumb report. Get the contact to talk."

Maxim smiled, quietly impressed. "That's very smart, Kenz."

I caught Kenzie's eye, saw his bashful grin and I knew. He was all-in on helping Maxim and Atlanta. This kind of hackery was his dream. I watched as he showed Maxim and Atlanta his phone and the app he used to access the dark web, enthusiastically outlining the process of finding and buying data with more of what remained of his crypto."

"Bobbie will get mad," I reminded him. "Just like Olga said. Think about it – your mom is already unhappy you're spending your crypto on hacked data."

I felt I owed it to Bobbie and Zara not to lead their son into further trouble. At the back of my mind, however, a terrible logic was emerging. None of us were saying it out loud, yet I'm sure we were all thinking the same.

If Czar Ilyin got his hands on the unicorns, what might he unleash? I'd experienced just a small sample of what their psi powers could do. I balked at the thought of an army of psi-powered teens in the control of a power-hungry dictator.

Within three hours Kenzie paid for, downloaded and had sifted through millions of random phone records from phone accounts registered to nations in the Third Russian Empire. Using the technique he'd described to us, he'd come up with a shortlist of six names. All six were tagged in someone's contacts as 'K-FDN.' He handed the list of names and numbers to Atlanta.

"This guy?" Maxim hooked a thumb at Kenzie. "A genius."

From a drawer in the living room he took an unopened pre-paid cell phone. I guess all criminals keep a stash of burner phones but it was still surprising to see Maxim help himself, as if he owned the place. Was housekeeping really the only thing our old buddy did for Carillo?

Maxim called the first four names over speaker phone, while we held our breath. Later, Atlanta told me how the conversations, which were all in Russian, went.

"Hello, this is Petyr Mikhailovich Sobchak from the Department of Operational Quality Control. I've been instructed to deliver a report on the recent operation concerning General Anatoly Petrovich Krylov."

None of the agents he spoke to denied the operation. All were taken aback at being contacted out of the blue by such a brusque-sounding officer. None were prepared to answer questions, or confirm anything. One hung up on the spot, saying only 'Nyet."

"Keep going," I urged. "Before one of these four gets the idea to phone one of the last two!"

Maxim dialed again. The next name on the list was listed on the website of St. Petersburg University as a geneticist, the only scientist of the six. This man replied cautiously but when Maxim pushed with a follow-up, seemed willing to talk. Yes, the operation had been a success. The team had been able to locate the target. He'd given up the information easily. How? They'd offered both carrot and stick. The target had 'chosen wisely."

"And the final 'delivery'?" Maxim demanded. "Was this also efficiently made?"

"Oh, very much so," the agent confirmed, proudly. "I wrote the protocol myself, you know."

"That's correct," Maxim said, smoothly. His eyes closed in calm concentration. "We have you registered as the inventor."

"It took less than the three minutes I'd planned. To be precise, two minutes and forty seconds."

"Excellent work," Maxim said. "Glory to the Empire, God save the Czar."

"Glory to the Empire, God save the Czar."

Maxim hung up. He folded his arms and began to stride about the room. "So now we know. Krylov is dead. They killed him. That was the 'final delivery.' Before he died, he gave up the camp's location. Sounds like they promised to pay him off. The drunken idiot believed them."

Kenzie scratched his head. "It actually worked. Honestly, not sure I believed it would."

Maxim had already moved on. "This pretty much nails it – the visit to a bioresearch center is a cover. Three days from now, Ilyin is going to the camp."

"Only one reason for that," Atlanta said.

I agreed. "He's going to take the unicorns for himself."

Atlanta corrected me; "For the empire."

Maxim shrugged. "For Ilyin it's the same thing."

"In which case…" I could scarcely believe what I was hearing myself say. "We need to get those kids out before Ilyin shows up."

THIRTY-FIVE

THE PLAN

"*We* need? We?" Maxim sounded delighted. He threw both arms around me and briefly, hugged me tight. "Finally! The real Padi is back."

I couldn't help blushing, at Maxim's touch and at his sudden approval, which I wasn't sure was deserved. I'd been trying to find a way out of this for me and Kenzie. On some level, I still was. My instincts were screaming at me to run far away and never return. Yet the harsh reality of our situation was sinking in, slowly. Help Maxim or try to run? Either way our options were limited.

Fly to Mexico and then beg their police to help us? We had no way to know if they were compromised by Chekists. Almost certainly, they were. We could end up being disappeared. Get help from Bobbie and Zara? After what happened to Olga, I wasn't prepared to risk their lives. Just walk away from it all? *How?* We'd still have to run the gauntlet at Border Control in Cuba, Mexico and the USA. Even if there was any chance of us being allowed to walk away with the information now in our heads, it left Maxim and Atlanta and all those K-Foundation kids in the lurch.

I didn't yet understand Maxim's plan, but if he said he needed a minimum of three people then that's what he needed. *This* Maxim, the guy who wanted to free his psi-powered family, I recognized at once. Laser-focused, determined not to let anyone be the weak link in his scheme.

Yet, every so often since it had happened, I'd flashed back to the feeling of being inclined. As badly as the memory creeped me out, I understood at a visceral level that if Maxim's mind could reach mine while I was in the chopper, I'd be able to fly it. At least for a short time. The major variable was *how long* I'd be able to tolerate being inclined. Because – and I cannot stress this enough – it feels very super-gross to feel your arms, legs, fingers being moved under someone else's control. The over-riding urge is to kick out that invader. The more I thought about it, the more I understood why Maxim had chosen to simply demonstrate inclination rather than discuss. I would never have believed it was possible. But now the cells of my body knew what it felt like and there's no arguing with cells.

I knew I could help. I knew that without me this couldn't work, not in time. It didn't seem like I had a lot of choice. I knew we couldn't risk power like theirs in the hands of Czar Ilyin. That evil bastard has been murdering his way across a continent for more than twenty years. The K-Foundation children deserved to be free, not enslaved by leaders bent on using their powers for military ends. Obviously I was sympathetic, but I was also scared out of my skull. All I could think about was *why me*? Why did any of this have to land anywhere near me?

Maxim had managed to win over Kenzie. The way he'd used his hacking skills (and crypto – wow!) to solve the mystery of what had brought Ilyin to Cuba was truly awesome. Doing Maxim favors was as addictive as it ever had been. The way he looked at you afterwards was hard to forget. Like you were his savior. Yes, we were jittery, but Kenzie and I had come round to the idea of joining the rescue mission.

Over the next half-hour Maxim and Atlanta laid out the entire plan. Once we'd flown, perfectly legally into the private section of Holguin Airport, our first step was to steal a Mil Mi-8. The fifty-year old Russian transport helicopter was in a scrap yard near Bayamo.

"Steal?" Kenzie blurted, "I thought the narcojunior was handing you the keys?"

"Beto's *contact* is giving us the access codes. Let me and Atlanta worry about the rest."

Kenzie's eyebrows remained raised, but we let that go. Now that we had an inkling of what Maxim and Atlanta were able to do with their minds, different rules applied; rules we didn't yet understand. All we could do was trust that Maxim knew what he was doing.

That thing about not being able to read my mind — truth or bullshit?

I projected this thought directly at Maxim, watched his face closely for any reaction. Nothing. He'd called me a 'latent.' Did that mean I was susceptible to mind control yet unable to hear his 'sent' thoughts, or to have him read my mind?

"Next we fly the chopper to within a klick of the camp. It's in the Sierra Maestra mountains so potentially tricky. Anyhow, we've studied the satellite photos and found a spot. I've flown the mission lots of times in the flight simulator. It's a two-person job. One to fly and one to distract the air-traffic control. For this stage, you're just passengers."

In the next phase of the plan we'd split up. From here, everything about the plan was nerve-rackingly daunting.

"After we've left for the camp, you will be in charge of the chopper, Padi. You'll be safe inside, in case anyone comes snooping. At least, you'll be all right until the military show up."

I froze. "Military?"

"Cuba's dictator is in Ilyin's pocket. So yes, if the wrong person at the scrap yard notices the chopper's missing, the Cuban military may well show up."

"Seems pretty likely to happen."

Maxim nodded. "Eventually. That's why we'll take the chopper at night. Should buy us a few hours, until dawn."

"And when the military do show up and you're not back...? It's just me against them?"

"They won't shoot. They'll want the hardware back. You stay inside, doors locked, quiet as a mouse but with your hands on the controls, ready for when we return."

"But that's a worst-case scenario," Atlanta pointed out, as if that was somehow reassuring, which it wasn't. I could already think of a few worse scenarios.

"Meanwhile, me and Atlanta will hike to the camp. The perimeter is surrounded by stun mines. If you trip the lasers, you activate all the mines in the vicinity. The electric shock is bad enough to make you pass out."

I winced. Suddenly, hanging back inside a bulky Soviet helicopter was preferable. "Sounds nasty."

"We'll take the stun mines out with an EMP, an electromagnetic pulse. It'll blast any electronics in a small area with enough electromagnetism that they'll be disabled, for about ninety seconds, maybe more, maybe less. We'd need to test the equipment, to know how long. That's where you come in, Kenzie. I'm hoping you can make us an EMP generator. We have the kit and instructions but we're short on time."

Kenzie gave a confident nod. "I'll figure it out."

"After the stun mines there's an electrified fence. We'll toss the EMP generator over the perimeter for when we need it later. The next stage, Atlanta hands me over to the camp guards. We'll say they caught me in Havana. That's how we'll get in."

Now I was the skeptic. Maxim's psi powers were stronger than Atlanta's, so how could Atlanta overpower him? "They'll believe that Atlanta caught you?"

"Atlanta always scored better than me in tests. Krylov's people don't know half of what I can do. That's how I was able to escape."

"Seems sus, either way."

Maxim shrugged. "They'll be suspicious, but they'll let us in, probably put us under guard while they verify the story. That's all we need. Once we're inside they can't stop us. The whole camp is run by guards who use their blocking powers to control the kids. Atlanta and I don't have the drug in our system anymore. Even if they inject us, it'll take ten minutes to take effect. Ten minutes is more than enough."

"Then what?"

"We round up the kids and bring them to the fence. Activate the EMP, disable the fence and stun mines. We bring the kids to the chopper. You start it up, get everything ready."

"That's all? Just start the engine?"

Maxim nodded. "On our way back from the camp I'll incline you to do the basic checks, start the engine. When we reach the chopper, I'll take over as pilot. We fly back to Mexico and land on a quiet beach of Cozumel. Then maybe Padi takes a flight back to D.C. from Cancun, neatly avoiding the Chekists waiting for you at Tapachula airport."

"Wait, what do I do?" Kenzie asked. He sounded confused, like things were getting away from him. "Apart from help make the EMP generator?"

"You go home, Kenz. Before we leave. You get on your flight to Mexico City and then to DC."

"But… the airport?"

"The Chekists are hunting for a pair of gringos, a girl and a boy, not a boy on his own. This is better. Your moms stay happy, no more worries they'll show up here."

Kenzie said nothing more, but it didn't take a mind-reader to notice he was unhappy.

THIRTY-SIX

PLAN B

The mission was a night-time thing, so we figured it'd be good to go nocturnal. That afternoon, however, I couldn't sleep. I checked in on Kenzie to find he was awake, too. He was studying instructions Maxim had downloaded weeks ago, about how to make a home-made EMP generator.

"Max's stocked up on all the kit. No reason not to get on with building this thing," he said, sounding a little despondent, "since I won't be going on the mission. Makes no sense for me to go nocturnal."

I found a spot on his bed that wasn't covered with printouts of scheme for the build. "Sounds like you wish you were going."

"Obviously."

I paused. At this point, I'd have taken any solid excuse not to get involved. Was Kenzie trying to impress me? Or was he actually that reckless? "It's risky. If we get caught or even delayed in Cuba, your moms will find out. And they will *not* be happy."

"Roni," he said, eyes imploring me. "Don't you get it? My moms will be just as upset if anything happens to you."

"They'll be upset," I agreed, "but they'll be able to deal with it. It's different for a parent."

"Well… there's also your actual parents," he reminded me, gently. "You won't see them but I'm sure they still care for you."

I couldn't deal with that right now so I shut down the emotions bubbling beneath the surface and changed the topic. "What d'you think of the plan? In general, I mean."

"The plan? It's risky AF. But then I haven't been 'inclined,' so what do I know? If Maxim and Atlanta can do the things they claim, I guess it could work. At least until they reach the camp. After that, who can say?"

"You're right. According to Max, the camp guards are all psi-powered, too."

"They grew up in that world. Only they know if they can overpower those folks."

We reasoned that Maxim wouldn't risk going in at all if he wasn't confident. But I was still nervous. The plan struck me as unnecessarily complicated. Why go through the charade of pretending to have Atlanta hand Maxim in? Why not just use the EMP to break in and out?

"Because the EMP would need to be recharged. It only works one time on each charge. That takes time and testing," Kenzie said, then briefly paused. "If I went along, I could do it. Which seems like a really simple workaround. Weird that Maxim didn't think of it."

"Maybe," I said. "Or maybe it's the best plan in the world – for three people. You know how monomaniac he gets. All this time he's been waiting for one more 'unicorn' to escape and make it over here. He's been one hundred percent focused on a three-person plan. It's only since you and I arrived that he's started to think about using normies. Yet he's still hung up on a team of three."

"'Normies'? Max said that?"

I sighed. "Actually no. I said it. He didn't like it. Asked me to say 'non-telepath.'"

"They say 'non-telepath,'" Kenzie said, pointedly.

I blushed. He was right. It had slipped out. Yet I couldn't stop from wondering. If psi-powered humans existed then the rest of us were – what? Normal, yes, statistically. Lesser, too? Maxim seemed to think so, even if he rejected any comparison with Magneto. I asked Kenzie if he understood the reference.

"Holy crap. He compared himself to Magneto?"

"Only by saying he's not like that."

Kenzie put down the sheet of instructions. "We could be in trouble, if he is."

"Is Magneto the one that wants to kill every other person in the universe?"

"That's Thanos. Avengers. Different universe. Magneto wants mutants like him to rule the world."

"Oh. I get it. 'Superpower supremacist,' Maxim said."

We were kidding around but the truth is, I already had an inkling it might lead somewhere bad. Whatever misgivings I had were swamped by the more urgent prospect of the entire 'unicorn' cohort falling into the hands of Czar Ilyin. Like it or not, right now the world was finely balanced in a three-way nuclear glare. Where it came to psi-powers, according to the leaked documents in Vault 7, Krylov had been selling to a bunch of different regimes. It was another kind of power balance. With Krylov out of the way and the camp's location compromised, Ilyin's grab for the entire operation would change that. It'd tip the scales in his favor.

Based on how Ilyin used the TRE's military muscle, it didn't bode well for any of their neighbor nations. More cities reduced to rubble by missiles, more agricultural and factory produce seized, more citizens shipped off to the distant regions of the empire to be enslaved in grim factories that polluted the air and the ground, while their children were sent to re-education centers to be brainwashed into worshipping the Czar. Anything I could do to stop *that* was worth the risk. It would potentially save the lives of millions.

Kenzie felt the same. "My moms would understand," he acknowledged. "But if we do tell them and they're ever questioned… I don't know. Could be real bad."

"Better than never knowing what happened to us."

We agreed that all options sucked. But we had no time to find an alternative. Maxim's mission plan dominated our thoughts. Sleep was out of the question. The more we discussed it, the harder we agreed: Maxim's plan was a hot mess. We needed something simpler, stealthier, even if that meant risking a fourth member of the team.

I gave Maxim and Atlanta until eleven at night to sleep and then woke them up with my idea.

"No," was his immediate response. "Bad enough to risk you, Padi. Me and Atlanta don't have parents to mourn us. We can be totally focused on the mission. Kenz can't help but think about his moms. Could be a fatal flaw."

Predictably, Kenzie objected. "Bro, all I'd be doing is hiking to the camp and then charging and discharging the EMP. You got Padi flying an ancient Russian transport helo, when she's never been inside one – yet I can't even mess with a battery?"

"Not flying it; guarding it and starting the engine," Maxim corrected.

"Much simpler if you and Atlanta just sneak in and out of the camp," I told Maxim. "No need for theatrics. Just a quick, simple heist. When you get back, Kenzie will have recharged the device. Then you just walk out."

Atlanta nodded. "She has a point. Also, what if something goes wrong with the EMP generator? With just you and me there's no margin of error. But Kenzie could repair it."

Maxim was silent, fuming.

"Even in the dark, I can find my way from the perimeter to the dorms," continued Atlanta, with supreme confidence. "It'd take, what, five minutes to wake all the kids? We could be back at the fence in another five. Eight minutes, max. Another twenty to hike back to the chopper. Thirty at most. The whole thing can be done in an hour."

Eventually, Maxim began to speak, albeit grudgingly. "The weakest part of the plan is how long it'll take for the Cuban military to track us down. Once we steal the chopper the guys at the scrap yard will report the theft. The military will start searching the sky for us. Which means we'll have to fly low, below the radar. But eventually, they'll lock on to us, because when we get to the mountains I'm not risking flying too low. Their surveillance can detect heat. The Mi-8 will light up pretty strong. They'll scramble jets or helicopters from the air base at Santiago. That's forty-five minutes flying time from where the camp is. The less time we take the better."

There was a stunned silence before Atlanta said aloud what we were all thinking. "Then one hour isn't enough."

For the first time I saw Maxim look actually crestfallen, disappointed with himself as he recognized the glitches in his plan. "You're right. It's not enough. I have to stay with the chopper, so once you're inside the camp, I can fly it closer. That'll save twenty minutes, with no need for you to hike back with a bunch of sleepy kids."

Kenzie frowned. "Why not land nearer in the first place, shave off another twenty minutes?"

"A beast like the Mi8? It'd wake up everyone in the camp. Even landing a klick away is pushing it."

We were all quiet for a moment, until I broke the

silence. "Maxim needs to stay with the chopper, fly it closer. Let me go in with Atlanta, help wake up the kids, bring them out of the camp and back to the chopper. Me."

All three turned to me. In a low voice Maxim said, "Wow, Padi. Then you'd really be stepping into the arena. Are you good with that?"

I thought about my mom and dad and what they did. The shame of their actions was on our family, forever. But if I did this, if I did something to stop one of the most evil people in the world from growing more powerful, perhaps I'd finally wipe away the stain of their treason.

THIRTY-SEVEN

THE PREP

It all came down to how fast we could hike through the cloud forest near the camp. The EMP generator was Kenzie's priority, infiltrating the camp was down to me and Atlanta. Flying the chopper was now Maxim's one and only job.

We disagreed about how to prep the hike. Maxim wanted us to spend hours hiking through the nearby woods at night. But I remembered the last hike I did and how for two days afterward I'd been reduced to hobbling and groaning.

"In your mind you're still running the old plan," I pointed out. "The one where you go in a few weeks or months from now, whenever your third telepath makes it here. That world is gone, Maxim."

"Padilla is right," Atlanta agreed. "We can't let ourselves get tired."

"Exactly. We should rest and load carbs, ready to go all-out for an hour."

On the other hand, I didn't want to just sit around eating spaghetti marinara. There had to be more we could do. Kenzie didn't want help with building the EMP generator – Maxim's interference on its own was as much as he could take.

I suggested that we memorized the speediest hiking route from studying satellite maps. There were a number of visible trails, with some switchbacks that'd get us lost if we made a mistake. When a clear route emerged we tested each other until we had it down. After that, Atlanta drew us a map of the camp. In Maxim's original plan for three K-Foundation escapees to be the raiding team, no map was needed. With me going along, this was another change.

"In total there's twenty-five other kids aged between one and seventeen. Two are under age five. We'll have to carry them," Atlanta said as I watched them add detail to the map. "In baby-backpacks. We'll wear them to the camp and then give them to the strongest kids there."

I took the sheets of paper on which Atlanta had drawn the plans, preparing to memorize them. "I've been wondering about something. Why'd do call Maxim 'Jaguar'?"

"It's his camp name. Krylov banned us from using the names our mothers gave us. I should call him 'Maxim,' probably."

"When you say 'camp name,' is that connected to the names of the towns your birth mothers came from? Like 'Santiago' for Maxim and 'Camaguey' for you?"

"No, camp names were more like aliases. They didn't want us using the names our parents gave us. Partly to prevent what happened with Masha – they didn't want our parents trying to rescue us."

Each new detail I learned about the Krylov camp seemed to be more appalling than the last. I noticed Atlanta watching me, apprehensively, and held back the horror and pity that were welling up inside of me.

The K-Foundation kids were raised not even knowing their own names.

"I… I'm sorry. I assumed that if Maxim knew his real name, then you…"

Atlanta's expression hardened. "Yeah well, not everyone has a crusading mom, like Masha."

I hesitated, but pressed ahead. "Then 'Atlanta' is your camp name?"

Through gritted teeth they replied, "It's my only

name."

I got the message at once. "Last name?"

Atlanta shrugged. "No real last names. Krylov doesn't want us to know who's related to who."

"But I thought Maxim had a younger brother?"

"Yes. Masha told him about Sacha. Most mothers don't dare to do that. Like I said, she was special."

I thought for a second or two. "Then Masha was Sacha's mom, too?"

"His egg-mama, yes. I already told you – a lot of two-dubs have two mothers. Maxim and Sacha had the same mother but a different surrogate."

"And their father?"

With a grimace, they shook their head. "Unknown."

Sighing deeply, I said, "And Masha… she…?"

Atlanta seemed to be reading my mind. "She left Sacha behind, yes. He was too little to run with them, just a toddler. He was still being looked after by his birth-mama, anyway. You can't judge Masha – what was she supposed to do, take Sacha from the only parent he knew? It was different with Maxim, he was older, already spending all his time in the main camp. Any mother would rescue their child from that future, if the chance came along."

"Then 'Santiago' isn't Maxim's real last name?"

"No. 'Camaguey' isn't mine either. They're the names of the towns our birth mothers are from."

"Oh, that's right, you said that," I mumbled, distracted by the sheer grimness of what they'd just told me.

Birth mother. A horrible reminder that Masha's eggs had been taken when she was just fourteen, to be fertilized and implanted in a surrogate. I wondered if either had even consented. Krylov probably didn't even see any need to ask. After all, the Czar's army routinely used rape and torture, even against their own soldiers. They had no interest in any human rights except the Czar's.

"Are you related to Maxim?"

Another shrug, this time with touch of ruefulness. "Maybe."

Carefully, I asked, "So – Max could never be your boyfriend? Because you might be related?"

Atlanta gave a gentle laugh and took a deep breath. "That. Plus he's a jerk. But mostly because I prefer girls."

"Got it," I said. Then like an idiot I asked, "Anyone in particular?"

Atlanta's lips twitched, holding off a grin. "Well, we've only just met…"

It was an awkward few seconds. "I didn't mean me."

"Relax, I'm kidding. It's kind of obvious you're into boys. You can't even decide which one. The answer is, yes, there's someone. She's still in the camp."

"Coati?"

"What? No. Is that what you thought, because I need to get Coati out?" Atlanta snorted. "Jump to conclusions, much?"

"What's your girl's name?" I said, hurriedly trying to smooth things over.

Atlanta sobered at once. "Puma. And she has no clue. I don't even…" They took a raggedy breath then released it all at once, as if saying the girl's name alone was a major release. "I don't even know if she likes, y'know, femme people."

I understood at once. For Atlanta, this was all personal. It would have been cool to keep on talking about their past but they switched the topic. I guess we had more urgent priorities. Atlanta offered to test my knowledge of the camp's layout. Afterwards I studied for another hour and we went again and again, until I made zero mistakes.

Meantime, Maxim wandered from me and Atlanta to Kenzie, checking in. After a while we heard curses from the next room, where Kenzie was testing the device he'd built. By then the sun was rising and we were getting droopy. We shuttered all the windows and retired to the bedrooms. It took me another couple hours to sleep.

I was so, so wired. What was I doing, what was I thinking? Had I lost my mind? To believe that we could fly to Cuba without the permission or knowledge of Kenzie's moms, who'd been so kind to me, steal a Russian military helicopter, fly a military helicopter, infiltrate a top secret camp and rescue a bunch of kids? The CIA or whoever, that's who should do this. Why couldn't they? Why did it fall to us? But I was beginning to understand what was at risk. Any official rescue effort could be seen as an act of war. Whereas our plan was so bonkers, no one would expect it. I imagined Ilyin raging at the idea that four teenagers could fly out of Mexico and block him from stealing a prize like the K-Foundation.

Most definitely, we'd be the Czar's enemies for life.

I reminded myself that Chekists were already waiting for us in Tapachula. Staying off the Czar's radar? It was already too late. It came down to this – if I wanted a chance to grow up in a world free of the Czar's 'Mind Game,' if I wanted to help twenty-five kids avoid a life of modern slavery, then I had to stop fretting. Zone in on the mission and nothing else.

Exhausted, I finally dropped off and slept until one in the afternoon. When we woke Atlanta gathered us for some stretching exercise to help us stay limber for the hike. We played a yoga instruction video and all four of us followed along. I helped Maxim cook a huge pan of chilaquiles for the carb loading. We'd be leaving in less than twenty-four hours.

I tried not to think what Bobbie or Zara would say if they knew what we were doing. Every time an inside voice encouraged me to panic, I thought about how soldiers must feel when they're about to go to war. All the hundreds of thousands fighting back the forces of the Third Russian Empire. If I didn't do this now, how would I live with the knowledge that *I* could have made the difference that stopped Ilyin adding a slave-army of telepaths to his war machine?

Kenzie finally did a successful test of the EMP device. He made it using a capacitor taken from a camera's flash unit, a toggle button, insulated thick copper cable, enamel-coated wire and a high-current momentary switch, which he'd jimmied together using duct tape and a soldering iron. Unfortunately he blew out the TV, so no more yoga or any kind of entertainment.

Atlanta and I headed for the beach for some exercise, also to get out of Kenzie's hair. He'd started yelling at Maxim to stay away, too.

"You want me to do this or do you want to piss me off so badly I burn your stupid fricken' 'science project'?"

Amazingly, Maxim agreed to stick to my modified plan. At T-minus sixteen hours, where T was the time we had to be at Mexico City Airport, we helped Maxim to close down Carillo's hacienda. Next, we hopped into the Toyota Corolla and headed back to the nearby private airfield, from where we took off in Sandra-the-*narca's* Cessna. She flew us to Holguin, Cuba. Atlanta, Kenzie and I clutched our US passports, ready to land, doing our best impression of a couple of *yumas*. Maxim, I noticed, brandished a Mexican passport. We arrived into Holguin amid a blazing golden sunset, at around seven. Even the Border Control guy was part of the Carillo operation and calmly stamped visas into our passports. This part of the plan went off without a hitch. This part. Not much else.

THIRTY-EIGHT

MIL MI-8

We took a cab to Bayamo. Maxim passed a few bills of Cuban pesos to the driver of a handsome, powder-blue 1957 Chevy Bel Air. At each step of the plan I'd catch glimpses of how thoroughly he'd been preparing. For example: he'd stashed everything we'd need for the mission at Carillo's hacienda ahead of time, including a duffel bag containing cash – US dollars and Cuban pesos.

But Kenzie and I were a brand new element in a hastily re-worked plan. Could it still work?

From what I could tell, Kenzie was refusing to let himself worry, was focusing totally on the EMP device. It had to work twice without fail. There was a lot riding on his part. *Just leave me to get on with it* seemed to be his approach.

Bathed in the rosy hues of sunset, the Cuban countryside flashed past us as the noisy old Chevy trundled along a pot-holed freeway. At first, it didn't seem all that different to rural Mexico. Then I'd spot a farmer using a scythe to harvest crops, or an ox to plough a field. It was like a window to the 19th century. Maxim checked his watch, over and again. Despite his calm demeanor I saw tension in the tightness of his jaw.

The cab dropped us in the main square at Bayamo, Plaza del Himno. It was a jewel of a town, old but bright-colored buildings with colonnaded arches flanking all four sides. Painted in shades of peach, yellow, blue and turquoise, they dazzled in the late afternoon sun. Lush gardens with red and orange tropical flowers adorned sections of the center, like in any old Mexican town. In fact it was a lot like Mexico, except for the music. Cabs bumbled along, their stereos booming the dembow beat of reggaeton. In some upper room off the plaza, I heard someone practicing conga drums.

We settled under the ceiling fan in a nearby restaurant and ordered grilled sandwiches as we waited for the sky fully to darken. The food arrived along with a trio of elderly men, one carrying bongos and two with battered old guitars. Touring the tables, they took requests. Maxim handed their singer some cash. They performed for us, a few songs, alternately lively and romantic, some of which sounded familiar. As he listened, a wistful air settled on him. He occasionally smiled or sang along with them, yet his underlying sadness didn't budge.

It made me wonder about that year he'd spent alone in Havana, fifteen years old and having to survive in a world he'd been prevented from knowing. It must have been a tough year. Despite this, Maxim seemed to feel something for the island. How long was that after he'd lost his mom? It seemed like he blamed himself for her death.

I wanted to reach for his hand, to say something that might comfort him, but I didn't; I was afraid to do that in front of Kenzie and Atlanta. We hadn't been together long at all, yet our team had managed to achieve a fragile unity that I was afraid to disrupt. I wondered if these were our final hours as blameless citizens of the free world. No two ways about it – once we committed to stealing the chopper, our lives would change forever. Despite the summertime Caribbean heat, I shivered.

We'd each brought a rucksack to Cuba. Between us we had the kit Maxim had been buying up carefully and then stashing; EMP device and spare flash capacitors as well as tools for last minute repairs, a hand-held metal detector, glow sticks and also ski masks, rubber-coated gloves, night-vision binoculars that fitted into the palm of one hand and even night-vision headsets. The headsets were kids' toys but fine for what we needed.

At nine-thirty, Maxim led us to the edge of town, to an industrial estate. Graffiti was everywhere, political slogans like *Venceremos*, *Nuestra Victoria Para Todos* or the Cuban flag, but also some weird drawings that resembled zombies or aliens. The scrap yard stood at the end of the row and occupied the whole of a block. Like all other businesses in the estate, its doors were closed and the barred metal gates locked. Beyond the gate I spotted the silhouette of a guy smoking a cigarette as he mooched, a chunky weapon slung casually over his shoulder.

"AK-47 Kalashnikov," Maxim whispered, after a peek through his small night-vision binoculars. "Semi-automatic. Better he doesn't fire it at all. If only we'd had more time to prepare. Two more weeks and we would have had body armor."

He broke off. The sleepy-town atmosphere had started to lull me somewhat, but noticing that AK-47 woke me right up. We hedged out of sight of the guard until twenty minutes later, he wandered away.

Kenzie raised an eyebrow. "Think our boy's on a pee break?"

Maxim ignored him. He darted across to the main entrance, typed in the access code he'd been given by Carillo's contact, and pushed at the door. It opened. Seconds later we were inside the darkened building. Atlanta took a glow stick from a rucksack and snapped it. After a minute the glow lit up surroundings, enough to make out two corridors and a few doorways.

I panicked that we were making too much noise, then realized I was hearing the sound of my own heart pummeling the inside of my rib cage.

"Remember to breathe," murmured Maxim. He pulled ahead of the group.

Kenzie and I made to follow but Atlanta held us back. They didn't explain why. I guessed Max and Atlanta were in telepathic contact. It was hard to keep from feeling slightly resentful. I wasn't jealous exactly, or maybe I was, but their connection was undeniable. However much Maxim insisted we were part of their team, Kenzie and I were destined to be on the outside. Another minute went by and then Atlanta turned to us.

"Count to thirty, slowly. One Mississippi, two, etc. Then follow. Down that corridor, through those doors at the end." Handing me the glow stick, Atlanta took off after Maxim.

I began to count. Kenzie watched. When I reached the count of thirty we followed Atlanta. At the end of the corridor we found a set of double doors, which led to another corridor. At the end of that was a door to the outside. It was open. About fifty yards ahead I spotted the streaking light of a slowly-waving glow stick. We set off in its direction, almost tripping over the prone body of the guard. I raised the glow stick over him and scanned for any sign of blood, but there was none. No gun, either.

Kenzie said, "What the hell?"

I was about to lean over and check the guard's pulse, when Kenzie hissed, loudly. The distant glow stick was now waving, frantically. We stepped over the fallen guard and jogged across the yard, towards where Atlanta was signaling. As we drew closer the outline of a hulking Russian chopper became visible.

One door was open. Maxim was inside the cockpit, familiarizing himself with the controls. Seeing me approach he said, "What'd I tell you? *Super fácil.*"

"What'd you do to the guard?" I said, dreading his response.

Maxim's grin widened. "Him? Ketamine."

Kenzie blurted, "Fuck sake, Maxim!"

"What? I came prepared. Atlanta distracted him and I stuck the guy with a needle." My relief must have showed because suddenly, Maxim barked out a laugh. "Did you think I put him to sleep with my mind?"

"How would I know?" I snapped. "It's not like you catalogued your powers."

"Jaguar," Atlanta growled, obviously irked by his flip attitude. "There'll be a second guard. Probably taking a dump somewhere. We need to leave."

Maxim stood and opened the chopper's passenger door. It appeared to be heavy, but from the way it slid and clunked into place I could see it was well-oiled. Kenzie, Atlanta and I climbed inside as Maxim resumed his pre-flight checks. But then he did something that set my nerves jittering. He took a folder off the co-pilot seat and began flicking through it.

"What's happening right now?" I spluttered. "Are you *literally* reading the manual?"

"It's fine. I'm checking it's the same model I saw online." He turned. "Hop on up here with me?"

So I did, strapped myself into the co-pilot seat, all the while staring ahead and above at a terrifying array of switches and dials. Maxim's right hand landed on a giant joystick while his left hand hovered over a lever closer to the ground.

Pointing out the instruments he told me, "Cyclic on the right, collective on the left. Pedals." He nodded. "Ready."

I wasn't ready. A sudden and deafening clatter roared above our heads as he fired up the rotor blades. Carillo's little puddle-jumper, which Maxim had flown for the demo, was a hummingbird next to the Beast. The Mil Mi-8 was a groaning metal dinosaur that shuddered and rattled as though its screws were trying to unwind themselves. I was sure I could hear every bolt in the rotor falling apart. Despite the shocking volume of noise, the helicopter somehow stayed in one piece.

"Teeny tiny pressure on the collective," he said, as if reciting a nursery rhyme. The chopper began to lift, maybe a foot off the ground. "Teeny bit of pedal to raise the nose…" The nose of the chopper titled upwards for a second, then swung down so fast that I thought the blades were about to carve the ground. At that second he pulled on the collective and we seemed to be yanked into the air.

Through the side-window behind Maxim I caught a glimpse of what looked like a fire cracker. Then I realized – it was machine gun burst. They were shooting at us. The chopper's rotor was so loud we couldn't hear the gun but a few bullets smacked into doors, inches away from where Kenzie was sitting. The craft lurched backwards, still dragging us into the sky.

"Too much nose," Maxim observed. "It's a little different than what I practiced."

He sounded unruffled, like he was still playing in the simulator. I gripped the edges of my seat as the craft wobbled from side to side. Maxim couldn't seem to keep us level. Bullets clanged against the wheels. It was like a sick-making fairground ride that goes on way too long. After what felt like ten minutes but might only have been one, he finally seemed to get the helicopter on an even course. The ground beneath us turned black as we left behind the lights of Bayamo.

I allowed myself to relax. "My gosh. And you thought I'd *ever* be able to do that?"

"If you let me incline you, absolutely. I studied so

you wouldn't need to. Would you like to try?"

I couldn't tell if he was joking.

We flew in silence for the next hour. Maxim's focus was on navigating and flying the craft, for which he was using not only the Mi-8's control panel but also a navigation app on his phone. As we neared the landing site he shouted, "Crap! Forgot to put on the night goggles."

I hunted in his rucksack for the headset, then urged him to sit absolutely still while gingerly, I placed it over his eyes.

"Switch them on!" Maxim yelled. "I can't see a thing!"

Well, *now* I was shaking like a leaf, fingers fumbling at the edge of his headset in search of the on-switch. The craft pitched. Adrenaline shot through me. I was close to panic. Through the fog of terror I heard Maxim say, "Let me incline you. You need to allow it!"

I closed my eyes and tried to remember how I'd switched off my mind (it'd felt that way anyway) in the little Toyota, when he'd done it before. But I couldn't do it. Taking his hand off the cyclic, he pushed my hand away. The chopper yawed to the left and began to roll. Everyone screamed. I was close to blind panic, when Maxim finally located the switch for his night goggles and we began to straighten up.

"Everyone, night goggles and gloves on RIGHT NOW," yelled our glorious leader.

Shaking, I gripped the edge of the seat. I couldn't let myself be inclined for a measly minute. The whole plan was about to go up in smoke.

Get. A. Grip.

Five nerve-wracking minutes later, the chopper hovered over the landing site. It was a forest clearing, a flat section surrounded by higher ground so dense and devoid of shadows, it seemed to be thick with trees.

Just then, I heard what sounded like a low airplane. There were no lights in the sky. The sound came closer. It seemed to be coming from very high in the sky. Then I noticed a shadow overhead, a dark shape in the starlit sky.

It was a reconnaissance drone. They were already onto us.

THIRTY-NINE

EXFILTRATION

Luckily the guard at the Bayamo scrap yard had proved inept at shooting us down, what with our Russian helicopter being quite the tank. But Maxim's fear that they'd report the theft and we'd be caught on radar seemed to have happened pretty quickly because now there was a drone stalking us. Next, aircraft would scramble from Santiago's airbase. They might already be in the air. There was no way we could risk a hike through the woods, not even one klick. Maxim had to get the chopper in the air again and put us down right beside the camp.

Atlanta was irate. "We can't keep changing the plan!"

Kenzie and I focused our energy on clambering to the rear of the chopper. "Are we screwed?" he muttered to me. I replied, "I think we might be royally screwed."

My panic attack of a few minutes back had momentarily thrown me. If I couldn't find a way to let Maxim incline me, our mission was doomed. This was exactly what I'd been afraid of since it'd happened. I didn't want anyone else's thoughts controlling me. It went deep, like a phobia; hard-wired. Grisly thoughts crossed my mind. What might happen if they caught us? Would Kenzie and I wind up in some grim Cuban prison? Would Czar Ilyin have us extradited from Cuba and sent to a penal colony in Russia? What if the K-Foundation was guarded with weapons – would we be gunned down like the guard at the scrap yard tried to do?

I was mad at Maxim. His grand plan turned out to be riddled with holes. Most of all I was mad at myself. This whole thing was beyond stupid. What had possessed me to get involved?

The chopper swept into the air again as Maxim flew closer to the camp, scanning for a place to land. He found another spot but the Beast wasn't even on the ground, when he yelled above the rotor's roar, "Use the rope ladder! I can't get it any lower."

We were at least ten yards from the ground. Below were some trees whose canopy was dangerously close. I unbuckled and put on my rucksack, then looped the fabric of the baby-carrier from my neck so the carrier lay on my chest. Kenzie slid open the door and stood by the opening as I tossed out the rope ladder.

Maxim called to me. When I turned to face him I saw the pleading in his eyes. "Padi, you got this. I believe in you, always did. Don't be afraid."

I turned away, unable to respond. Before I stepped onto the ladder, I surveyed the ground below. With the night-goggles it was hard to perceive depth. After a few yards everything just went black. Maybe it was Maxim's pep talk or maybe some reckless streak, but somehow my fear was receding. The moment had arrived, my part of the mission had begun. Fear was pointless now. I had to put all my energy into it, forget about what might go wrong. Then, over I went.

The ladder swung violently as if in a storm. Maxim was having difficulty keeping the chopper still. At the time I cursed him, but what did I know? Until you've tried it, you cannot imagine how hard it is to balance a helicopter in the air. I finally landed and was immediately knocked off my feet as Atlanta landed on me, then the ground. A minute later, Kenzie was down, too.

Maxim flew the chopper away at once, casting

around for another place to set down. Only Atlanta's telepathy could reach him now, but I had no idea how long their range was. We had to hope it'd be enough.

Using the satellite map on their phone, Atlanta guided us to the camp. It was less than two hundred yards away and the trees were widely spaced so at times we were able to jog, but it was dark so we had to take extra care to dodge fallen branches and ditches. After a few minutes Atlanta stopped, pointing at a light shining from within the trees about twenty yards away.

"The perimeter."

We approached the light, cautiously. It was fixed to a tree about twelve yards from a fence that extended in both directions through the woods. Beyond the fence were several one-story buildings and a basketball hoop. There was no sign of movement, which was odd. They had to have heard the huge racket made by the chopper. I prepared myself to run into some camp guards. When I turned around Kenzie was kneeling over his rucksack, preparing the EMP generator. Atlanta had a handheld metal-detector wand and was waving it around, searching for stun mines. When they found a cluster they called Kenzie over.

"I'll count down from three," he said. "Three, two, one…" There was a fizzing sound as he activated the device. "GO!"

I sprinted at the fence. Reaching it, I leapt forwards with both hands outstretched and braced myself for a giant shock. The rubber gloves and sneakers did their job. After a moment I landed neatly on the other side.

Atlanta was beside me a second later. "Remember where the lil' kids dorm is?"

I oriented myself from a giant mango tree next to a nearby basketball court, landmarks Atlanta had made me memorize, then pointed to the building next to the basketball court.

Atlanta nodded. "That's it. Let's go. If we run into a sentinel, leave them to me."

"Sentinel?"

"Camp guards. Adult two-dubs who turn traitor. They stay here to remind us it's a prison."

We set off, moving stealthily, sticking close to any trees. Few lights were on but enough that we might be spotted in the open. We made it to the nearest door. Atlanta held it open for me while I checked that the coast was clear. I signaled, we pressed ahead. Two minutes later we were inside the dorm.

The kids were already awake, sitting silent in the darkness. No-one said a word. They began to shift, climbing out from under the sheets and still in total silence, searching for and putting on their shoes. I watched, awestruck. It was like a weird ballet. In the corner I noticed a toddler standing up in a cot. I dashed across the room in case the kid began to cry. He gazed at me with huge eyes, confused and then for some reason, shocked. Yet without taking his eyes off mine, the baby eventually held up both arms in the universal language for 'carry me."

I took off the baby-backpack, set it on the floor, swept him up, dropped him into it then lifted it onto my shoulder around fifteen kilos heavier. It was so strange to see a toddler respond to me that way. The way the entire room responded to us, in fact. Like witnessing a hive mind at work. Luckily, they seemed happy to see us.

One of the older kids, I'm guessing he was around five, took my hand and tugged. I got the impression he was trying to communicate telepathically with me and puzzled at my lack of response. He seemed to want to head for the door. Atlanta was busy picking up the older toddler, who was standing next to a normal bed. The fourth kid, who was the oldest of the four, seemed to be waiting for them. But after a second, he turned and paced over, joining me by the door. Calmly, he placed one hand in mine.

Okay, I thought, holding onto both boys. *Guess I'm taking these three then?* A few minutes later, I understood why.

With all the little kids gathered up, we proceeded to the other dorms. I guessed that they were telepathically chatting to each other. It was the only explanation that made sense of their silent, yet eager compliance. It was confusing. Maxim had told me their psi powers were blocked in the camp, by the guards. Maybe basic communication was allowed? Or perhaps it worked some other way. There was obviously a lot Maxim hadn't explained about their telepathy.

In the next dorm we found the boys. They'd evidently been warned ahead of time also, and were dressing in silence, putting on shoes in the dark.

I shook my head in wonder. *Maybe we can actually do this?*

Out of the blue, a teenager with shoulder-length hair swung for Atlanta, yelling furiously, "Atlanta? Go fuck yourself!" Two others leapt into action. They piled onto the one who'd attacked Atlanta and pinned him.

I whispered, "What's going on?"

Atlanta cut me off. "Ignore him, he's being a jerk."

The boy that Atlanta had trapped managed to shout, "No! Don't trust Jag…" before the other two clapped hands over the kid's mouth.

I froze. It didn't take a genius to figure out what the trapped teenager been about to say.

"Don't trust Jaguar."

SOLO

I pulled Atlanta aside. "He's not too happy to see you."

Through gritted teeth she whispered, "Yeah. That's Coati. This place is a nightmare for queer kids. We all had to hide it. Coati and me, we took care of each other."

"Oh." I sensed there was a whole thing behind this statement but it wasn't the time. "He doesn't seem too eager to come along."

Atlanta looked grim. "Can't leave anyone behind. Especially not Coati."

"Even if he wants to stay? Is it about the addiction?"

"Coati's not sixteen yet, so no morpho in his system. He's doing it to spite me. Like I said, he is angry 'bout the way I left. It's fair."

The two little boys whose hands I held became instantly tense, gripping my fingers. Meantime, Coati got hustled through the main door by his two captors. I fired a WTF? look at Atlanta, who blanked me then shushed the entire room – not that anyone had made a peep since the outburst by the complainer – and sidled towards the door. Peering outside for a moment, Atlanta signaled me that someone was out there and then reached into a rucksack for something I had no actual clue was there – a taser gun.

Ignoring my shocked gasp at the sight of Atlanta holding something gun-shaped, they slunk into the corridor. A moment later I heard a strangled cry followed by the slump of someone falling to the floor.

From outside I heard Coati begin to howl. I have no clue how he got away from his captors. A minute later there was another noisy struggle as once again Coati was muffled.

Simultaneously, the two little kids released my hands. The bigger of the two fixed me with a solemn stare and for the first time, spoke aloud. "Atlanta says 'hide.'"

There was only one door. I was out of there and into the corridor before I had time to plan an escape. Heavy footfall rushed towards the older boys' dorm. With no more than a quick backwards glance at Atlanta, who was plucking taser wires out of an adult woman writhing on the ground, I sped off in the opposite direction. I rounded two corners and then pressed myself into a doorway to catch my breath. That's when I remembered I still had the toddler on my back. He'd not made a peep, but all the same I reached around, stretching a hand to gently touch his cheek.

"It's okay baby, you're with me. I'm Roni. Everything gonna be fine."

Silence. The poor baby was probably trying to send a telepathic message. Too bad I was a normie. I pressed my cheek to the wall. From a couple of corridors away came the booming voice of an adult man.

"Mess around and find out, Atlanta. Your last stint in the hole is gonna seem like paradise compared to what we'll do to you."

A scuffle followed and some juicy curse words as Atlanta was overcome. Two seconds later I was stunned to hear the tiny child in my backpack lisping into my ear.

"Thtay hidden."

I blinked, urging my shocked brain to recall the

floor map of the camp.

"Beathe," advised the baby.

It felt faintly ridiculous to be taking instructions from a one-year-old, who I was supposed to be rescuing. The advice, however, was smart. After a few drawn-out, calming breaths my heart was no longer trying to jackhammer its way out of my ribcage. An image of the camp's layout began to form in my mind. I spun around to orient myself to face what had been the top of the map. Kenzie was waiting for us, due east, just outside the perimeter. If things had gone according to plan he'd be clearing a path free of stun mines using his own hand-held metal detector. Once he reached the fence he'd recharge and prepare the EMP device to zap one section. It'd been faster for me and Atlanta to go over with the protection of rubber gloves and sneaker soles, but for all the kids to get out safely, we needed a section of non-electrified fence.

The older girls' dorm was back in the direction I'd come. Briefly, I thought about going there but decided against. Now that the guards seem to have contained Atlanta, they'd gone quiet. The same gruff voice that'd threatened Atlanta was now ordering the teenagers back to their beds on pain of a beating if anyone was too slow. Any minute now, the guards would probably round up the under-fives and take them back to their own dorm.

It was strange that they hadn't come after me. Why not? I spotted a door that I recognized from the camp layout. It was a classroom. I sneaked inside and headed for the teacher's desk, hoping it was the type with a drawer pedestal. I got lucky – the desk had two pedestals. Between them was just enough space for me to kneel and lower my chin almost to the floor, so the baby in the backpack didn't bump his head.

"We're going to stay here very quiet now," I

whispered. "A quiet, *quiet* baby. Yeah?"

The baby didn't reply. I stilled myself, listening to their regular little breaths. Had the kid fallen asleep? I wondered if Atlanta had done that with their power, at a distance. Maxim had been scornful of my suggestion that they could put people to sleep at will but what if he'd lied? That kind of power in the wrong hands could be incredibly dangerous. Was this why Coati had tried to warn me not to trust 'Jaguar'?

Atlanta, if you can hear me, I'm hidden. What now?

No reply. So much for being a 'latent."

A few more minutes passed. Whatever they'd done with Atlanta had been achieved quickly and with little fuss. Somehow it hadn't occurred to them to search for an accomplice. Still no sign of a search – for me or the baby. I thought about Jaguar in the chopper outside, watching the radar for a sign of any approaching cavalry. We couldn't have much time left before the Cuban military showed up. I began to fret. I *had* to get these kids out. How was I going to do it, alone?

I crawled out from under the desk. Gingerly, I checked the corridor outside through the small panel window in the door. All seemed quiet. Baby was still snoozing, judging by his relaxed breathing. I sneaked out and padded noiselessly back to the older boy's dorm. No sign of any disturbance. I tried the door. This time it was locked.

Frantically, I peered at the keypad beside it. It needed a three-digit code. My heart was sinking as I calculated the odds, but as I examined the keypad, I noticed that the impressions of three numbers were slightly faded. The entire unit seemed pretty old, like it'd been new when this kind of lock was originally invented. A combination of only those three digits? That hugely narrowed the possibilities.

On the twelfth attempt I cracked it. The boys

inside were already waiting by their beds, ready to leave. From the shadows, the tallest of them pointed at the fastening of my baby backpack. "I can take over."

I glanced around, searching out Coati, who'd tried to warn me about Jaguar. He was in his bed, mouth stuffed with some kind of fabric, his hands and feet bound. Even with the night vision goggles I could see him seething.

A tall, brown-skinned guy with dark, tightly-curled hair, approached and gently reached for the baby. "My name's Bobcat," he said, softly. "Let me carry him, now." Bobcat was one of a half-dozen, non-white 'two-dubs,' including the baby, who looked to be of Asian descent.

Uncomfortably, it dawned on me that K-Foundation children being born to people of color, was probably a conscious decision. Although I knew these kids were bred for their telepathic abilities, there was something even more disturbing about their ethnicity being brought into it. From before their birth, these children were destined to be deployed as agents in particular parts of the world, their facial features and skin color used as a way to help them blend in with the population.

Thinking about this made me so anxious that unfastening the buckle of the baby carrier, I fumbled and almost dropped the baby.

"Whoa, take it easy!" Bobcat exclaimed.

I stepped away, shaking. Bobcat noticed at once. He finished securing the baby onto his back, then took my hand. "You're doing great. Just breathe. What's your name?"

"I'm Roni," I replied, voice trembling.

He grinned at me, warmly. "All good, Roni."

I tried not to think about how futile this was. Even if we managed to get away, what possible chance did

Maxim have against an organization that had been breeding kids like him for decades, who had a network of buyers across the world, run by some of the richest, most powerful and evil people on the planet? What was I even thinking, getting involved with this?

Bobcat's voice finally got through to me. "Roni. Let's go fetch the girls now. Kay?"

Quaking, I managed another nod. In almost total silence and still in darkness, Bobcat led us out of the boy's dorm and towards the girls'. Inside we found the same scene but this time, no dissenters. Everyone was sitting quietly on their beds, shoes fastened. All Bobcat had to do was signal them and they stood, ready to leave.

My curiosity piqued then and I tried surreptitiously to peer at the three oldest girls, wondering which one was Puma, Atlanta's crush. All were pretty good-looking, but one girl stood out. The kind of girl you'd kill yourself if you fell for, because you'd know it was hopeless. Puma appeared to be Asian, maybe descended from people in the far eastern territories of the Third Russian Empire. A real beauty. *God help Atlanta, if that's her*, I thought.

Holding my breath, I followed Bobcat back to the little kids' room. As he tapped in the code, he muttered, "Sentinels are so stupid. They actually believe we can't get out of this room."

"Do you know where we're taking you?" I asked.

Bobcat shrugged. "Doesn't matter. So long as it's far away from here."

"We have to find Atlanta," I began, then abruptly stopped as he hushed me.

Then we all heard it – from the east, a distant, low drone, the blended din of what sounded like dozens of helicopter blades thrumming in unison.

FORTY-ONE

BREAKOUT

A wave of panic surged all the way to my fingertips, which seemed to go numb. I tried to inhale and couldn't. The two little boys hugged my legs, tightly. Their hands found mine at once, a gesture of such simple trust that it enabled me to relax, just a pinch.

These kids depend on me.

Right now, I was their only chance out of that place. Even if that chance looked slim at best, we had to try. Still holding on to the little boys, I wound my way to the front of a straggling line of kids. I led them out and lengthened my stride until they had to jog to keep up. I peeked occasionally at the walls or corners, checking for security cameras. There didn't seem to be any. The whole vibe of the place was like one of those cheap, tacky camps for folk who want to avoid their kids all summer – with added security perimeter. Stupidly negligent, given the value of what they were trying to contain.

In the plan we'd pre-selected the optimal exit – a classroom with French doors that opened onto the basketball court, on the opposite side from the sentinel's quarters. From there a wooded path led to the fence, where we'd left Kenzie. We slipped out easily. In single file and sticking close to the shadows in case any sentinel happened to check their windows, we proceeded to the fence. There was no mistaking the sound of approaching helicopters. The sentinels had to be aware. I guessed they'd be getting dressed in a hurry and first checking the dorms. When they found them empty, where would they go? Atlanta would know, but I could only hope the sentinels wouldn't head straight for the same fence as us.

I couldn't see the choppers yet, not even with the night vision goggles. The goggles were basically a kid's toy but Maxim, with his binoculars and radar, ought to be able to pinpoint the helicopters. Where was he right now?

I scanned along the line of K-Foundation kids. How many of them had we managed to round up? It was too dark to count properly, but there should have been twenty-four. We'd had to leave Coati tied up when he threatened to holler, obsessed by the idea that we were heading into a trap. I felt guilty, especially with what Atlanta had told me about gay kids not being safe in this place. But what could I do? Every second counted and the others hadn't been willing to force him to join us. Had the other boys bullied him?

I tried not to think about it, because if so, then I was complicit. Atlanta was still somewhere inside, too. I had to hope that they'd escape and drag Coati along, too. Because there was no time for me to go back for Atlanta.

When we reached the fence I gathered everyone around.

"Hi everyone. I'm Roni. I came here with Atlanta and Maxim. We're here to get you out. Bobcat, can you help me to count everyone?"

"Sounds like you've already been rumbled," said one teenage girl, throwing a sullen glance in the direction of the approaching fleet of choppers.

Dozens of eyes regarded me with something between pity and contempt. A very tough room.

From beyond the electrified fence I heard Kenzie's voice. "Are you guys ready? I'm gonna use the EMP again." He returned then, a silhouette beside one of the perimeter posts. "It'll disable this section, between these two posts. I've run a test – the electricity reboots in one minute and forty seconds. Get ready. You need to be quick."

I instructed the kids to spread out along the section of fence. We had to pray that Maxim could get the chopper in the air and come find us. Or else pretty soon we'd have twenty-some kids panicking and running around in the forest. Not easy for the Chekists to round up either, if they were to arrive any time soon. But it wasn't the result we wanted, either.

As if on cue, somewhere in the shadows nearby, the Beast roared into action. Its thunderous rotor blades swallowed the noise of the approaching fleet. It sounded as though every bolt in the crate was shaking itself loose. Spying its looming hulk rising unsteadily from the woods, I got down on my knees and urged the five-year old boy to piggy back me. One of the bigger teenage boys offered the same to the slightly older little boy who'd taken my hand, but he refused. The bigger boy scooped him up instead, preparing to launch him high onto the fence.

Kenzie shouted, "Three-two-one-GO!"

We leapt onto the fence. It juddered as twenty-some little kids and teenagers clambered over, grabbing ahold of each horizontal wire in turn. I was grateful for my rubber gloves, but some of the kids were wincing as the wires dug into their palms. I emptied my mind of anything but climbing and leaping free on the other side, from as high as I dared. When Kenzie cried out a warning that time was almost up, I looked up in horror. One of the two little boys was still on the fence, climbing fastidiously down.

Standing beneath him I yelled "JUMP!" The current must have reactivated then because he let go at once, too shocked to cry out. Just as he landed on my face I felt someone else slide behind me, breaking my fall.

One of the older girls sprang into action. It was Puma, I noticed. She shoved me out of the way and bent her head to face and announced, "His heart's stopped." She began pumping the little guy's chest in the classic *Stayin' Alive* rhythm.

I stood aside, too stunned to react. Lights turned on inside the camp, sentinels were spilling out of the buildings. Two sentinels rushed toward the fence. From this point, I couldn't clearly make out any single speaking voice. The clatter and rumble of the Beast dominated all.

I pulled two glow sticks from my rucksack, cracked both and began frantically to wave them, painting neon-green threads of light in the air. Anything we could do to help Maxim find us. The older teens began nervously to corral a few younger ones who were getting twitchy. Most nervously watched the fence behind us, watched the sentinels glaring at us as they waited for someone to switch off the power. Probably hadn't been done recently, because whoever had been sent to do it was taking their sweet time.

As the chopper descended no more than fifty yards from the fence, the air around us began to whirl with stiff drafts. Out of the corner of my eyes I glimpsed two sentinels climbing the fence. The instant they landed on the outside, they'd be mere seconds behind the slowest of us. Three older kids in our group loitered by the fence, ready to tackle the sentinels. I hesitated, then yelled at the top of my lungs for them to join us. They ignored me. I pointed the remaining kids toward the Beast, which was now touching down somewhere in the woods, around fifty yards away. With Kenzie leading the charge, we made a dash for the chopper, following beams of yellow light that broke around the trees.

Maxim was waiting there, both feet on the threshold of the cockpit, ushering the first arrivals into the passenger section. He waved me closer and then leaned toward me and spoke directly into my ear.

"Where's Atlanta?"

I turned my mouth to his ear "Captured. There's a kid who was unconscious after the fence. One girl stayed to revive them. Three others stayed to hold back the sentinels. I… I think maybe they're all over sixteen?"

I didn't need to say more – he understood at once. Three older kids, probably all addicted to whatever the controllers mixed in with the drug that blocked their powers. They'd chosen to help us escape, but they weren't coming along.

Maxim grabbed my forearm, frowning. "You mean we're leaving six people behind, including Atlanta?"

Stammering, I admitted, "S-seven. Coati refused to come."

For two seconds, I withered under the intensity of his glare. He pointed firmly at the passenger section, then drew my head close again. "Stay with them. Get ready. Into the co-pilot seat, hands on the cyclic and collective, foot on the pedal, like I showed you. And let me incline you."

Stricken, I pulled back. "Why?"

"Why? Because they're coming," he said, staring at me like I was clueless. "The sentinels are on their way. And this needs to be in the air when that happens."

I felt emptied out as I processed this. "You want me to… to take off? To fly?"

"I'm going for Atlanta. And any others I can bring." he shouted, turning away. "Bobcat, Kenzie, on my signal, drop the rope ladder." Then he leapt to the ground and sprinted off into the darkness.

I peered into the forest, stunned and shaky. The helicopter shuddered, its rotor blades spinning. My whole frame trembled as with both hands, I clung to the edges of the door. I couldn't will myself into the cockpit.

I can't fly this thing.

Inclination. Every fiber of my body wanted to reject it. All those kids were going to be recaptured because of me.

FORTY-TWO

REMEMBERING

Bobcat gawped in disbelief. "Did Jaguar say he was going to incline you? What's wrong with him? That's not a thing."

I nodded uncertainly, equally bewildered. "*What?*"

"I don't know *what* you're talking about." Bobcat turned to the line of sleepy kids that were clambering into the rear of the helicopter. "I need to make sure these all strap in good." He halted suddenly, shot me a pointed look. "Wait, tell me the truth, is this serious? *Inclination?*"

"Absolutely. Maxim inclined me. It's very much a thing."

"Jaguar inclined you," he repeated, amazement spreading over his face. "Then Coati wasn't lying."

"About inclination? No. Is that bad, is it bad if he wasn't lying?"

Bobcat bent low, both hands on his thighs as he took a few deep breaths. Hopefully just recovering his wind, but maybe trying to calm his anxiety? I couldn't tell.

"Okay, okay. Coati wasn't lying about the inclination. I believe you," he nodded, breathing slowly. "It's just, I've never seen it done. I thought Coati was making it up, and pretty much everything I know about inclination comes from him. Can't say I'm an expert, but from what Coati told us, Jaguar can incline a person over a long distance. If he knows them well, that is. If they're close. You've done this before, have you?"

Was he wondering just how close Maxim and I had

gotten? *Good question if so*, I thought. Myself, I was split on the matter. Not close enough, was how I felt most of the time, when any part of him brushed against me or I found myself remembering the timbre of his voice and its subtle, expressive range, when I caught myself staring at the nape of his neck and the way damp strands of his hair stuck to it, when I contemplated the way his eyes closed when he'd played the piano, as if in brief moments locating a peace that eluded him in the rest of his life. I very badly wanted to watch him play piano again, I realized suddenly and far too late, because our time together was almost over, compressing like a collapsing tunnel and me racing to be present at the very end.

Yet something within me, the secret voice, which told our ancestors that the rustle in grass was caused by a snake, not the wind, that part of me warned that maybe he'd already gotten too deep under my skin.

"Maxim, me and Kenzie go back a ways," I replied, after a moment. "We were kids together, in happier times. And yes, I've done this before, like I said."

Bobcat seemed persuaded. "Then you know it's possible. Whatever you did last time, do it again."

I imagined the air around me humming with telepathic messages. Did it work like radio, I wondered? Did some activated part of a tee's brain act like a biological transmitter or receiver? I had to admit it – I envied their ability to read each other's minds. Could they also read feelings? If so, they'd be able to read the abject terror of their stand-in pilot, aka *me*.

The K-Foundation kids were settling now, visibly calmer as they filled up the passenger section. Above me the rotor whirled slow and steady. I made myself turn to face the cockpit, those two empty pilot seats taunting me. Nausea radiated through my body, my knees buckled and I grabbed at the walls for support.

No way I can be responsible for flying this. Can't control the balance. I'll flip it. The rotor will carve up the forest. The chopper will explode. I'm going to kill everyone.

"Maxim says to get into the pilot chair," shouted Bobcat.

I peered into the cockpit again, unable to move a limb. Some part of me stood aside, observing myself with detached pity. *I'm having an out of body experience,* I thought.

So climb into your body. The reply seemed to come from outside of me and for a moment, I felt untethered from reality. Who'd said that?

Watching from his passenger seat, Kenzie unbuckled and approached the cockpit. Gently he placed a hand on each of my arms. "Hey, it's all good. You drove that car, blindfolded. You can do this."

I turned to Kenzie. Unable to speak, I gave a single shake of my head. A frightened look crossed his face for a second. Then Bobcat was at his side, too.

"Please. Let's go. Jaguar has to reach *your* mind out of all the others here. So focus on something that you know for sure he'll recognize."

I heard myself say, "*The Forgotten Village.* I have the download on my phone. Kenzie, do you have earbuds?"

A hopeful smile touched the edges of his lips. "Better than that. I'll plug your phone into the helo's sound system."

Bobcat appeared baffled. When I finally moved towards the pilot chair, his features relaxed in relief. "Bring the rope ladder" he instructed Kenzie. "I'll stand by to throw it out."

In position in the pilot's seat, I focused on recalling exactly how Maxim had gripped the cyclic and the collective. As my fingers wrapped around the controls, the vibrations of the craft went through me. The slightest shift of my wrist would do… something.

I don't even know what these controls do. It was the most badass thing I'd ever attempted and by a country mile, the craziest. And yet I did it, like I was born to it, because I had to try. Someone had to and when it came down to it, there was only me that could.

Kenzie slid into the co-pilot seat and waved his phone at me, as if in encouragement. He found somewhere to plug in the phone and scrolled through his music downloads. I caught sight of Maxim's phone screen, which was mounted on a stand next to the pilot's seat. It appeared to show several aircraft fanning out.

Pointing at the screen, I turned to Kenzie. "Are they close?"

He leaned across to check Maxim's phone screen. "Yep. The helos are encircling us. Can't land, so I guess they're waiting for us to take off."

"Then we're toast?"

After a second or two, Kenzie shook his head. "Nah. The Czar didn't go to all this trouble just to shoot down his precious cargo of unicorns."

I swallowed hard and fastened the seat belt. From the moment I'd mentally climbed back into my body, gradually fear had melted away, leaving only a light-headed sensation.

Confidence felt *light*, who knew?

From behind, Bobcat loomed over me with an air of skepticism, but confidence was a shell around me by now and I dismissed him. "You should get into the back with the rest of the precious cargo."

Kenzie finally located the track and hit 'play.' Music filled the helicopter and wrapped around me. *The Forgotten Village.*

I closed my eyes and inhaled, deeply. I cleared any remaining commotion from my mind, focused in on the music. If I could locate the memory of precisely how it'd felt just to let go, the way I had when I'd driven the car, then maybe this was possible. In my left hand, I gripped the collective. But nothing happened. I sensed a crack in the confidence I'd built, a dangerous fissure.

"Send it through the headset," I instructed Kenzie. "I need to hear it even louder."

My thoughts raced as I battled to prevent my resolve from collapsing. I became hyper-aware of Kenzie beside me, willing me to make it work, Bobcat somewhere behind me, all the other kids. If I couldn't clear my mind, each and every one of them would be failed. The failure would be all mine.

This is what you get for trying to be a hero, idiot. You and a whole bunch of kids going up in a fireball. Nice going, hero.

Kenzie placed the headset over my ears and gave my shoulder an encouraging squeeze. He lifted my right hand, placing it lightly on the cyclic. "Take your time, Padi."

I screwed my eyes shut and began to breathe deeply. The track came to an end and then looped. I let go of thoughts of the kids, of what was at stake, handed everything over to something greater than me. You could call it prayer, you could call it despair. Whatever. I let go of all that responsibility and just allowed myself to exist in the moment, free. That's when I felt myself relax. I listened only to the music. Let it transport me back to that rehearsal room all those years ago, both Kenzie and I watching Maxim as he bent over the keyboard, dropping his fingers with precision at every bar. Remembered the feel of drumsticks in my hands, the quiver of the high-hat when I tapped it with a brush.

How had I ever given this up?

My left hand closed around the collective. And then

my muscles moved. By themselves. In the next few seconds I was twisting the end of the collective, hearing the rotor speed up. I felt myself raise the collective, very, very gently. My hand seemed to know by itself just how much. Absolutely nothing tentative about it. The helicopter began to lift.

"Woo, Padi, you're doin' it!"

My left foot leaned slightly on the left pedal. We rose a little higher. I opened my eyes for a second, saw that we were now level with the tree canopy. Kenzie laughed in delight. "Yeah, go Padi!"

My right hand gripped the cyclic and pushed it forward. A powerful vibration went through the chopper. Somehow I ignored it, shut my eyes again and kept going.

Focus on the music.

More collective. We rose higher and faster, steady as a balloon.

"Oh shiiit," Kenzie groaned. "They're *everywhere*. We're surrounded."

I didn't dare to watch. Controlled from afar, my hands and feet kept everything in equilibrium. And I just kept on listening to the music.

FORTY-THREE

THE DREAM THIEF

We're in a monstrous titan of flying metal, rotor blade thundering above our heads. Below us, the wheels brush the tree canopy. A rope ladder trails from the open door, falling all the way to the forest floor. Circling us in the air I count the lights of five smaller helicopters. When they don't immediately fire on us, I finally begin to believe that Kenzie has it right: they're saving us for the Czar. Where we go, they will follow. I wonder about what'll happen if we try to leave Cuban airspace.

Talk about being stuck in a moment. Close my eyes today and I'm still there, in the cockpit of the Beast, hands on the cyclic and collective, foot poised above the pedal. You will never know what it is to have mastery of a machine the way I did that day. Even if you should learn to pilot a Mil Mi-8, which frankly I doubt will happen, you'll be piloting it with your own mind. I was not. In my memory, I am one with the machine, I'm part of it. Not a bystander. Like the collective, I'm another cog in the machine. As my limbs fly the helicopter my mind wanders free, detached, observing myself. It's an out-of-body experience.

There's a drag on the craft as we take on weight. My muscles adjust instantly, a little more pressure here, a lean there. And then slowly, we're rising.

Beside me Kenzie is crowing, "This is the GOAT!"

Two minutes later Atlanta climbs into the chopper. They tap me on the shoulder. "Nice job, Roni. Hang on just another minute. Jaguar's almost here."

Hearing Atlanta, I have a faint memory of something I urgently wanted to ask. But it's elusive and then it's gone. I feel myself emerging from the trance. That last minute is the hardest. Somewhere in the last ten seconds the psi connection snaps. I become vividly, luminously conscious. And I'm back in my body.

Still detached from my immediate surroundings, over my shoulder I glimpse a girl climbing in. It's Puma. She's followed by one of the older boys. *Thank God!* Still no sign of Maxim.

It is *my* right hand on the collective, *my* left hand on the cyclic. Can't even touch a pinky to the helicopter controls without consequences. But even a few precious minutes in control seemed to have given my muscles a hint of the memory they needed to make the Beast hover in place. *Very* odd. Something that took pilots weeks of training had become as natural to me as riding a bike.

Then Maxim reappeared at my side, shooing Kenzie out of the co-pilot seat. He strapped in and flashed me a broad grin. "Top drawer flying, Goose. Now let the master take over."

I felt the control shift to him. Relief flooded through me, grounding me even deeper in my own body. I began to shake.

"It's normal to feel weird," he shouted, above the din. "Just breathe easy."

We climbed higher. The helicopter's nose pitched forward as Maxim cranked up the speed. The military helicopters arced into a turn, preparing to follow us. One of them seemed suddenly to lose control. It wheeled into a spin as we whooshed above it, clearing it by mere yards. We heard an explosion behind us, then another. A few of our passengers cheered the first, but not the second.

I turned to Maxim. "What happened?"

Hands firmly on the controls, he faced straight ahead and answered me in a flat, detached tone. "I clouded him. One of their pilots is a latent. We got lucky. Now we might actually make it out of here."

"You…? You 'clouded' his mind? So you… you killed him!"

"No. He killed himself. And a couple of the others."

I cringed, appalled. "Then… could you 'cloud' my mind too?"

"Don't knock a good mind-cloud. That's how I got Atlanta out of the camp without being seen."

"You didn't answer my question."

Maxim seemed disappointed, but said nothing more.

I was silent for a moment, then remembered what I'd been trying to ask of Atlanta.

"And Coati?"

Maxim shot me a hard look, then gave a quick shake of his head.

The weight of this loss slowly settled onto me. I tried to glance into the rear of the chopper to find Atlanta but they were tucked into the side somewhere, hidden in shadows. What did this mean for Atlanta? Their relationship with Coati was evidently complicated, given what I'd seen in the brief minutes the two had been reunited, even if freeing him had obviously meant a lot to Atlanta. Why hadn't they brought him? Had he straight-up refused? I couldn't help but wonder if deep down, Atlanta agreed with Coati about trusting Jaguar. And what did that mean for me and Kenzie?

I turned these thoughts over as the Beast flew hard and fast, heading north, increasing the lead we had on the three helicopters that had remained in pursuit. Maxim piloted with fierce concentration. I didn't dare shift from my seat so instead stretched around, straining to catch Kenzie's eye. When our eyes met, it was to exchange a long, anxious look.

So... Maxim caused people to die in a gruesome fireball. But he was fighting for his life, and the other kids.' That qualifies as self-defense, right?

Except that this wasn't convincing, even to me. Did the Czar plan to kill these kids? Almost certainly not, or it'd already have happened. Everything we'd done was because Maxim refused to live as a slave and he wouldn't allow it to happen to the others, either. This had been his intention all along, ever since he escaped the K-Foundation. Maybe this had been the plan from the start, ever since he first dreamt of escaping the camp.

I thought about reports I'd read about how the Czar's soldiers treated civilians in countries they invaded, shooting handcuffed men, women and children. About the rapes, the mutilations, the torture. The rumors of secret gulags to which citizens of occupied countries had been transported, to work as slaves, like back in Stalin's day. About children stolen from their families and gifted to childless couples in the TRE, their identities erased so they'd forget their parents. About how Ilyin raised statues to the most violent war criminals and flew his flag everywhere.

The idea of Maxim and all the K-Foundation kids under the orders of a butcher like Ilyin, was horrendous. But these Cuban pilots weren't to blame. Why did they deserve to die?

My curiosity had led me, sleepwalking, into a Second Cold War covert operation. No time to think about the ethics of war – this was personal. Killing Olga, killing Masha, abducting my childhood friend for a life of slavery, all this made it personal for me. For Maxim it was all that, times a thousand.

From the radar on Maxim's phone I could see that we'd pulled one klick ahead of the military helicopters. We were headed for Havana.

"We're going to touch down real soon. Have your bags ready, you and Kenzie. Get ready to hop out."

Maxim pointed at the duffel bag on the floor of the cockpit. "There's twenty thousand American in there. Take three straps, that's three thousand. For your travel. Grab a taxi, head for the airport. Leave on the first flight to Mexico or the USA. Cuba's not safe."

I was about to ask where the cash came from, then stopped. Did I really want to know? What would I do if he told me it belonged to his *narco* buddy? Instead, I reached into the bag and pocketed three straps, each of ten hundred dollar bills. It was the most cash I'd ever touched. My attention went back to the radar, the helicopters on our tail, to the approaching coastline.

"What will you do? With the kids, I mean."

Maxim adjusted the craft's yaw "We'll land somewhere else. By the time they catch up we'll be gone."

"You said Cuba's not safe."

He shot me a brief, wary glance. "They won't find us."

"You're staying?"

"I have a way off the island. But we'll need to hideout awhile, first."

"You really did plan this," I said, in awe.

Wistfully, Maxim smiled. "Didn't count on you and Kenzie showing up in Tapachula. That was all you."

"So you honestly *didn't* send the message, *'Remember The Forgotten Village?'*"

"No. I already told you that. But I'm really, really glad you did. *Remember*, that is."

"Then, who?"

He paused. "Could be Auntie Olga."

"No, we ruled her out."

"Then I can only think of one other possibility, the people who rescued my brother. The Atlas group."

"Atlas, as in Elena Atlas?"

His eyes tensed in suspicion. "How'd you know that name?"

I blinked. Ahead, the lights of Havana glowed. "Long story. Remind me to tell you sometime. What about your brother, why didn't they rescue you too?"

"Long story," he echoed, then sighed. "Remind me to tell you sometime."

Our eyes met in sadness. I asked, "Will we see you again?"

It was dawning on me that once we jumped out of the Beast, Kenzie and I would be hitting the road, fast. There'd be no time to exchange contact details. Now that the Chekists were onto Tapachula, it wasn't safe for Maxim. I wondered what he'd tell Carillo about taking care of Hacienda Narcojunior.

"I'll send you a message through your podcast. I'll use a codeword so you know it's me."

A *codeword*. I turned over possibilities from recent shared memories – mamey ice cream, Blue Dolphin, Carillo, Mi-8, the Beast. Too many that might reveal important information.

"How about '*Dream Thief*'?"

Maxim nodded, a little surprised. "The name of the album with *The Forgotten Village*. I like it. Good. Then, expect a call from the Dream Thief."

"What if I need to call you?" I was already beginning to worry that Chekists might track us back to DC, show up at Bobbie and Zara's, snatch us off the streets and torture us for clues about what'd happened in Cuba.

"Oh, I'm going to message you real soon, don't worry. But first I have to get these kids off the grid."

He leaned on the pedal, pitching the nose down as we began to descend. The Beast was headed for a patch of dark near the coast.

"I'm putting down next to Playa Bacuranao. Head for the coastal road, pick up an airport taxi returning from Varadero. They can't accept US dollars but they'll take you to exchange money at the airport. But first, tip the driver with a hundred US and make it clear it's not the fare but a personal thanks for being so reasonable."

"Hundie tip, got it."

We descended further and I unbuckled. Kenzie had worked his way back to the cockpit and lifted my backpack from the floor. He handed it to me. I checked to see that my passport and phone were still there. Nothing else really mattered. Ahead, an occasional flash of white surf came into view, where beach lights lit up the ocean.

Maxim pointed. "That's the *playa*." He nodded at me. "Get ready."

"Bye, Maxim," Kenzie said, offering a fist to bump. "Take it easy."

I leaned down and kissed Maxim's cheek. "Bye, 'Jaguar.'" A weird moment to flirt, perhaps, but I gave in to an impulse.

He winked. "It's 'Dream Thief' to you."

Bobcat unbuckled, stood up, swung open the door. I scanned the passenger section for a final glimpse of Atlanta. They sat in a corner with both arms wrapped around two little kids, who'd fallen asleep leaning against Atlanta's chest. When I saw that right next to them was Puma, I grinned. Waving, I touched my temple in a salute. Atlanta managed a tired smile.

The helicopter landed bumpily, skidded for about thirty yards. Bobcat gave me a shove and I tumbled out. I landed on my left shoulder and rolled a couple of times before tumbling to a stop. A second later he tossed out Kenzie. Without even properly coming to a halt, the Beast swept into the air.

I heard someone – probably Bobcat – yell out "Take cover!"

Then Team Jaguar were gone.

FORTY-FOUR

LEAVING HAVANA

I used our cash to book us some eye-wateringly expensive last-minute flights, then returned to meet Kenzie at the airport snack stand. There were rows of the same three types of snack and four flavors of soda – lemon, orange, cola and malt. There was just one type of beer. All were Cuban brands. It was kind of soothing, how little choice there was. I asked for two beers, expecting at least the usual ambiguous smirk, but the guy handed them to me without even blinking, let alone checking my passport. I was so relieved that I forgot to get chips.

Kenzie handled his beer, impressed. "Nice. You think they'll sell us cigars, too?" The surrounding shops sold pretty much nothing but Cuban cigars, rum and other souvenirs.

"Probably. But you'd be fined for taking them to the USA."

I handed him two boarding passes. His eyebrows shot up. "CDMX via *Miami*? We fly into the US and then out again and then back again?"

I grimaced. "Yup. Direct flights to Mexico City were all booked. And we have to fly into D.C. from Mexico City on our original booking, since your moms will be expecting us on that flight."

He seemed crestfallen. "No flights to D.C. from Miami?"

"Booked up. Maxim said to take the first available flight out of Havana. Also, I refer you to my previous statement about where we were actually supposed to fly in from."

Boarding passes between thumb and forefinger, Kenzie held my gaze for just long enough to understand. "I get that you don't want Bobbie and Zara to know we went to Cuba. But…" He flipped open his passport to where the Cuban visa was stamped. "They're going to find out."

"Bruh, it's so much worse than that."

He fixed his attention on the boarding passes, head bowed as he realized that I was right.

"The time for telling them about Cuba, was when you called them from Hacienda Narcojunior. You only admitted that we were waiting in the home of some friends of Maxim, nothing more."

"Obviously I didn't say more than that, and by the way, that was bad enough! But yeah, my moms would go ape-shit if we told them we were in Cuba."

"Better not let them see your passport, then."

He looked up, dazed. "I'm in a lot of trouble."

I clapped a hand to his shoulder. "Stay positive. The Cuban authorities haven't put us on a no-fly list yet, or else I couldn't have bought the ticket."

"You don't know that. What if they're waiting for us at Border Control?"

Kenzie was right, it was definite possibility. I couldn't think of a way out of that one. Meanwhile he was descending into further gloom.

"Lookit," he said, pulling me away from the nearest other passenger. "We arrived on a private jet in Holguin. Three gringos and a Mexican national, Maxim. They'll have logged us into the system. Then they find out that a stolen helo is raiding a top secret camp for kids with psi powers. Can't be too long before they put two and two together and get Maxim, you and me. Put a stop on our passports and we're stuck here."

"It's less 'two and two' and more 'differential

calculus.' Think about it – it is a *huge* secret that the 'unicorns' even exist, so that's one piece of the puzzle the regular Cuban police won't have. Four teenagers arriving on a private plane to Holguin won't automatically raise suspicion."

He wrung his hands, nervously. "They wouldn't expect four foreign teenagers to be stealing and flying an ex-Soviet helo, maybe. But what if there's CC footage from the scrap yard?"

It was a fair point, but I still thought Kenzie was being unnecessarily paranoid. "If that happened they'd put a stop on passports. We wouldn't be able to book our flights. And, see?" I waved my boarding passes. "No problem."

"The booking agent didn't look at you weird or anything?"

"Not even a little."

Kenzie gave a grudging nod. "It'd take tight intel to find us so fast, that's true. And this is Cuba. I mean, it all seems fine, but isn't the country supposed to be poor and all?"

"Exactly. And the K-Foundation is classified. They'd have to put our arrival at Holguin with Atlanta and Maxim yesterday, together with the raid on the camp. Why would they? There's literally nothing to connect us."

"Maybe not right away, but eventually, once word gets out from the camp that they saw Max."

I shook my head, confidently. "No. They saw Atlanta, they saw me. But not Maxim. He clouded their minds."

Kenzie balked. "He did *what*?"

"Clouded their minds," I repeated, more calmly than I felt. "That's what he told me, anyhow. It's how he got one of the military pilots to flip a helicopter."

His amazement turned to dismay. "Maxim caused

those pilots to crash?"

Come on, I thought. *Don't pretend like you didn't know.*

Kenzie cracked open his drink and took a long sip. I did the same. The beer can was frosty-cold and the beer crisp and a little sweet. It tasted fantastic, my first legal drink in a bar. Too bad it'd be years before I could do the same back home.

"So – what, was the pilot a latent, like you?"

"Our side got lucky." I grimaced. "The pilots, not so much. By the way, one of the two-dubs from the camp, Bobcat, was very surprised to hear about inclination. Said it wasn't a thing, until I told him that yes, most definitely, it was a thing."

He didn't follow, so I explained. "I think maybe only some two-dubs can do it. Maybe just Maxim."

It was too soon though and I wasn't thinking straight yet, hadn't fully thought through the implications of what Maxim had told me about the Atlas group. But we'll get to that – one day.

Kenzie reflected. "Yikes, Then I guess to Maxim, latents are basically back doors to hacking humanity." He made a 'boom' gesture with his hands. "That's a lot of power, Padi."

Grimly, I nodded. "Yeah. I know."

We were both quiet for a minute. I was fairly certain he was thinking the same thing as me: *Did we do the right thing by helping Maxim?*

"We had to help," Kenzie said, answering my unspoken question. "Maxim is, well he's Maxim. Doesn't always play by the rules. Knows what he wants and always has a plan to get it. But Czar Ilyin, that man is a monster, hands-down."

Emphatically, I agreed. Yet I didn't at that time share with Kenzie the one point of data I had, which tallied firmly in the 'we did wrong' column: Coati, the solitary kid in the camp that had refused to go. The one who called out, '*Don't trust Jag…*' only to be cut off by the others.

Maybe it was just a personal grudge. Or maybe not.

"*Maxim is, well he's Maxim*,' Kenzie had said. But none of those K-Foundation kids had called him that. They called him 'Jaguar.' A boy they'd known between the time he was dragged back to the camp after years of freedom in DC, up until when he'd escaped. Three years. The Maxim we remembered, a serious, earnest boy with goals and unlimited focus. A guy with few friends, perhaps not even really us, when it came down to it.

Kenzie asked, abruptly, "Do you think we were ever his friends? Or just part of his music project?"

I thought it over. "Maybe yes, maybe no. But I do know that music means a lot to him. The music we shared, especially. We were more than a project, I'm sure of it."

Or else how could he have reached my mind so much more easily, when I focused on *The Forgotten Village*? I didn't tell Kenzie this last detail, however. For some reason I wanted to hang onto a memory that was just mine and Maxim's.

Still, I kept thinking about what Kenzie had said – *Maxim is Maxim*. Well, not quite. He was also 'Jaguar.' And who was 'Jaguar'? Truthfully, we had no clue.

I finished my beer and picked up my backpack. The lines for security were starting to lengthen. Beyond was the dreaded Border Control. Just then a message dinged on my phone – a new comment on the podcast.

`Dream Thief loves Telegram. #tapachula. You'll know.`

Kenzie plucked his passport from his rucksack, placed the boarding pass between its pages and took my hand. "Ready?"

I squeezed his hand. "Let's get out of here."

A Message From The Author

Thank you so much for reading *The Mind Game*. If you enjoyed the book, it'd mean a lot to me if you'd leave a lovely review and tell your friends about the book, too. Spreading the word is the best way to support authors whose books you enjoyed. ☺

Sometimes it's hard to believe that I had the idea for this all the way back in 2006, even before *The Joshua Files* was accepted by a publisher.

While the first book of that series was still with my literary agent, I started to write a book set in a secret camp in Cuba, where telepathic kids were bred and trained to be sold as spies. I actually had a contract to publish *Jaguar's Realm* but decided to go with a 5th *Joshua File*s instalment instead. Later I was busy writing *Emancipated* (as M. G. Reyes), *Gemini Force One* and other books. My series about telepathic spies went back into the drawer.

In 2022 I felt it was time to return to my telepathic spies. Instead of opening with the story of their escape, I imagined those characters further down the line. In a fictional world where a Russian empire was acting aggressively as in our real world, what would those young telepaths do, what could they become? Inspired by crime and mystery podcasters, I developed 17-year old investigative podcaster, Roni Padilla, as my new fictional hero.

Hope you enjoyed reading as much as I enjoyed writing *The Mind Game* and please look out for the sequel *False Flag* later this year!

About M.G. Harris

Born in Mexico, Maria Guadalupe "MG" Harris grew up in Manchester, England. She's been a massive *Doctor Who* and *Blake's 7* fan since childhood.

Her writing addiction began with B7 fanfic. Before being published she was a molecular biologist followed by a stint as an Internet entrepreneur.

MG has authored three book series for young readers. *The Joshua Files* (Scholastic Children's Books UK), which was translated into 17 foreign languages, *Gemini Force One* (Orion Children's Books) and a young adult crime trilogy, *Emancipated* (Harper Teen, as M.G. Reyes), as well as a novel for the *Doctor Who* universe – *Doctor Who - Doom's Day: Extraction Point* (Penguin RH).